鈴木光司

DARK WATER

KOJI SUZUKI

Koji Suzuki

‖VERTICAL.

Published by Vertical, Inc., New York.

Originally published in Japan as *Honogurai mizu no soko kara*
by Kadokawa Shoten, Tokyo, 1996.

ISBN 1-932234-10-1

Manufactured in the United States of America

First American Edition

Vertical, Inc.
257 Park Avenue South, 8th Floor
New York, NY 10010
www.vertical-inc.com

DARK WATER

CONTENTS

PROLOGUE

Whenever her son and his family came down from Tokyo to spend time with her, Kayo would take her little grand-daughter Yuko out on early morning walks. They always made their way to Cape Kannon, the easternmost tip of the Miura Peninsula. It was just the right distance for a stroll, the walk around the cape and back to the house measuring less than two miles.

On the spacious observation platform provided for a panoramic view from the cape, Yuko would point far out to sea at whatever had aroused her curiosity, excitedly tug on her grandmother's hand, and buffet her with a flurry of questions. Kayo answered each of them patiently. Yuko had arrived the day before—she was on summer vacation—and was to stay for another week. The prospect of spending time with her granddaughter was, for Kayo, simply exhilarating.

The view of the furthermost recesses of Tokyo Bay beyond the Tokyo-Yokohama industrial area remained hazy. You rarely got a clear view all the way across, for Tokyo Bay was larger than people thought. In contrast, the mountains of the Boso Peninsula seemed to rise up immediately across the Uraga Waterway, and a high and distinct ridge snaked from Mt. Nokogiri to Mt. Kano.

Yuko let go of the railing and stretched her arms out as if trying to grasp something. Cape Futtsu, whose long, slender sandbar lay on the opposite side of the bay, appeared to be almost within reach.

The imaginary line that connected Cape Futtsu and Cape Kannon was the threshold of Tokyo Bay, and a stream of cargo vessels proceeded in and out in two neat columns through a corridor of water. Yuko waved to the lines of freighters, which looked like rows of toy boats from where she and her grandmother stood.

The tide flowed rapidly in the shipping lane, and striped patterns sometimes appeared on the water. High tide flooded the bay with water from the open sea, and the low tide emptied the bay. Perhaps for this reason, all the debris in Tokyo Bay was said to wash up at Cape Kannon and Cape Futtsu. If Tokyo Bay was a huge heart, the capes jutting out on each side functioned like valves filtering out waste from the seawater that circulated by the gentle pulse of the tide.

But it was not just the circulation of the sea. The rivers Edo, Ara, Sumida, and Tama all supplied fresh blood to Tokyo Bay like so many thick arteries. The variety of trash washing ashore ranged from old tires, shoes and children's toys to the remains of wrecked fishing boats and wooden doorplates bearing addresses from as far away as Hachioji. Some of the things made you wonder how they ever ended up in the sea: bowling pins, wheelchairs, drumsticks, and lingerie...

Yuko's attention turned to the pieces of driftage bobbing amid the waves.

Driftage can spark the beach-comer's imagination. The sight of a motorcycle's side cover can conjure up the image of

a biker skidding off a pier into the sea, while a plastic bag stuffed with used syringes has a whiff of crime. Each item of debris has its own tale to tell. Any particularly intriguing thing you may come across on the beach is best left untouched—because it begins to tell its tale to you, as soon as you pick it up. Fine if the story is heartwarming, but if it curdles your blood, things will never be the same.

Especially if you love the sea, you ought to be mindful. You pick up what looks like a rubber glove and find out it's really a severed hand. That sort of thing could keep you off the beaches forever. The feeling of picking up a hand is probably not too easy to shake off.

Kayo would say such things matter-of-factly to frighten her granddaughter. Every time Yuko begged for a scary story, Kayo responded by weaving a tale around a piece of driftage.

The young girl would probably ask for scary stories on every morning walk in the coming week, but Kayo had plenty of stories to tell and then some. Ever since she'd picked up that thing by the sea, one morning twenty years ago, when she'd just started taking her walks, her imagination had only been growing more active. Now, she could freely draw forth from articles of driftage the bizarre tales that littered the water's edge.

"No treasures?" Yuko wanted to know if nicer things ever washed up, perhaps from some faraway land, instead of just the scary stuff.

11

All kinds of vessels, from tiny boats to giant ships, busily plied the narrow sea-lanes down there in the bay. Why shouldn't a chest of gems plop from a ship's cabin into the water now and then? So reasoned Yuko.

"I wouldn't say I've never found any," Kayo replied ambiguously.

"May I have it?!" Though Yuko didn't know exactly what this treasure was, her desire for it was spontaneous.

"I *could* give it to you," said Kayo, hinting that the offer was conditional.

"If what?"

"If you'll keep me company for the whole week, on my walks."

"Of course I will!"

"Then you shall have your treasure on the morning of the day you go back to Tokyo."

"Promise?"

To seal the bargain, they performed a pledge that was popular among children. Perhaps Yuko wouldn't like the treasure—or even agree it was a treasure. To make sure the girl wouldn't feel cheated, Kayo needed to keep weaving more tales, so that the setting where the words had sprung would be vivid in Yuko's mind.

For Kayo, one thing was certain. In the long life that Yuko had ahead of her, the moment was bound to arrive when the treasure would reveal its worth.

FLOATING WATER

Thinking again about drinking the tap water, Yoshimi Matsubara held the glass up to the fluorescent light in the kitchen. Rotating it just above eye level, she saw tiny bubbles floating in it. Tangled up with them, or so it seemed, were countless particles of dirt that could have come in the water or been a deposit at the bottom of the glass. She thought better of taking a second gulp and with a grimace, poured the water down the sink.

It just didn't taste the same. It was already three months since they'd moved from their rented house in Musashino to this seven-story apartment building that stood on a landfill, but she still couldn't get used to the tap water. She'd take a gulp out of habit, but the strange odor, which wasn't even like chloramine, attacked her nostrils and almost always kept her from finishing the glass.

"Mommy? Can we do fireworks?" It was her daughter Ikuko, now almost six years old, calling from the sofa in the living room. She hugged a bundle of miniature fireworks that a friend at nursery school had been kind enough to share with her.

Barely registering her daughter's pleas, still clutching the empty glass, Yoshimi was picturing the path their water had to take from the Tone River. As she tried to trace the route in her mind, wondering how it differed from the flow of water back in Musashino, an image of tar-black sludge came to her. She did not know exactly when the apartment's site had been filled, nor in what way the water pipes wound from island to island. But she did know, from a map charting the history of Tokyo Bay, that the land they lived on didn't exist in the late '20s. The thought that the uncertain ground beneath her feet had as its foundation the dregs of several generations enfeebled her grip on the glass.

"Mommy!"

It was dusk on a Sunday in late August. Urged on by the deepening dark, Ikuko pleaded with her mother. The water still hadn't been turned off when Yoshimi turned to face the living room.

"There's nowhere to set them off..."

The park by the canal in front of their building was closed for construction work, and since there was absolutely nowhere else in the neighborhood that was suitable, Yoshimi was about to tell her daughter no. Then she realized they'd never been up to the roof of their apartment building.

Mother and daughter proceeded to the fourth-floor elevator hall with a box of matches, a candle, and a plastic bag containing the fireworks. They pressed the up button and waited for the elevator, which arrived with a painful groan.

When they got in, Ikuko said, imitating an elevator attendant: "Welcome, madam. Which floor do you require?"

"Take me up to the seventh, please," Yoshimi played along.

"Very well, madam."

With a slight bow of the head, Ikuko turned to press the button for the seventh floor, only to find that she couldn't reach it. Yoshimi giggled at her daughter's plight; on tiptoe and with her arm outstretched as far as it would go, the best she could manage with her straining index finger was the fourth floor. By this time, the elevator doors were starting to close automatically.

"Too bad," Yoshimi said, and hit the button for the seventh floor.

"Huh!" Ikuko sulked.

The grainy feel of the elevator button lingered with Yoshimi, and she unconsciously wiped her forefinger against her linen skirt. Every time she used the elevator, the black, blistered surfaces of the floor buttons made her feel gloomy. Someone had used a cigarette to scorch the buttons for the first through the seventh floors. Although the NO SMOKING sign right next to them remained unscathed, none of the originally white buttons had escaped. Whenever Yoshimi wondered what could motivate such behavior, she felt chilly. It probably had something to do with repressed anger against society—and who could be sure the frustration wouldn't be vented on people someday? What terrified her most was that this man (she'd somehow decided it was a man) used the elevator of the very apartment building they lived in. As a single mother, worried about the worst, she couldn't shake off her anxiety. Still, she'd had enough of men and didn't ever want to live with one again.

During the two years she'd lived with her husband, she'd never once felt protected. When they separated four and a half years ago, and when a year later the divorce became official, she felt relieved, frankly. She just couldn't adapt herself to living with a man. Perhaps it was a Matsubara family tradition. Both her grandmother and her mother had followed the same path, and for the third generation now, theirs was a two-person family of just mother and daughter. Ikuko, who held Yoshimi's hand now, would in the years ahead likely get married and become a mother, but Yoshimi somehow knew the marriage wouldn't last.

As the elevator stopped and the doors slid open, Tokyo Bay spread out in front of them. They stepped out into the corridor and saw four apartments to the left and four to the right of the elevator, but none of them showed any sign of occupancy. The fourteen-year-old apartment building suffered from the after-effects of the burst economic bubble.

A few years earlier, when, out of the blue, a project to construct a high-rise complex in this area had come up, this apartment building and other mixed-occupancy buildings in the neighborhood had been subjected to a bout of land speculation. But the neighbors resisted being chased out, and while the coordinators fumbled, the Bubble burst and the construction project disappeared into thin air. About half of the forty-eight apartment units in the building had been purchased, but could not easily be resold; twenty were eventually put up for rent at considerably less than market value. Yoshimi, who caught wind of this from a friend in the real estate business, had always dreamed of having a view of the sea, so she grabbed the opportunity, leaving the rented house in Musashino she'd lived in for so long, and transplanted herself onto the completely different environment of reclaimed land. She simply couldn't abide staying in a house that still reeked of her husband, and also, now that her mother was dead, childcare-friendly Minato Ward seemed more convenient for a single mother and her daughter. The publishing company Yoshimi worked for was in nearby Shimbashi, and the best thing about it all was that she'd be able to devote time saved on the commute to her daughter.

Upon moving in, however, she found that a lot of the owners had purchased their units as an investment. They had never moved in, and by now most of the units had been transformed into offices. Inevitably, the building almost emptied out at night. Some five or six single people lived there as tenants, while the only family in the entire building lived on the fourth floor—in Yoshimi's unit number 405. The super had told Yoshimi that a family with a daughter the same age as Ikuko used to live on the second floor, but had moved away the year before due to some tragedy. From then on, the apartment building had seen no children until Yoshimi and Ikuko moved in three months ago.

Yoshimi surveyed the deserted seventh floor for a stairway leading to the rooftop. There it was, immediately to the right of the elevator; the roof would be only a floor above. Holding her daughter's hand, Yoshimi climbed up the steep concrete stairs. Next to the elevator engine room, there stood a heavy looking iron door. It didn't appear to be locked, and when Yoshimi tried turning the knob and giving it a push, it opened with surprising ease.

It wasn't spacious enough to be called a rooftop. It was a cramped place measuring no larger than forty square feet, fenced in with a waist-high handrail, with concrete pillars rising up from the four corners. Yoshimi would have to keep her eyes on her daughter if she approached the edge—the weight of your own head seemed enough to pull you over if you dared peer down.

In the gentle breezeless dusk, on this pier into the air, Yoshimi and Ikuko lit their fireworks. The red jets stood out in the deepening darkness. Below them to the right, the dark waters of the canal flickered with light reflected from the streetlamps, and opposite was the nearly completed Rainbow

Bridge to link Shibaura with Daiba. The top of the suspension bridge, outlined with red signal lights, sparkled like real fireworks.

Yoshimi took in the view from on high, and Ikuko held aloft her little sparklers and cried with delight. It was when the score of sparklers had all turned into charred cinders, and the two prepared to go back down, that they discovered it, both at the very same moment. They had had their backs against the wall of the penthouse, which housed the stairwell and atop which sat the building's water tank; but in the small drain that ran at the bottom of this wall was what looked like a handbag. It didn't look like it'd been dropped, but rather, placed there on purpose. After all, who'd come to a place like this and lose her bag?

It was Ikuko who picked it up. No sooner had she let out a faint cry of surprise than she'd dashed over to it and grabbed it. "It's Kitty," she noted.

It was hard to see in the dark, but against the glow of the street lamps from down below, the Kitty motif was indeed visible on the cheap vinyl bag. The bright red vinyl surface squished and changed shape in her hands.

"Give it to me," scolded Yoshimi. She reached for Ikuko, who was trying to unzip the bag to see what was inside, and succeeded in taking the bag away from her.

Yoshimi's mother, when she was still healthy, used to take Ikuko on walks in the hills around Musashino, often to come home with some discarded item. It was only natural for a woman of Yoshimi's mother's generation to feel that modern folks threw things out too soon. That was that. What Yoshimi couldn't stand was the thought of her own daughter scavenging through garbage, and she had frequently gotten into arguments with her mother about it. In bringing up Ikuko, Yoshimi never tired of hammering into her a simple rule about picking things up. Whatever it was, you didn't take it if it didn't belong to you. Every time Yoshimi said this with a solemn look, her mother would react with a grimace: "Now don't be such a stiff..."

Having taken the bag away from her daughter, Yoshimi didn't know what to do with it. Through the surface came a lumpy feel of its contents. Yoshimi, something of a hygiene freak, decided without even opening the bag that the best course of action was to go talk to the superintendent about this. She was going to his ground-floor office right away.

The superintendent, Kamiya, was a long-time widower who'd been the building's live-in super for ten years, ever since he'd retired from a hauling company. Although the job didn't pay well, the accommodations were free, and it was an ideal arrangement for an old man living on his own.

No sooner had Yoshimi handed him the bag than Mr. Kamiya unzipped it and emptied the contents on top of the office counter. A bright-red plastic cup bearing the same Kitty motif as the bag. A plastic wind-up frog whose legs were designed to flap. A little bear with a beach ring. It was clearly a three-in-one bath-time toy kit.

Ikuko cried out and started to reach for the toys, but yanked her hand back when her mother glared at her.

"How very odd," the superintendent mused. What puzzled him was not that someone had left a bag on the rooftop, but that a toy set that obviously belonged to some child was found on the premises of this building.

"You could display a notice and try to find the owner," Yoshimi suggested. Perhaps the owner would see the bag and claim it.

"But the only child in the building is little Ikuko—right, Ikuko?" the old man sought the girl's assent. She was gazing intently at the Kitty bag and red cup from where she stood beside her mother. It was only too obvious from her expression what outcome Ikuko desired. She wanted it: the bag, the toys. Annoyed by her wistful look, Yoshimi grabbed her by the shoulder and forced her to step back from the counter.

"You did mention that a family used to live on the second floor..." ventured Yoshimi.

Kamiya looked up in surprise and said: "Ah, yes."

"Didn't you say they had a little girl of five or six?"

"Indeed. Yes. But it's been two years."

"Two years? I thought you said they moved out last year."

The super hunched his back and began to scratch his ankle audibly. "Well, yes. They didn't move out until last summer."

Yoshimi remembered being told by the super, when she moved in three months ago, that a family who'd been living on the second floor had moved out of the building the previous year because there'd been some misfortune in the family. Yoshimi was guessing that it was they who'd somehow left the bag up on the roof.

Yet, neither the bag nor its plastic contents looked like they'd been exposed to the elements for a whole year up on the roof. The Kitty bag—which was without a speck of dust or grime, as brand-new as if it had just been purchased from the store—refuted the idea that it could've been abandoned for so long.

"All right then. I'll try displaying it on the counter for a while to see if we can find the owner."

In this way, the super sought to end the conversation. After all, it was only some cheap bag, and he couldn't care less if they found the owner or not.

Yoshimi, however, did not move from where she stood in front of the counter. Instead, she fingered her curly chestnut hair, debating whether to come right out with what she had on her mind.

"If the owner doesn't turn up, Ikuko, then you could have the bag, couldn't you?" Mr. Kamiya offered and smiled at Ikuko.

"No, that wouldn't be right. If the owner doesn't turn up, please dispose of the bag," Yoshimi turned down the offer with a resolute shake of her head. She then left the super's office, pushing Ikuko from behind as if to get her away from some contagious object.

Yet something troubled Yoshimi as they rode up in the elevator. She had avoided the subject of the so-called tragedy that was supposed to have befallen the family. After all, she did not want to appear the kind of person who entertained herself by talking about other people's misfortunes. But the question needled her and she longed to know the exact nature of that family's misfortune.

The next day was a Monday. Yoshimi spent longer than usual combing her hair that morning. From the living room she could hear the theme song of a children's television program. This melody served as a time signal, indicating on this particular morning that she still had plenty of minutes to spare before setting off for work. She would take Ikuko to the nursery school by nine o'clock, then catch a bus from the school for a twenty minute ride to her office in Shimbashi. The time and energy required to get to work here was truly nothing compared to what her commuting hassle used to be. It really made the move here worthwhile. Had they stayed in Musashino, she wouldn't have been able to put Ikuko into nursery school, and certainly couldn't have worked. She could always find another job, but it was unlikely that she'd ever find anything as good as her present position in the proofreading department of a publishing company. The job not only allowed her to devote herself to the world of the printed word, which was one of her passions, but there was no overtime and little need to associate with other people. On top of this, the pay was quite adequate. Ikuko came into the room with a pink ribbon and asked her mother to tie back her hair with it. The knot she had just tied had come loose and Ikuko's hair draped down, almost covering her shoulders.

As she touched her daughter's hair, she found herself surprised at how unmistakably the child had inherited her genes. It was strange that such an obvious fact should not have occurred to her until now. Their two faces looked identical in the three-sided mirror before them: the same chestnut-colored curly hair, the same white skin, and the same freckles under both eyes. One face belonged to a woman in her mid-thirties and the other was that of a little girl turning six.

"Noodles..." She remembered a boy once looking at her in high school and announcing that her hair looked as if someone had dumped a bowl of noodles on top of her head. She hated everything about herself in those days, her natural curls, her face, her freckles, and her skinny body. How many boys told her how passionately they felt about her in high school? It never occurred to her to count. She had no idea what they saw in her, and had to conclude that her criteria as to what constituted beauty were totally at odds with others. Everyone remarked on the beauty of her cute little face, freckles and all, and her natural brown hair, a rarity among Japanese. She simply didn't understand. When the boys caught on to her indifference, they began to make fun of her auburn hair behind her back. There were a lot of girls who knew how to handle things better, saying what they liked without the slightest risk of backbiting. Hiromi, a classmate in junior high school, was a typical example of that type.

With her hair now tied up, Ikuko said a quick "thank you" to her own reflection in the mirror rather than to her mother, and dashed back into the living room to watch television. Yoshimi could detect no trace of her former husband's physique or manner in Ikuko's figure. That at least was a blessing. She had never once found anything enjoyable about the physical union of man and woman. Her only word for it was "agonizing." Yet there is never any shortage of talk about sex in the world. She simply couldn't understand it. Perhaps some insurmountable barrier separated her from other people. They differed on everything from what constituted beauty and ugliness to definitions of pain and pleasure. The world as she perceived it was largely at odds with the world as others saw it.

When her husband learned of his wife's unwillingness to

accommodate his needs, he would often resort to solitary measures, casually tossing the tissue paper under the sofa. She once got some of the fluid on her fingertips when she'd inadvertently picked up a ball of tissue the following morning. The image of his idiotic expression of bliss came to her mind, leaving no room for the desire to understand. At such times, her entire body would shudder with extreme loathing and scorn.

The familiar voice of a female television announcer from the living room reminded Yoshimi that it was time to set out.

Ikuko thrust the door open and ran towards the elevator to press the down button before her mother. Once out of the elevator, they could only leave the building by the main front entrance by passing by the super's office. The red bag was on the counter. Yoshimi and Ikuko caught sight of it simultaneously. The Kitty bag that they'd found on the rooftop the evening before lay on the counter with its zipper closed, and with a notice on top. It read:

> Wanted: any information as to owner.
> Kamiya, superintendent

Though the super seemed to have acted on her suggestion, Yoshimi somehow thought it very unlikely that the owner would turn up.

Far from bringing a respite from the intense summer heat, the onset of September saw temperatures soar to record levels. During three days of abnormally intense heat, the bright red bag sporting the Kitty character was still visible on the black counter in the super's office. When Yoshimi saw the bag as she passed by every morning and evening, she found herself the victim of an inexplicable obsession. The bright-red bag seemed to symbolize flames. Then, as if to prove her notion true, the moment the bag was removed from the counter, the sweltering heat of late summer suddenly showed signs of receding. Had the owner turned up to claim the bag? Had the super simply disposed of it of his own accord? It no longer mattered either way. The bag no longer had anything to do with her. Another source of anxiety had arisen to take its place, however. She was suffering from work-related depression. After an interval of six years, she had once again to proofread the new novel of a writer of violent fiction she remembered only too well. Her boss had handed her the proofs as soon as she had arrived for work that morning.

The job involved finding errors in the manuscript. To do this, Yoshimi had to read meticulously through the work over and over again. Six years ago, she was completely unprepared for a manuscript by the same author that ended up traumatizing her. So great was the shock that she'd been pushed to the brink of a nervous breakdown. The brutal scenes depicted in the work etched themselves into her consciousness and even tormented her in the form of nightmares. She was on the verge of seeking psychiatric counseling in an attempt to rid herself of the adverse affects of working on the novel. She suffered waves of debilitating nausea on several occasions, lost her appetite, and shed eight pounds. She was also frequently unable to distinguish between illusion and reality.

She complained to the editor in charge of the project, demanding to know why the company handled work from such an author. With a haughty attitude, the editor, a young man still in his mid-twenties, explained that they were in no position to complain. The author's work sold well and that's all there was to it.

The remark only reminded Yoshimi once again just how high the barrier was that separated her from other people. She found it incredible that people were prepared to pay good money to read such a disgusting novel. The crowd that swarmed on the other side of the barrier had minds that functioned based on completely different principles than hers. As if that weren't enough, she was shocked the following year to come across the same book, though one issued in paperback by a different publisher, on her husband's shelves at home. The moment she set eyes on it, she was overcome with a sensation akin to terror, followed by the image of her husband enjoying gory fantasies aroused by the book. It deepened her resolve to divorce him.

Yoshimi caught sight of the red Kitty bag again the next Saturday morning. This time, she unexpectedly found it in the garbage facility provided for the apartment tenants. She had gone to put out some non-burnable waste and had lifted off the lid of the large polyethylene garbage bin. The red bag had been wedged between two black plastic bags. Although she did momentarily stop and stare at the bag, it was far from difficult to conclude how the bag had got there. The super had thrown it away in the belief that there was no likelihood of the owner ever turning up. As if nothing had happened, Yoshimi dumped her own sack crammed full of sorted waste on top of the red bag and covered the garbage bin with the lid.

That should have been the end. The bag was to be carted off in a garbage truck with the rest of the incombustible waste destined to form new groundwork for a landfill.

On the first Sunday in September, Yoshimi and Ikuko had gone to buy a few things at the neighborhood convenience store. They found that fireworks had been significantly discounted now that the summer season was nearly over. In fact, the price was so low that Yoshimi could not reasonably refuse Ikuko's pleas on grounds that fireworks were too expensive. The disappearance of the remaining fireworks from the store shelves would signal that the lingering embers of summer had finally gone out. Fond as she was of summer, even Yoshimi could not resist the allure of these last goods on the shelf, for there was something poignant about their impending disappearance. So Yoshimi found it perfectly natural when Ikuko said that she wanted to play with fireworks again that evening.

The two of them made their way up to the rooftop at exactly the same time in the evening as they had the week before. The instant she touched the knob to open the door of the penthouse, she was beset with an awful sense of foreboding. She felt an image in red flicker somewhere in her consciousness. As she pushed the door open, she found herself instinctively looking towards the right. Her line of vision locked onto its target in an instant, as if she had known all along that it would be there. An object of livid red highlighted the dark gray of the waterproofed surface of the rooftop. Despite the same poor visibility as the week before, the blazing red sped to the eye through the gloom.

"Oh..." Yoshimi stood with her mouth open and her entire frame rigid. She shrank back without a word, groping wildly with her hands behind her for her daughter. Ikuko, however, ducked in a flash, evading her mother's arms, and rushed over to the Kitty bag, which was placed exactly where it had been the week before.

"Stop!" Her voice trembled as she called her daughter back.

There was no explaining the dread she felt. Just as her daughter was about to pick the bag up, Yoshimi caught up with her, and swept the bag from her reach. The Kitty character on the side squished out of shape as the bag rolled over several times on the concrete. No question, it was the same one. The bag with the Kitty motif that they had discovered on the rooftop one week ago, the bag that had sat for three full days on the counter in the super's office before being thrown out unclaimed in the polyethylene garbage bin along with other garbage, that bag was here in front of them now. Undeterred, Ikuko reached out once again to where the bag had rolled. Yoshimi hit her hard.

"I said NO and I mean it!"

Her heart pounded violently in fear. She did not want her daughter to touch it. It was her instinctive loathing of strange objects. Ikuko stared wistfully at the bag and then looked up at her mother's face. Turning back to the bag, her face puckered and she burst into tears.

So much for fireworks. Yoshimi stroked her daughter's shoulders with a circular motion to comfort her as they went back into the penthouse and closed the door behind them. Nothing on earth would have induced her to lay a finger on that bag. She didn't want to bring it back to the super, and she never wanted to come up to the rooftop again.

More than anything else, she wanted to know how such a thing could possibly happen. The bag had been in the polyethylene garbage bin, so how on earth could it have made its way back up to the roof? Her temples ached. "Made its way back" had been an unconscious choice of expression—as if the bag had a life of its own.

As soon as they returned to the apartment, Yoshimi tried to put the chain on the door, but found that she had no control over her hands. Her legs also trembled. As she tried to remove her sandals, one flew awry and knocked down a pair of Ikuko's boots. Ikuko's expression was reproachful as she set the sandals and boots straight; her face clearly betrayed a hankering for that Kitty bag.

Yoshimi emerged from the bath first and began drying herself with a bath towel. She could hear her daughter's muffled voice coming from inside the bathroom. Her daughter would not leave the tub until she had put away the toys she played with in the water. She had also been brought up to always remove the plug after a bath.

With a bath towel wrapped around her chest, Yoshimi took a carton of milk from the refrigerator in the dining area and poured herself a glass. She made it a rule to drink a glass of milk before going to bed. It kept her bowels regular. Ikuko still showed no signs of getting out of the bath when Yoshimi had finished drinking her glass of milk. She bent down near the door and was about to tell Ikuko to get out of the bath when she heard her daughter talking to herself. She could only catch snatches.

"That's 'cos I'm playing all by myself... but... bear... no fair... It isn't yours...mi..."

The "Mi..." caught Yoshimi's attention as probably being the name of Ikuko's friend. But, as far as Yoshimi knew, none of Ikuko's friends at the nursery school or in the neighborhood where they used to live in Musashino had names beginning with "Mi." Who on earth was Ikuko having her imaginary conversation with then? Ikuko did have a classmate called Mikihiko, but she always called him by his surname instead.

Yoshimi opened the bathroom door. The "unit" bathroom was one of those comprising a bath and western-style toilet. A plastic washbasin floated on the water in the cream-colored bathtub. In the center of this basin was a small drenched towel that rose up in the form of a column. It somehow resembled a wayside *jizo* statue, but one with its head tilted to one side. Having soaked the towel and wrung it into this shape, Ikuko now seemed to be talking to the towel as if it were a playmate. A trickle of water dripped from the tap into the bath, linking the opening of the tap and the surface of the bathwater with a slender column. As the little washbasin floating in the bath came into contact with this column of water, it tilted a little and started spinning.

"Ikuko, what are you doing in there? Come out at once."

Immersed in the bathwater, Ikuko had her back to the door when she answered her mother.

"My friend loves taking a bath all by herself. She never, ever gets out."

Yoshimi asked herself again who on earth her "friend"

might be.

"Never mind. Just get out," she told her daughter.

Ikuko put the washbasin in the sink and stood up with a swoosh. Yoshimi wrapped Ikuko in a bath towel and held her. Despite having been immersed in the tub for so long, Ikuko's shoulders were strangely cold to the touch.

Ikuko fell asleep on her futon, with the picture book she had been reading open in front of her. Yoshimi debated whether to stay up for a while and read, but finally decided to turn the light off and go to sleep. She fell asleep as soon as she pulled the light summer sheet over her chest.

She had been asleep for about two hours when her consciousness began to edge its way back up from slumber to wakefulness; her casually extended hand could no longer detect that familiar warm presence at her side. Yoshimi's body rolled frantically to and fro. Sliding her hand along her side, she could feel nothing. She was wide-awake in an instant. Half sitting up, she groped the surface of the futon where Ikuko had been sleeping, and began calling her daughter's name. The tiny nightlight at the foot of the futon was enough to reveal the emptiness of the small room: Ikuko wasn't there.

"Ikuko! Ikuko!" Yoshimi tried shouting louder.

This kind of thing had never happened before. Ikuko was a deep sleeper. Once she had snuggled down to sleep, she always slept soundly through to the next morning without ever waking up during the night. She would rarely get up to go to the toilet.

After checking the living room and dining area, Yoshimi was about to check the toilet, but the bathroom light was out so Ikuko obviously wasn't there. Just then, she heard the sound of tiny footsteps in the passage outside.

Yoshimi dashed to the door, where she noticed that the door chain was not fastened. Did she forget to fasten the chain when they returned from the rooftop, or did Ikuko unchain the door?

Unconcerned about being clad in nothing more than her negligee, she rushed out into the corridor outside. She could hear the sound of the elevator moving. The elevator hall was halfway down the corridor. She stood there and watched the floor numbers light up in succession. The fifth-floor lamp went out and the sixth-floor lamp came on. Then the sixth-floor lamp went out, the seventh-floor lamp blinked on, and it stopped. The elevator had gone to the top floor, where no one lived. Someone had just gotten off on the seventh floor. In that instant she suspected that that someone was Ikuko. That suspicion was being confirmed in her mind. Ikuko could not bear the thought of the red Kitty bag being left out there on the apartment rooftop, Yoshimi concluded. She must have been desperate for that bag. At the same time, though, Ikuko knew better than to believe that her mother would allow her to pick up something that someone else had thrown away. That's why she had waited until her mother was asleep before heading for the apartment rooftop. Although Yoshimi doubted that Ikuko had the courage to overcome her fear of the dark, she pressed the elevator button to call the cage back down from the seventh floor. The elevator stirred, made its way down to the fourth floor, and flung its doors open. Yoshimi pulled the sides of her negligee close together over her chest as she entered the elevator. She pushed the button for the seventh floor, only to feel the elevator plunge softly downward, contrary to her expectations. Yoshimi took several steps away from the door, until her back was against the wall of the elevator. She brought her clenched elbows together to cover her chest more closely.

"Oh dear, someone's getting on."

That someone, thought Yoshimi, must have called the elevator from one of the floors below before she pushed the button at her end. Whoever it was had to be on the first floor, actually. No doubt it was one of those men living alone on the fifth or sixth floor coming home drunk. It was already past one o'clock in the morning. Her horror of being harassed by a drunk made her resent the cramped elevator itself, which offered her no means of escape. As the elevator began its descent, the scorched buttons began to light in succession.

The elevator came to a sudden halt. She looked up at the row of numbers indicating the floor. It had stopped at two.

...Why the second floor?

She braced herself. She'd never get used to riding elevators late at night; it was a nerve-wracking experience. The doors opened, but no one was waiting for the elevator. Yoshimi gasped, made her way slowly forward, then peered outside, scanning both sides twice. The dark deserted passage seemed to stretch on to infinity. Obviously, there was no one there. Who on earth then, had summoned the elevator? The doors started to slide shut automatically. Yoshimi stepped back reflexively. Yet, the second before the door had shut completely, she was quite certain that she sensed a presence steal swiftly into the elevator. Maybe it was just her imagination, but temperature in the confined space of the elevator seemed to have dropped suddenly. She was not alone in the elevator; there was something else with her. She felt someone's breath on her abdomen, the kind that turns white on a cold winter's day.

The elevator made its ascent, then stopped at the seventh floor.

When she reached the landing of the staircase leading to the rooftop from the seventh floor, Yoshimi turned on the lights of the penthouse. Two fluorescent tubes on the ceiling flickered to life. Encouraged by the light, Yoshimi bounded up the staircase to the rooftop.

She pushed the door wide open and left it there so that the fluorescent lighting would spill out to the roof.

"Ikuko!" she called.

No matter how much she strained her eyes, she couldn't locate the small figure she sought. She looked down from the western edge of the rooftop, but the light of the streetlamps along the road did not show the dark stain that would signal tragedy. She heaved a sigh of relief. Ikuko hadn't fallen to her death. The northern, southern, and eastern sides of the building all had balconies protruding on the seventh floor. Even if Ikuko had fallen, the fall wouldn't be fatal.

…Where did she go?

Yoshimi's stomach threatened to rise to her gorge. Who knew? Ikuko could be somewhere in the apartment. Was it too much to hope? Such thoughts passed through her mind as she looked back at the penthouse. The white fluorescent light spilled out onto the rooftop. Immediately above the penthouse sat the creamy-skinned overhead water tank, held aloft by a turret of iron poles. Bathed in light from beneath, the coffin-shaped body protruded straight up in the center of the clear night sky, holding water within its walls. This was where the household water was collected and stored before being fed to each of the apartments below.

Two cord-like objects could be seen swaying in the shadows of iron poles that supported the overhead tank. Straining her eyes further, Yoshimi was just able to make out a tiny shadow playing under the tank. It puzzled her that she could only see the shadow, but not the object casting it. The image she began to conjure up in her mind was that of a little girl crouching directly beneath the overhead water tower.

"Ikuko, is that you?"

There was no reply. To search the top of the penthouse, she'd have to scale the perpendicular aluminum ladder set in the concrete wall of the penthouse. It was a climb straight up of more than six feet that would fully engage both her hands and feet. Though such a climb, crawling spider-like up the side of a wall, would normally be difficult for someone of Yoshimi's delicate build, she hauled herself up, fueled by the desperate desire to get a look at what was up there. No more than halfway up, she looked down to gauge how far she had climbed. She spied a dark object lodged in the darkness of the drain that ran the length of the penthouse wall. It was just where it had been the night before, where she had swept it from Ikuko's grasp and caused it to roll away. Yoshimi's mind began to race in confusion. Something didn't fit. She was missing some essential point.

It couldn't have been Ikuko!

Her right foot almost missed a step as this realization came to her. It could not have been Ikuko who'd come up to the seventh floor in the elevator; her daughter was too short to be able to reach the button for the seventh floor. A shiver ran down Yoshimi's spine. As she looked up she saw the shadow gaining greater substance. There could be no doubt that someone or something was up there. She heard the joints in her legs crack from the strain.

…If it wasn't her daughter, who was it?

She only needed to heave herself up a little further to have her entire face level with the upper edge. Yet her courage failed her. All kinds of images flashed one after another in her mind's eye. Her body stiffened, making it difficult to climb up or down.

At that instant, she heard the voice that she most longed to hear, calling out from directly beneath her.

"Mommy."

Yoshimi's strength nearly left her. Her exhaustion was so great that it was all she could do to keep her hands and feet from losing their hold on the aluminum ladder. Her jaw pressing against her left arm pit, she saw Ikuko standing there in pajamas.

"Mommy? What are you doing up there?"

There was a hint of reproach in Ikuko's tearful question.

In the morning, she led her daughter by the hand to the elevator at the usual time. Once in the elevator, she noticed that the straining sound of the elevator cable was subtly different from how it had sounded late last night, although she couldn't articulate the exact change. All she could say was that the light of day had brought a totally different nuance to the noise. Yoshimi unconsciously tightened her grip on

Ikuko's hand.

Yoshimi had spent a sleepless night during which she had repeatedly asked herself whether Ikuko had lied, or whether her own behavior had been the impulsive result of an obsessive delusion.

Ikuko had insisted that she'd been in the bathroom when her mother had inexplicably dashed out of doors. "You can't imagine how hard it was to go up the stairs to the rooftop by myself! What on earth were you doing there?" her daughter had said.

Seeing her mother clinging to the wall of the penthouse, Ikuko's heart pounded violently as if to prove that she'd just rushed up the stairs. The anger in her voice came from the terror of having been left alone. As an infant, she would always cry hysterically if she ever woke up to find herself alone. She couldn't possibly have been feigning all this. It must have happened just as Ikuko said it had. Yoshimi had rushed out into the passage without thinking that her daughter might have gone to the bathroom without turning the light on. The numbers on the elevator floor indicator had put the notion of the rooftop in her head. In the absence of any other possible interpretation, she had to take her daughter's word for it. While she was ashamed over having behaved like a possessed woman, something still failed to convince her. Why did the elevator stop at the second floor? There had been nobody there. Yoshimi remembered quite distinctly the presence that had sneaked into the elevator. She remembered the moment the warm air had turned chilly inside the elevator.

As soon as the elevator doors slid open on the first floor, Yoshimi took in the morning sun as it streamed all the way to the center of the lobby. The powerful rays of the sun seemed to banish the morbid aura of the night before. She spied the super ahead of her, broom in hand.

"Morning, ma'am," he greeted her with a broad smile.

Yoshimi tried to walk past, avoiding his gaze and with only a token greeting. But changing her mind, she stopped and said, "Excuse me."

"Ah, if it's about that bag..." he offered.

"No, it's not that." There was something else on her mind that Yoshimi didn't know whether to ask him or not.

He no longer held his broom upright, and his hand hanging casually by his side, he turned to Ikuko and asked affably, "You'll be on your way to nursery school, then?"

"It's nothing to do with me, I know, but you mentioned that the family that used to live on the second floor suffered some kind of tragedy. What exactly was it that..."

Yoshimi let her inquiry trail off unfinished. The super reined in the cheery smile, contriving an expression more suited to recounting the misfortunes of others.

"Ah, that? Well, it all happened two years ago. The little girl was about the same age as little Ikuko is now. She was playing somewhere around here and went missing, you see."

Yoshimi placed her hands on Ikuko's shoulders and pulled her daughter closer to her.

"When you say that she went missing, do you mean she was kidnapped?

The super leaned his head to one side. "I don't think it was done for a ransom. You see, the police turned it into an open criminal investigation."

As long as there was a possibility that a kidnapping has

been committed with a view to financial gain, the police conducted its investigation with utmost secrecy. But as soon as the possibility was ruled out, they usually launched a public investigation and announced it to the media. That way they could obtain more information faster.

"So you're saying that they..."

The super shook his head. "They never found her. For nearly a year, the parents never gave up hope that she'd return. In any case, when there was that move to buy up the apartments, it was Mr. and Mrs. Kawai on the second floor who objected most. They felt that if the apartment block were demolished, their daughter would have no place to return to. But in the end, they probably did give up hope. At any rate, they moved to Yokohama last summer."

"They were called Kawai, the family?"

"Yes, that's right. Mitchan—that was the little girl's name—she was a lovely little girl. There are some evil people in the world, and that's a fact."

"Did you say 'Mitchan'?"

"Her name was Mitsuko; we called her Mitchan."

Mi, Mitchan, Mitsuko...the imaginary playmate that Ikuko was talking to in the bath. It all began to take shape, to fit into place, with that name. That column-like figure that Ikuko had fashioned out of a soaked hand towel and set up in the middle of the washbasin, the figure resembling a road-side *jizo* statue that Ikuko had chattered to like a friend, the figure that her daughter had called Mitsuko.

Yoshimi felt the blood drain from her face. Placing her hands on her temples, she sought support against the wall, and slowly let out a deep breath.

"Is anything the matter?"

She tried to deflect the super's concern by glancing at her watch. There was no time to explain. If they didn't hurry they'd miss their bus. She gave a slight bow in the direction of the super and quickly left the lobby.

To learn more, she could take advantage of the odd spare moment at work to go through the newspaper archives on microfiche. Even without an exact date, she was sure to find an article concerning the disappearance of a small girl named Mitsuko Kawai without difficulty if she looked meticulously through the newspapers from two years ago. From what the super had said, it seemed clear that Mitsuko hadn't been found. She had probably either been abducted by some pervert or had fallen into the canal. Either way, the poor girl no doubt lay dead and undiscovered somewhere.

About eight o'clock in the evening that day, Yoshimi had just turned on the hot water for a bath when the telephone rang. She let the water run and hurried into the living room to pick up the phone.

It was from the super's office. "You'll have to forgive me. I've gone and sprained my left ankle."

The super's remark made no sense to Yoshimi, who was at a loss to reply with anything but an "Oh." She had no idea why he was calling. It was only after giving an account of how he sustained the injury to his foot that he finally got to the point.

"There's a delivery for you."

She finally caught his drift. The super would often accept her home deliveries because she was seldom home during the day. Usually he brought the deliveries up to her. What he was driving at was that his sprained ankle prevented him from doing so. If the package required urgent attention, he wanted to ask if she'd mind coming down to his office to collect it herself. She knew whom the delivery was from, and it was nothing that couldn't wait. Still, she thanked the super for his trouble and, before putting the phone down, told him she was coming right away.

Upon reaching the super's office, she saw that there was a cardboard box on the counter. The super stood with his elbows on the box. As she thought, it was from her friend Hiromi. Hiromi had a daughter who would be starting elementary school, and she had kindly taken the trouble to send Ikuko the clothes and shoes that her daughter had outgrown.

She found the box surprisingly heavy and could understand why it had been too much for the super with his sprained ankle.

"Is your ankle all right?" She affected concern by drawing her eyebrows together.

"Nature's way of telling a foolish old man he's not as young as he used to be." The super laughed as he said this and betrayed signs that he wanted her to ask him how he had sprained his ankle.

However, Yoshimi's interest lay elsewhere. During the day, she had gone to her firm's archives to look through all the newspapers dated between July and October of the year before last. She had not succeeded in finding any article that reported Mitsuko's case. Yoshimi found "the year before last" not precise enough for her liking. She wanted an exact date.

She didn't really expect the old man to remember, but

she tried asking all the same.

"Just a minute," he replied as he checked inside the counter, bending down awkwardly. He brought out a thick battered notebook and thumped it down on the countertop.

The cover bore the words "Superintendent's Log" in thick black felt pen. Apparently he was in the habit of recording each day's events in the logbook so he could furnish his employer with some kind of report. The super muttered to himself as he licked his finger and turned the pages.

"Yes, here we are. Look."

He turned the notebook upside down and slid it across to her. The page was dated March 17th two years ago. It was now September, so, to be precise, they were not talking about something that happened two years ago, but rather, two and a half years ago. Even the time of day was recorded in the notebook. The authorities had concluded that there was no further justification for handling the disappearance of Mitsuko Kawai of apartment 205 as a case of financially motivated abduction and consequently turned the investigation into an open inquiry, at 11.30 p.m. Yoshimi committed the exact date and time to memory. As she was about to return the notebook to the super, an image of that flesh-colored overhead water tank flashed through her mind, though she didn't know why. No doubt the image had come through an association with some word or words. What had set it off were the following words, written higher up under the same date heading of March 17th.

Cleaning operations performed on intake tank and overhead tank. Water inspection conducted.

There it was—the overhead tank.

This was the same overhead tank that floated like a giant coffin in the starry night sky. The cleaning operations in question had been performed on the same day Mitsuko Kawai had gone missing. Two cleaners hired by the building management had come and worked inside the water tank.

Yoshimi let out an inaudible scream.

"The water tank..." Yoshimi paused to take a breath. "Is the lid of the tank usually kept locked?"

The super tilted his head to one side, puzzled as to why Yoshimi had turned the conversation to the water tank. But when he saw the entry in his own log about the cleaning operations, a look of satisfaction registered on his face.

"Ah, this? Yes, under normal circumstances, it's kept carefully locked."

"When is the tank opened? Only when it's cleaned?"

"Of course, of course."

Yoshimi put her hands around the cardboard box. "Has the tank been cleaned since?"

"Ehh, we don't have a maintenance association here, so it's..."

"Has it been cleaned?" she repeated, unable to bottle her impatience.

"Well, it's about time they got down it again. It's been two years."

"I see."

Lifting the box, Yoshimi staggered backwards and reeled out of the office. So unsteady was her gait that it was a wonder she made it back to her apartment without stumbling.

Being careful not to touch the water in the bathtub, she pulled out the plug and watched the water level drop gradually. She no longer felt like taking a bath. Ikuko had plaintively asked again and again why they couldn't take a bath that day. Her persistence had seemed unending; only a minute ago had she finally fallen asleep. To all appearances, the water looked perfectly clean. Yet Yoshimi couldn't but picture the particles floating in it.

She opened the kitchen cupboard, took out the bottle of sake she kept there for cooking, and poured herself a glass. Although alcohol did not really agree with her, she felt that she was not likely to get any sleep without it that night.

She made an effort to think about something else. The novel by that writer of violent fiction, the novel she was proofreading at work, would do as well as anything else to occupy her thoughts. What she needed to do was to recall some of those appalling scenes and thereby sever the chain of associations. Yet this just wasn't possible; the swelling images always converged on one point. The red bag with the Kitty motif that was found on the rooftop, the missing child Mitsuko, the fleeting shadow under the tank, the mysterious stop made by the elevator at the second floor. The evening before, a thin stream of water had linked the bathroom in their apartment with the overhead water tank on the roof. Immersed in the bathwater, Ikuko had been talking openly to Mitsuko as if she were actually there. All this led to a sole conclusion. Yoshimi forced herself to block out this train of thought with a scene from the novel she'd been proofing. In that fictitious world thick with the stench of gore, a punk had been abducted and confined by a rival gang, who were subjecting him to a series of brutal beatings, when purely by coincidence... Yes, that was it: she should think of it as a coincidence. The overhead water tank just happened to be cleaned the very day little Mitsuko disappeared. How absurd to think it could have been anything other than coincidence. Yes, now that she thought about it, every part of it could be explained rationally. In the case of the Kitty bag, neighborhood children had put it on the rooftop in some kind of ritual, out of some childlike fancy, perhaps to signal a UFO. No doubt the children had seen the bag in the garbage dump, retrieved it, then quickly returned it to the rooftop. The elevator had stopped at the second floor quite simply because someone living on that floor had pressed the button with the intent of going down. When the elevator started dithering at the fourth floor, however, he or she had clearly lost patience and decided to walk down the stairway. That was why there hadn't been anyone waiting when the door opened.

By forcibly disconnecting one event from another, Yoshimi sought to find a logical underpinning for each mangled fragment. Yet no matter how hard she tried to disrupt her train of thought, the severed fragments would instantly link up again, like some serpent growing larger every time it reconnected. She was already aware of the truth, but didn't want to accept it. The one and only possible conclusion. The inescapable conclusion.

There was no mistaking it, Mitchan was in that overhead tank on the rooftop.

She tried to suppress the thought, only to have the scene unfold in her mind. While the cleaners were away on their lunch break, the little girl had either fallen in the tank or been intentionally thrown in by someone. The decomposing corpse. The Kitty bag she clasped so tightly. The water-filled coffin. She had been drinking that water for the past three months. She had cooked with it, made coffee and chilled summer drinks with it. How many times had they soaked in hot bathwater that teemed with countless putrid cells? How many times had they washed their hands and their faces in it? More than you could tally.

Yoshimi pressed her hands to her mouth. The odor of sake mixed with an eruption of gastric juices. She made a dash for the bathroom, crouched down over the toilet bowl, and vomited. Her eyes were bloodshot. A stinging sensation burned the back of her throat and nose. She flushed the toilet, the water immediately streaming into the bowl before her eyes and swallowing up her vomit in its downward spiral. What remained was to all appearances clear water. The water that trickled down to cleanse the toilet bowl contained skin cells, which had peeled off; it teemed with little pieces of hair, fine, downy hair. Her feeling of nausea did not abate. Yet there remained nothing more to bring up.

As she wiped her mouth with toilet paper, Yoshimi coughed violently again and again from the choking sensation in her throat. She remained in her crouched position, waiting for her breathing to settle. It was then that she heard it. The sound of water dripping one drop at a time into the bathtub beside her. She thought she had turned off the tap tightly. Still, a tiny amount of water seemed to be leaking through. Her knees pressed against the floor, she clasped the toilet bowl with both arms. She frantically swallowed back the saliva, trying to prevent her delusions from becoming reality. Hallucinations! It was obvious. Hallucinations coursed through her very veins. She saw something that looked like the corpse of a little girl floating in the foul water that had collected in the bath. The face was purple and swollen to almost twice its original size. She tried to scream "Stop!" and fell back on the wet floor. A red plastic beaker floated near the breast of the corpse. A green plastic wind-up frog swam across the surface of the water, its front and back legs jerking busily. The frog bumped into the shoulder of the corpse, swam away, and returned to bump into the same shoulder, over and over again, each time gouging a tiny piece of flesh from the corpse with its plastic claws. The bright-red bag with the Kitty motif bobbed up and down, its strap held tight in the grasp of the corpse, the bone of whose clenched hands showed in places.

Apart from jerky gasps, Yoshimi had all but stopped breathing. The stench that assailed her nostrils was not unlike that of rotting kitchen waste. As she tried to avert her eyes from the putrefying corpse whose stench filled the bathroom, she struck her head on the door and collapsed in a heap, her cheek striking the chilly wooden floor of the corridor. She was quickly losing consciousness. A voice from far off that sounded like the chirping of a small bird penetrated the gloomy boundary between consciousness and darkness.

"Mommy! Mommy!"

Yoshimi's retina registered the form of Ikuko clad in baggy pajamas.

Her hand on the nape of her mother's neck, Ikuko's trembling voice turned to sobs. The tiny hand moved back and forth near Yoshimi's ear. This was Yoshimi's only reality, the warmth and tiny proportions of Ikuko's hand. The tiny body brimming with life was enough to banish her hallucination.

"Help me up."

The plea was but a hoarse whisper. Ikuko put her hands under her mother's arms and heaved with all her might. Once Ikuko had her mother sitting up, Yoshimi put one hand on the edge of the bath and managed to stand up on her own. The jumper skirt she always wore at home was soaked from the waist down. She glanced at the bath and found that countless droplets of water clung precariously to the gleaming cream curves of the bath. The awareness that she had been hallucinating hadn't been enough to fend off the hallucinations. Amid sobs, Ikuko looked up at her mother and simply murmured "Mommy..." It would take enormous emotional strength to be a good mother to her. Yoshimi felt ashamed of herself for her near collapse. Incited by her daughter's sobs, she too began to weep.

As they crossed the bridge over the canal, Yoshimi resisted the impulse to turn back and look at the apartment building. She carried a bag containing their valuables and a change of clothes. Each time she shifted the bag from one hand to another, Ikuko would also switch sides so as to keep a firm grip on her mother's empty hand.

Her behavior must have appeared very silly. Yet it was impossible to live even one more day in an apartment whose water supply was unusable. Tonight, if only for a single night, she wanted to sleep soundly. The water tank could be checked the next day. Convincing the super to have the tank examined, opening the lid, and looking in—these were things better done in the light of day.

The ground felt no more secure across the canal bridge than on the landfill. Yoshimi saw an approaching taxi with a vacancy light and hailed it. She helped Ikuko into the back seat and bent down to get in herself. As she did so, she caught a fleeting glimpse of the rooftop of the apartment building. There, dwarfed by the distance, loomed the flesh-colored water tank, high above the reclaimed ground. Was little Mitsuko still having fun splashing about in that sealed rectangular bath of hers? Whatever the case, Yoshimi wanted to sleep well. As she slid into the back seat, she gave the taxi driver the name of a hotel.

SOLITARY ISLE

1

He had often considered leaving the teaching profession. He was fed up with it all, the same routine year in year out; he simply wasn't getting anywhere in life. The urge to quit had been particularly strong this May. But then he had received his bonus payment and summer vacation beckoned, inducing him to think that teaching might not be so bad after all. He was prepared to give it a try for a little while longer. It had been the same the year before: he had been on the verge of quitting in May, only to reconsider, deciding in July to give it a go for a bit longer. Summer vacation was not only for the benefit of students; it also served as a perk for teachers who would otherwise seek employment elsewhere. He was absolutely certain that without summer vacation, he'd have given up this teaching lark years ago.

Kensuke Suehiro was going over all this in his mind as he walked down the corridor after his last lesson of the afternoon. He had entered the teaching profession eight or nine years ago right after graduating from one of Tokyo's national universities. That university had formerly been a "normal school" specializing in the training of teachers, which probably accounted for many of his classmates' intention to pursue the vocation. As for Kensuke, he'd been swept along by the prevailing current and had found himself in the teaching profession before he knew it.

As he stacked notebooks on his desk in the staffroom, he noticed a handwritten memo: "There was a call for you from Mr. Sasaki of Josei Junior High School."

Just reading the words "Mr. Sasaki" aroused fond memories. Sasaki meant a great deal to Kensuke. He'd been Kensuke's respected teacher and mentor. Sasaki had been the head of teachers in charge of seventh graders when Kensuke had been assigned to his first middle school post after graduation. That school was in Tokyo, and Sasaki, like Kensuke, taught science. Not only had Kensuke learned a great deal from him about natural science in general, but Sasaki had also supported and helped Kensuke in many ways, both privately and professionally. Sasaki had a distinctively original approach to teaching. Rather than stuffing the heads of his students with facts, he tried to draw out their latent capabilities by letting them experience natural phenomena for themselves. Some of these activities included taking his students on field trips to collect butterflies in the hilly marshlands or staying up all night with them to observe comets. It was when they ceased to be colleagues that Kensuke's passion for teaching began to wane. Sasaki, along with his distinctive approach to teaching, had moved on to another school. This alone had been enough to sap Kensuke's motivation. The transfer occurred five years ago, and for the past couple of years their relationship amounted to no more than the customary exchange of New Year's greeting cards. Nothing could have delighted Kensuke more than learning that Sasaki had called him.

Kensuke wasted no time in calling Josei Junior High School and asking for the headmaster. Sasaki had just assumed that post in the regular spring reshuffling of personnel. "This is Kensuke Suehiro. I'd like to..." The moment Kensuke had given his name, the voice at the other end answered unceremoniously, "Hey, it's me." Sasaki may have become a headmaster, but Kensuke was relieved that his old mentor had not changed his manner in the least.

"Please excuse me for my long silence," Kensuke apologized to his mentor, bowing unconsciously though he was talking over the phone.

"Sorry I called you during one of your lessons. It'd never have happened before, but I've lost my touch since I became headmaster. It was a lot more fun when I actually had classes to teach."

This remark was no doubt sincere. Sasaki was the kind of teacher much more suited to be in the classroom than on the careerist ladder. Kensuke wished he could transfer to Josei so he could work under a headmaster like Sasaki. A boss like him would relieve a lot of the job's stress.

"Say, how would you feel about going to Battery No. 6?" asked Sasaki point-blank, dispensing with pleasantries.

"Battery No. 6? You mean..."

"Yes, *that* Battery No. 6, the one under the Rainbow Bridge...the ghost island."

Kensuke found himself unable to speak. Little had he imagined that Sasaki had called to invite him to an uninhabited artificial island in Tokyo Bay that had held a special significance for Kensuke for the past nine years.

"How are we going to get there?" Kensuke sounded puzzled.

"Leave that to me."

"I think you'll find that the island is off-limits."

Sasaki lowered his voice to a whisper. "We'll swim there in the dead of night so no one's the wiser. Think your swimming's up to it?"

The Tokyo Metropolitan Government had restricted access to Battery No. 6 as a means of conserving it as a cultural asset.

"That's hardly the kind of suggestion you'd expect to hear from a headmaster. After all, you're a respected figure in the community."

"Respected figure!" Sasaki laughed. "You know how to strike where it hurts. But, come to think of it, you never had much nerve did you? Did you really expect that a pillar of the community like me would secretly go ashore in violation of the law? I'm talking about an on-site survey, okay, *an on-site survey.*"

"On-site survey..."

"Yes, the Minato Ward authorities have asked me to head an on-site survey."

Sasaki went on to explain what had happened. He had received a request from a special committee of the Ward Council to undertake a survey of conditions on Battery No. 6—the flora and fauna, the soil, and such. There was a note of pride in his voice as he described how it had all come about. It would have helped a lot and avoided much confusion had he explained all this to Kensuke at the outset. Although municipal officials and ward councilors were to take part in the survey, apparently there was room for others as well, and the city was looking for someone interested in natural science.

Sasaki's style never changed. He had to take the other by surprise first, and clarified only then.

"When is the survey due to take place?" Kensuke was

already asking about the schedule.

"Can I take it you're game?"

"Of course. I wouldn't miss it for the world."

Not only did Kensuke now have the opportunity to visit Battery No. 6, but also to do so legally. All he had to do was tag along. Now he'd certainly find out. The moment he set foot on the island, the bewitching creature that had dwelt in his mind for the past nine years would no doubt vanish.

Once Sasaki had given him the details about when and where the expedition was to get under way, Kensuke bowed deeply into the telephone, saying, "I'm really very grateful for this opportunity."

Sasaki's response to this expression of gratitude was hard to decipher: "Well, do your best."

2

The bewitching creature that had come to dwell on Battery No. 6 was a phantom by the name of Yukari Nakazawa. Phantom she was, but not one of the realm of spirits. Kensuke believed that Yukari Nakazawa was alive and well somewhere other than on Battery No. 6; and he hoped he was right.

He had first met her at about the same time of year nine years ago. He had been in his fourth year at the university and summer vacation had just begun. If not for the sound of that car horn, he would have never known that she existed. Until that instant, he had assumed that Toshihiro Aso had come alone on his visit.

Kensuke and Aso had been classmates in elementary and junior high. Both attended a well-known private school that assured its students passage all the way through college. When it had come time to enter high school, however, Kensuke found it impossible to deal with the traditional aspects of the private high and transferred out to a public school. In contrast to Kensuke, who was a reserved and introverted, Aso became not only captain of the rugby team, but also one of the school's academic stars. True to his childhood ambition, Aso succeeded in entering the department of medicine at his university. Although attending different high schools should have resulted in them going their separate ways, they continued to remain close friends for more than ten years. Though apparently complete opposites, the school hero and the dropout got on amazingly well with each other.

That evening, Aso had suddenly turned up at Kensuke's studio apartment in Azabu. It was already past nine, but Aso had brought a case of beer and invited Kensuke to drink with him. In under an hour, they had downed more than a dozen cans of beer between them. Aso drank so fast that he was already shuttling back and forth to the toilet to relieve himself. He could hold his liquor and wasn't one to get drunk on beer, but, upon consuming a certain amount of beer, he seemed to need to visit the toilet with increasing frequency to empty his bladder. His cascade hitting the toilet bowl, he peed sonorously like he meant for it to be loud. Once finished, he'd linger a while before flushing the toilet. It was during one of these momentary interludes of silence that Kensuke had heard the sounding of the car horn. Unable to resist wondering about the source of the honking horn, he went out onto the balcony and looked down on the one-way street below.

Despite being four floors up, Kensuke immediately realized that someone was honking at Aso's BMW. The BMW was parked right in front of the curb, making it impossible for a large minivan to negotiate the turn. Aso was going to have to go down there and move his car. But sooner than he thought this, Kensuke saw the BMW begin to back up. The car could not have moved by itself. There was someone inside. When Aso returned from the toilet, Kensuke asked him what was going on.

"Did you leave someone down there in your car?"

"Ha! No need to worry."

"Why don't you park your car in our garage and call your friend up?"

Kensuke's parents had built the apartment building on this site to replace their old home when the time had come to rebuild it. His family took the entire first floor of the building and rented out the three floors above. Although there was enough room for Kensuke on the ground floor, he preferred to live alone, and his parents let him have a single-room apartment on the top floor. His parents had their own parking space set aside in their private garden. It was spacious enough to accommodate at least two cars. A third car could squeeze in there with a bit of maneuvering. It was hardly necessary to keep someone waiting in the car out there at the roadside.

Without waiting for Aso's consent, Kensuke went down and moved his parents' cars to make room for the BMW. He then walked over to the BMW and knocked on the windshield, gesturing to the driver inside to park in the extra space. In the driver's seat sat a woman with a pale complexion and long hair.

This didn't surprise Kensuke very much. Aso often dropped by like this, leaving a lady in his car. But never for longer than half an hour. More often than not, he'd drop in and leave soon afterwards because he'd left so-and-so down in the car. That night, however, Aso had kept the woman waiting in the car for well over an hour. As far as Kensuke knew, this was the longest he'd ever dared to.

"I'm so sorry," Kensuke apologized to the woman on behalf of his thoughtless friend. He wanted her to know that if he'd noticed earlier, she'd never have been left alone so long. "Aso never mentioned you were waiting down here," he said.

Staring at the dashboard, she simply shook her head as if

embarrassed.

"Why don't you come up and join us?"

Although he was unsure how Aso would react, Kensuke thought it better to invite the woman into his home. She nodded and got out of the car. As she introduced herself, she spoke with a lisp:

"I'm Yukari Nakazawa."

As they walked along the passage and rode in the elevator, Kensuke could not stop looking at the woman, this Yukari Nakazawa. Aso had introduced Kensuke to many girlfriends in the past, but Yukari was quite different from all the others. First and foremost, she wasn't glamorous. Her petite body was well proportioned but she had only average looks, and she walked with downcast eyes in this terribly morose way. The red bag she carried under her arm looked so infantile that it would have made a schoolgirl blush. Her cheap-looking clothes had clearly been picked from a mail-order catalog. Yet her skirt revealed legs that were gorgeously slender, tapering down to firm and compact ankles. Kensuke found it difficult not to stare at her bare legs. Her entire appeal converged on her legs.

Aso was obviously not pleased when Kensuke returned to the apartment with Yukari. Peeved, he insisted that they were leaving right away. Kensuke appeased him, going out of his way to lighten up the mood and urging them both to stay and have a little more to drink. The situation became increasingly clear to Kensuke as the three of them talked together. Aso had wanted to avoid introducing Yukari to him. There was little denying that she did not compare with his past girlfriends. That must've been it. Aso indeed went haywire, perhaps feeling defensive, and began insulting Yukari.

"This woman has had no education to speak of, pal. She didn't even make it through high school."

"I knew she wouldn't be able to join our conversation. She's so stupid, everything goes straight over her head."

"As if that's not bad enough, she's up to *here* in some weirdo religious cult!"

"I can't show her around in public, can I?"

No matter how badly Aso trashed her, Yukari would only lower the corners of her mouth and look desolate, but show no hint of anger. She'd wait for hours on end in an illegally parked car if she were told to stay put. Women who would offer submissive loyalty in return for numbing brutality were an increasingly rare phenomenon. Kensuke could not for the life of him understand why Aso went out with Yukari. Surely there was absolutely no reason to be with her if he intended only to revile the poor girl. Yukari, too, could surely find someone more compatible than Aso.

It soon became clear that it was not to be the kind of pleasant chat among three friends that he had expected. The more Aso drank, the more vicious the abuse he heaped on Yukari. Unable to endure the torment any longer, Kensuke announced that the party had to end. He was doing the unthinkable; he was asking Aso to leave.

Kensuke walked them down to the car. Aso was already showing signs of being too drunk, so Kensuke sat him in the passenger seat. Yukari could drive. But Aso insisted that he was driving, and demanded a can of coffee. Kensuke ran to a nearby automatic vending machine and brought back cans of chilled coffee. He first handed a can to Yukari, who responded by taking a card from her bag and offering it to Kensuke.

"Please don't hesitate to drop by whenever you're in the neighborhood."

This did not escape Aso's attention.

"You stupid bitch!" he snarled, striking her hand aside and sending her calling card flying. Aso then grabbed her wrists and twisted her arms behind her back, forcing her head down. "He happens to be a good friend of mine. Don't you lure him anywhere nasty, get it?"

Yukari gave a small cry of pain and slumped onto the hood of the car. Aso did not move to help her up, but jumped into the driver's seat and started the engine. Adjusting her dress, Yukari went round the front of the car and got into the passenger seat.

"I'll be seeing you."

Aso directed a cheery smile at Kensuke alone, whereupon he drove off.

As soon as the car was out of sight, Kensuke began to scan the road for the card that Yukari had tried to give him. He soon found it among some shrubs in the garden. He read what was on the card in the light of a street lamp. Under the name of a religious organization that he'd never heard of, Kensuke read the name Yukari Nakazawa followed by an address and telephone number. It was not clear whether the address and telephone number were those of the religious group or those of Yukari. Kensuke put the card in his pocket and returned to his apartment. All through the night, he somehow couldn't still a feeling of excitement.

3

That proved to be Kensuke's sole encounter with Yukari Nakazawa. Yet, she became a phantom that was to dwell in Kensuke's heart. It was all Aso's fault. If Aso had never said it, Kensuke would have been spared the incredibly persistent image.

It was the end of August, almost two months after the day he'd first met Yukari. Aso called at the same time of day as he had then, but came alone this time—Kensuke made a point of confirming this before Aso could get past the doorway.

"Did you come alone?"

Aso nodded with a grave air. "Can I come in?" he asked meekly.

Kensuke got the impression that Aso had come because there was something pressing he wanted to talk about. Now that he thought about it, perhaps Aso had also come to talk about the same thing his last visit. Kensuke's thoughts turned to that evening two months ago, and, in hindsight, it seemed likely that Yukari's appearance had caused Aso to suddenly turn surly not because he had been seen with a woman who fell somewhat short of his standard of feminine beauty, but because her presence prevented him from saying what he had on his mind.

But this night, as it turned out, Aso hadn't come to say anything in particular, speaking instead as fancy dictated, reminiscing with Kensuke about their childhood days.

After an hour of this, Aso suddenly announced, "I'm off,"

and got up to leave.

"You can't be in that much of a rush. Stay a little longer," urged Kensuke.

Aso responded with a smile of derision, directed at himself. "There's no end to memories like that, eh? You're the only one I can talk to about those days. Great times. The good old days."

As he spoke, the look in Aso's eyes became distant, whereupon they plunged into another brief spell of reminiscing. That summer they spent together in Karuizawa... There was, of course, that time when they'd gotten lost in the mountains while walking along the unused tracks of the Kusatsu-Karuizawa line (it had linked the two towns until 1960), that time they'd resigned themselves to never returning to civilization alive. It was an experience they'd already rehashed numerous times since. They'd wandered off the track in the growing dusk, and there'd been nothing to do but spend the night outdoors. Kensuke, overcome with anxiety, could only moan and groan; Aso tried to give him courage by assuring him that if they just waited for morning and looked for the tracks, they'd be all right. It had been a night spent in fearful trembling. But looking back on the experience now, it had also been a night packed with excitement and rich in unspoken significance. Their friendship had deepened due to precisely that shared experience.

Aso's tone was different that evening. It was the first time Kensuke ever saw him wallowing so stubbornly, so sentimentally, in childhood memories. Possibly noticing the growing confusion on Kensuke's face, Aso suddenly snapped back to his usual self, brought an end to the reminiscing, and signaled his departure with an uplifted hand.

"I must be off."

It was only down in the car park, about to see him off, that Kensuke got round to asking, "How's Yukari getting on?" He was asking this not so much to ascertain her well-being as to find out whether Aso was still seeing her.

"How should I know? I dumped the bitch."

The answer only confirmed what Kensuke had expected. That kind of relationship could never have lasted long. Not only was Yukari obviously not Aso's type; not even she could tolerate such brutality for long.

"I'm sorry to hear it."

The impression of Yukari remained vivid in Kensuke's mind. For some reason, she fascinated him.

"Want to know where I dumped her?" called Aso as he unlocked the door of his BMW and climbed into the driver's seat.

"You mean there's a place you dumped her?" replied Kensuke in surprise.

After all, "dumped" simply meant "broke up with." No one used the word to mean tossing a woman in some sort of trash bin. Of course not.

"I found the perfect place. Want to know where?"

Aso's look became provocative. It was a pretty sick joke, but Kensuke decided to play along for a little while longer.

"Where was it you dumped her?"

"Battery No. 6."

Battery No. 6...the uninhabited island out in Tokyo Bay. In the wake of the arrival, in Tokyo Bay, of Commodore Perry's "Black Ships," Japan's feudal regime had created the islands to house gun batteries for protection against foreign attack. The only ones now remaining were Batteries No. 3 and 6. A breakwater now connected Battery No. 3 with Odaiba (Battery) Seaside Park, and only Battery No. 6 was still an island in the true sense of the word.

Kensuke laughed. Battery No. 6 was not far from a large refuse disposal site, and what was more, the island, which had been constructed to house a gun battery, had never once been used as such. It thus seemed the perfect place for dumping a girlfriend who'd outlived her usefulness. Kensuke couldn't help admiring Aso's sophisticated sense of humor. His jokes were good, very good.

"It's hot out there. Climb in," Aso said, apparently not having had yet his fill of conversation. Kensuke got in and closed the door, and Aso turned on the air-conditioning and began his story. It was a detailed account of why he'd dumped Yukari, on Battery No. 6...

Yukari was pregnant with his child. But the cult she belonged to forbade abortion. She had pressed Aso to marry her—a common enough scenario. Cult or no, this was the kind of story that Kensuke often heard from Aso.

"Is that why you dumped her?" intervened Kensuke, nudging Aso to get to the end sooner than later. If Aso was left to recount the story at his own pace, the whole joke would begin to sound too real.

"The stupid bitch showed me this picture."

Aso opened the glove compartment and took out a piece of paper folded into four. It bore a color illustration. Kensuke stared at the juvenile thing. It showed green trees growing luxuriantly under a sun painted in gold. Under the trees sprawled grown men and women surrounded by children at play. Dogs, cats, and even lions strutted contentedly among the trees. A closer look at the picture revealed that this earthly paradise was surrounded by the sea. Perhaps it was in the tropics; the trees were laden with coconuts. Kensuke guessed the author at once.

"Yukari drew this?"

"Yeah, this is apparently what you get when the stuff she believes in is put on paper. Peace, tranquility, no disease or old age, just life eternal. What do you make of it?"

Yukari was not much of a talker, and Kensuke could see how it must have been much easier for her to express her cherished ideal of paradise on earth as a picture rather than in words.

Kensuke just stared at the picture without answering Aso's question. After all, it wasn't the kind of question you could answer on the spot.

"Why don't we build our own paradise?" His hands clasped to his chest, Aso trilled grotesquely, mimicking Yukari. Then, dramatically jerking his face closer to Kensuke: "Nothing pissed me off worse in all my twenty-three years. That idiot just doesn't have a clue about how utterly miserable her notion of living on and on for all eternity is."

Kensuke sided with Yukari. "You're being too harsh. We're all different in how we look at things."

"Don't call me harsh! She tried to force her idealistic crap on me."

"So you went and dumped her on Battery No. 6, right?"

"Right. Banished her to a desert island, I did. I think I made the punishment fit the crime? If she wants to build a paradise, then she can damn well build it herself."

"But that island is off limits, isn't it."

"Took a rubber dinghy over there in the middle of the night."

Yukari didn't know that Battery No. 6 was legally closed to the general public and so had no qualms at all about their nocturnal adventure. They took the dinghy in the car, but it mostly fell to Yukari to inflate and to row the thing to their destination. Yukari would have followed Aso to the end of the earth without the slightest suspicion. Once they had landed on the battery island, Aso used chloroform to knock her out, leaving her unconscious while he made his getaway. The way he described abandoning Yukari on Battery No. 6, he made it all sound so simple.

Kensuke remained unconvinced. After all, a mere three hundred yards separated Battery No. 6 from the Marine Park. It was not too far a distance to swim. Even if you couldn't swim, many pleasure boats cruised by the island. All you had to do was stand on an embankment and shout to make your-self heard. Surely, he pointed out to Aso, Battery No. 6 was as easy to get off as it was to get to.

"No problem, I took all her clothes."

"You mean you left her there naked?"

"Look, I know her pretty well. She'd rather die than be seen naked in public. She's that sort of woman."

Kensuke was left speechless. He didn't know the whole story between Aso and Yukari, but he did know that they were in a relationship, and Aso must have felt something for her during that time. He didn't feel it was right, even as a joke, for Aso to be saying that he'd stripped someone naked

71

and left her for dead. Whether or not Aso was telling the truth, describing such an act to a third party was brutal enough.

The atmosphere was oppressive and Kensuke remained silent. Glancing furtively sideways, he noticed that Aso seemed to be on the verge of saying something but swallowing the words each time.

"I'd better be off then," he said. He shifted from Park to Drive mode and lowered his hand to disengage the hand brake.

It was as Kensuke opened the car door that he put his final question to Aso. "When did you do it? When did you leave Yukari there?"

"It must have been around the time of the Obon festival. The city was deserted, everyone gone home to the country."

Obon, when the ancestors returned... That made it about ten days ago.

Kensuke got out of the car and went round towards the driver's seat. Aso had the car window open, and his arm was dangling outside, his hand tapping the side of the car. He thrust this hand out in Kensuke's direction.

"So long," he said.

He'd extended his hand for a handclasp, and Kensuke took it reflexively. It felt cold to the touch. Cold, but clammy with perspiration. It was the first time Kensuke had ever shaken hands with Aso.

"Be seeing you," Kensuke said, and Aso nodded firmly, twice, before driving off in his BMW.

As he followed the car with his gaze, Kensuke was sure of one thing. There had indeed been a purpose to this visit, and so with the previous. Aso had come to say goodbye. The tone of his "So long..." and the cold feel of his hand came back to Kensuke. As his friend's BMW approached the intersection, the brake lights went on. Without signaling, the car turned left and disappeared out of sight.

4

For some time afterwards, Kensuke was troubled by a recurring fantasy. A naked young woman lurking in the deep recesses of some uninhabited island was arousing him mercilessly. Kensuke did not have a girlfriend at the time.

He often dreamed of frolicking in the woods. The flesh-colored trunks of trees resembling crape myrtle sprouted up like sinuous tendrils from the earth, none of them adorned with a single leaf. As Kensuke walked among them, his legs got entangled in the curling branches and he'd sink deep down into the ground. No analysis was necessary to see that the smooth tree trunks symbolized Yukari's legs. Another recurring dream Kensuke featured snakes writhing across the ground and transforming themselves into Yukari's legs. In the wilderness and in places that were clearly some island, Yukari metamorphosed into various plants and creatures and lived on.

Kensuke couldn't find out if the story was true by asking Aso. Even if Aso said, "I was lying," the story wouldn't just go away. The possibility that Aso's confessing it was a lie was the real lie would remain forever.

Kensuke tried dialing the number on the calling card that Yukari had given him, and got neither her parents' home nor her apartment, but rather, a sort of dormitory where the members of her religious cult lived. Kensuke asked the feeble-voiced woman who took the phone that he wanted to speak to Yukari.

"She's not here," the woman said, and that was all she

said.

Kensuke had expected Yukari to come to the phone without much of a to-do, so this stole his tongue. After a pause, he managed to ask, "Where may I find her?"

The woman replied simply, "I don't know."

"How long has Yukari been away?"

"I haven't seen her face the last couple of weeks."

When Kensuke asked her for Yukari's parents' number, she merely responded with a question of her own: "Ms. Nakazawa has a home?" The way she said it made Yukari seem like a vagabond with no family.

"So she doesn't have one?" Kensuke pressed.

"I wouldn't know," the woman responded unceremoniously.

Kensuke couldn't tell whether Yukari did in fact have no home or whether the commune had simply been given no information. He put the phone down. All he had been able to confirm was that Yukari had not been back to the dormitory for about two weeks now. The awful thing was that Aso's story was beginning to show signs of plausibility.

It did occur to him to visit Battery No. 6 and check for himself, but the Tokyo authorities had declared the place off limits. Kensuke was due to take the public employment exam in order to become a teacher, and could not afford to get in trouble with the metropolitan government. Besides, he didn't have the courage to make a clandestine landing on Battery No. 6 under cover of darkness.

He felt he needed to see Aso again to get to the bottom of the matter. If Aso hadn't been lying, Kensuke needed to do something before it was too late. He didn't know what sort of criminal charges accrued from stripping a woman naked and leaving her on Battery No. 6. He figured that if she died of starvation, prosecution was inevitable.

He was thus on the verge of contacting Aso when news came that he had been hospitalized in his alma mater's affiliate. A chest X-ray had apparently shown a patch on Aso's lungs. A bronchoscope, and tests, revealed that a particularly virulent form of cancer had claimed most of his body already. His brain was blighted too, and surgery was impossible. Even with some desperate chemotherapy, Aso had only two months or so left to live.

Strangely enough, Kensuke was left unfazed by the news. He closed his eyes and calmly let the fact sink in that the time had come. The happy days that they'd shared sped all in a jumble across his mind's eye, but the idea that "it was unbelievable" simply didn't occur to him—only the terrible pity of dying at twenty-three, Kensuke's own age.

Aso had probably sensed, even before he took the tests, that he didn't have much time left. And so he'd come that day to say goodbye. Given death as a premise, Aso's recent behavior made sense. Just as Aso had seen his own death looming, Kensuke had intuited that his friend's days were numbered, and had no doubt been bracing for this.

Ten minutes or so after he'd digested the news, Kensuke suddenly began to sob. It wasn't that he was sad; rather, it was because confusing emotions besieged him deep inside. After crying for some time, he felt an irrepressible desire to go and see Aso. It was Kensuke's turn to say goodbye.

Kensuke thought he'd chosen a slow time for his visit but, in addition to Aso's mother, there were a few others gathered there in the private room. Aso lay on the bed, in no condition to carry on a normal conversation. A man who'd come to see Kensuke in a car just a month ago now lay before him hardly able to breathe and wreathed in tubes. The cancer cells that riddled Aso's body had wrought so dramatic a change in so short a time. His left lung had completely ceased to function; apparently, the end would come when the phlegm accumulated in his windpipe.

Right before he left, Kensuke approached Aso's pillow, bent low, and asked in a gentle whisper: "Was that true, about Battery No. 6?"

Kensuke felt certain Aso wouldn't tell a lie on his deathbed. If he'd only shaken his head then, Kensuke's suspicion would have been allayed.

Instead, Aso smiled and nodded.

In disbelief, Kensuke tried again: "Are you sure?"

Aso nodded twice in succession. Kensuke thought he saw a look of satisfaction on Aso's face, but it could have been his imagination.

Placing his hand on Aso's, Kensuke told him, "Hang in there," and left the hospital room. No doubt, it would have been more appropriate just to say "Goodbye." Two days later, Aso was dead at the young age of twenty-three.

5

The assembly point was the lounge of the Dream Island Marina. Sasaki looked quite busy lapping his ice cream. Aside from him and Kensuke, the only one there was a metropolitan official named Naito; the councilors representing Minato Ward had yet to turn up. It was ten minutes past the appointed time of 10:00 a.m. Summer vacation had just begun, and on this weekday morning, many young men and women came to the marina. Whenever a young woman passed by, Sasaki's face would lift from his ice cream and follow the woman as she walked off. Kensuke poked him in the ribs with his elbow.

"Leader, it's disgraceful. At your age."

"Don't 'leader' me, okay?" replied Sasaki wryly.

"You told me this was going to be a serious expedition."

"Leave me alone, will you?"

Kensuke's sarcastic barbs were having their effect, and Sasaki waved his hand as though to chase away an annoying fly.

"Making a mountain out of a molehill" was a saying that existed to describe Sasaki. His trademark impulse to blow things up tenfold had been applied to the Battery No. 6 inspection crew, which in Sasaki's telling was to consist of the best scientific minds the city could muster. But Kensuke had arrived to find only Sasaki and a city official.

"Where are the other members?" the baffled Kensuke had asked, blinking.

Sasaki had given this excuse cringingly: "They're all

busy and called in one after another to cancel."

Naito, the city official, revealed a different story when Kensuke questioned him about the matter. Apparently, just one ward councilor and one city official were required for the inspections, but Sasaki had nagged them persistently to be taken with them. All Sasaki's talk about having been "commissioned by the ward council" and having "organized a survey team" had been barefaced lies. The truth was that Sasaki had tapped Kensuke so he wouldn't look too bad just tagging along by himself.

"Here comes Mr. Kano. We're ready to go." Spotting the representative of Minato Ward, Naito rose to his feet. Reflexively, Sasaki and Kensuke also stood up.

Waiting aboard the small cruiser tied up at the wharf were the captain and a single deck hand, also government employees. The team, now six members in all, motored out of Dream Island Marina under the bright summer sun at half past ten and headed for Battery No. 6, which was but a stone's throw away.

On their way they passed under four bridges. The girders of one of them, so low as to be almost within touching distance, blocked out the rays of the sun for a moment, and the whole weight of the thing seemed to bear down on them. As they passed under the fourth bridge, the Rainbow Bridge came into view and beyond it Battery No. 6. Kensuke recalled how he'd looked down at the island from the Rainbow Bridge's pedestrian walkway shortly after the bridge's completion. At the observatory, using the binoculars, he'd peered into the depths of the woods that overgrew the battery. Now, for the first time, he was seeing the island from approximately sea level.

As the profile of the island loomed larger, Kensuke was getting his hopes up. He was finally gaining access to the setting of a nine-year-old fantasy that had burgeoned and morphed with a will of its own. Battery No. 6, an irregular pentagon with a surface area of about twelve acres and a perimeter of about a third of a mile guarded by a stone wall sixteen feet high, apparently had a freshwater well on it despite its being a manmade island in the middle of the bay. Thinking that with water you could survive, for nine years Kensuke had kept Yukari alive on that walled island. He understood it was a ridiculous notion. Yet he couldn't discount that bizarre smile of satisfaction Aso had displayed on the threshold of death. Had Aso, his brain invaded by cancer, succumbed to his own lie? Or had he perhaps, hoping for a place to live after death, conflated the image of heaven with the uninhabited island?

Likely expecting to be fed, a large flock of seagulls circled the cruiser. Flying just above the surface, the birds skimmed Battery No. 6 and swept up high over it. As if shaking the gulls loose, the cruiser pulled alongside the landing on Battery No. 6.

6

While Sasaki, meticulously prepared, was armed with camera, video, and sketchbook, Kensuke had brought hardly anything at all except a pair of waterproof boots, which he put on instead of his sneakers prior to landing.

Sasaki hopped onto the wharf and cried, "Hasn't changed a bit!"

Kensuke, surprised, asked him, "You mean you've been here before?"

"Only once. Ten years ago, on a survey like this one."

Ten years ago..., mused Kensuke. That was a year before Aso's death.

"Look at that."

Sasaki pointed to a narrow gap in the embankment. Behind it spread a dim space overshadowed by the trees, while in front, where it was practically still the shoreline, what looked like a variety of parsley grew in profusion.

"Would that be parsley?"

"It's angelica. *Angelica keiskei*. Common on the Izu peninsula and Oshima island. Must have drifted no small distance! It was there ten years ago, too."

Sasaki expressed admiration for the vitality of the angelica plant, whose seeds had washed ashore from who knew where and taken root and grown with such vigor. Sasaki repeated several times that the most amazing thing about Battery No. 6 was the variety and vitality of the seeds that found their way to it, and that the place was a natural treasure chest well worth investigating precisely because it was off limits to the public.

While Naito and Kano proposed that they first conduct a summary survey by circling the island once along the embankment, Sasaki clearly wanted to head straight into the center. In the end, it was decided that the team should split up into two, and Kensuke chose to accompany Sasaki. The captain and the crewmember were to remain on the wharf. It was also decided that each pair, Kano and Naito touring the perimeter and Sasaki and Kensuke venturing inland, would carry a portable receiver. It wasn't a large island, with edges only a hundred yards or so long; they'd be heard if they shouted. But they had the receivers and there was no reason not to use them.

"See you, then." Naito and Kano waved to the others and got going, walking along the top of the embankment.

Sasaki and Kensuke stepped through the growth of angelica and headed into the dim interior. Every time Sasaki caught sight of a fascinating specimen of vegetation, he angled his camera, recorded it on video, or drew it in his sketchbook. There wasn't any plant Kensuke didn't recognize that Sasaki could not identify; the mentor was indeed proving himself a specialist of the natural sciences. The serious look in his eyes seemed to give lie to his usual jocularity, and Kensuke saw him in a different light again.

The soil, unused to the trample of human feet, was soft, and black liquid oozed out of the humus under their deliberate tread. If not for their boots, their feet would have been soaked completely a good while ago. Even the air was wet. Grasses and trees that were a rare sight in Tokyo thrived here, giving off an eerie odor for some reason and forming a hybrid copse unique to the island. When the sea breeze stirred the treetops, sounds fluttered down all around them, and from time to time Kensuke would not know where he was. He had pretty much forgotten about Yukari. The island was just too different from the site of his fantasies.

The deeper they went, the thicker the gloom—and Sasaki spoke less and less. He wasn't peering through his camera and video as frequently, either. Facing this way and that, he finally halted.

"How odd," he muttered.

Kensuke, who'd been following Sasaki, also stopped. "What's odd?" he asked.

Sasaki just let out a sort of grumble and didn't explain, lost in thought. They both stood still for some time, neither of them uttering a word.

"Are you all right?" Kensuke looked concerned as he broke the silence.

"The clump of angelica back at the landing looked just the same. But the further in we go...something's odd."

"You mean, it's different than before?"

"I can't put my finger on it. Sure doesn't feel right though."

Hearing this, Kensuke looked around him nervously. He thought he was getting bad vibes, too. Apparently, back in the '20s, Battery No. 6 had been rumored to be a sort of haunted isle. Just recently, a windsurfer practicing at the Seaside Park had passed from view behind the island and disappeared for good, board and all—or so Kensuke had heard. Recalling such stories, Kensuke didn't feel too good.

"Let's go on, shall we?" urged Kensuke, intending to

muster courage, but his voice trembled somewhat.

"No one's supposed to have come here in ten years..." Sasaki mumbled to himself, as though to confirm the fact, and resumed walking. Naito had told them aboard the cruiser that the Minato Ward Council was participating in the survey for the first time and that there hadn't been a comprehensive field investigation in ten years.

Kensuke remained silent.

Sasaki stopped again. Looking up, he cried, "This forest's nurturing something!"

"Why not? Don't trees always sustain nearby life-forms?"

Sasaki pointed diagonally ahead. "That's a persimmon tree. The one beyond it is a medlar. Last time I was here, there weren't any fruit-bearers."

No sooner had he said this than Sasaki started running ahead.

"Wait!" cried Kensuke.

But Sasaki only gained speed, and it was all Kensuke could do to keep up. Dripping with sweat, he was about to give up the chase when the view changed suddenly and he found himself in a clearing about thirty feet wide. The place seemed to be the center of the island, the woods appearing equally thick on all sides. To the north the Rainbow Bridge towered against the sky. It was jarring to catch sight of a modern structure from the center of an island that resembled an uninhabited jungle. It was as though the dimensions had come unhinged and Kensuke had wandered into an alien world.

The noonday sun drenched the grassy clearing with its

rays. Cicadas chirped loudly. It wasn't hard for Kensuke to come up with a word to describe the clearing: it was a garden. Tomatoes, eggplants, cucumbers, and other summer vegetables had been planted in a neat configuration. It was impossible now to deny that there was some force at work here other than nature. These vegetables had been planted according to some will for some purpose. This wasn't a case of seeds washing ashore sprouting naturally on their own. Kensuke and Sasaki looked at each other and verified the impression with each other.

"Look, over there." Sasaki jerked his jaw toward the east end of the clearing. Three slender strips of wood stood atop a mound of earth.

Walking over to take a closer look, they saw that the strips were tablets. Of the ink-lettered characters only two were legible, both of them what you'd expect on a tablet, while the others had completely worn off. What were the tablets doing there? Could they have come drifting to Battery No. 6, too? Why were they staked so firmly into the ground then?

"What do you think?" spoke Kensuke.

The mound of earth under the wooden strips suggested only one thing to both men.

Sasaki said it: "It's got to be a grave."

Ants were squirming in columns on the rounded heap of earth. A grave… It just couldn't be anything else.

Just then, the portable receiver that hung from Kensuke's shoulder sprang to life.

"Kano here. Do you read me? Over."

"We read you," replied Kensuke, his finger on the transmit button.

"We've spotted a small dark figure on the western embankment. It disappeared into the woods and must be heading toward the middle. Please exercise due caution."

"What?"

"It was probably just an animal."

"A dog maybe? A cat?"

"No," Kano refuted him without pause.

"Why are you sure?"

"We're not sure. We tried to go after it, but it scrambled into the woods at an amazing speed."

"Western side?"

"Yes."

"Roger and out." Concluding the transmission, Kensuke looked at Sasaki's face and awaited his decision.

"Come."

Sasaki started walking toward the western woods, where the thing was reported to have vanished, and Kensuke followed closely behind. The two men stopped at the edge of the clearing and, taking care not to make any noise, scouted ahead. They couldn't hear anything yet, but the thing was coming their way through the thicket right in front of them. Kensuke held his breath and waited for something to appear.

A mosquito hummed annoyingly close to Kensuke's nose while he waited in a crouch. If he didn't move at all, he'd be feasted upon where his flesh was exposed. Having to stay in that crouch and make fidgety little movements at the same time was indeed tiring.

The grass in the bush ahead seemed to sway. Soon, the approaching presence became audible through the branches being thrashed away. And then, all of a sudden, a small black thing jumped out at Kensuke.

Before he knew, he was lying face up on the ground. The impact of something hard striking his jaw from below had almost knocked him out, but his two hands had instinctively caught hold of the thing. A beastly roar went up next to his ear, and an instant later, he felt a searing pain in his arm. He had no idea what was going on. He felt a weight upon him, and when it lifted, he opened his eyes to see against the blinding summer sun a small dark silhouette that was flailing its limbs in Sasaki's arms. The creature that Sasaki had pulled off him was a boy perhaps seven or eight years old.

Kensuke managed to sit up but remained in a state of disbelief. The boy was howling, not in any human language, but like a wild beast. The shrieks contained a frantic appeal but were totally incomprehensible and filled Kensuke with terror. The boy had no doubt bitten him. There were drops of blood on the arm where he'd felt the pain. Kensuke stood up, pressing down on the spot with his hand. Just then, Kano and Naito came dashing out of the woods behind. No sooner had Kano caught sight of the boy in Sasaki's restraining arms than he fetched his receiver to get through to the captain of the cruiser.

"Prepare to depart... Contact the police..." The instructions Kano issued in rapid succession registered only as fragments with Kensuke.

He felt dizzy. He tried to reason out what had just happened. The boy must have been glancing behind him as he ran. Not noticing Kensuke's presence right ahead, he'd banged his head into Kensuke's jaw. But why a boy, on this island?

Kano and the others were asking him for his name and address. Tossing his head wildly, he only let out inchoate shrieks and supplied no information. Hearing the cries, which weren't in Japanese nor any foreign language, Kensuke felt dizzy again.

7

The boy sat on the cruiser's deck floor with just his head poking above the side. He was gazing intently at the island. There was no expression on his face. Leaving your natal land usually elicited a special surge of emotion, but the boy didn't seem to know how to express such sentiments. The moment they'd taken him aboard the cruiser, he'd quieted down, and now for some time he'd sat there without once budging.

There was nothing to do but call off the survey. Their top priority was to take the boy back to the city and to hand him over to the proper authorities. Unable to conceal their excitement at the unexpected catch, Naito and Kano exchanged theories about the boy's provenance and stared unabashedly at him as at a wild child who'd been reared by wolves.

No one else had a clue. But Kensuke could paint a reasonably good picture of what had transpired on Battery No. 6 in the last nine years. One look at the child's face was enough to make everything clear. The refined small nose, the clear glacial eyes, the thin lips—though obscured by a mass of overgrown hair, all of the boy's features bore an irrefutable resemblance. It was in third grade that Kensuke and Aso had first met and gotten to know each other. The profile of the boy who sat before Kensuke now was the living image of his former classmate. Without a shadow of a doubt, this was Aso's son by Yukari Nakazawa.

Aso had lied. He hadn't stripped Yukari naked and deserted her on Battery No. 6. The absurd scheme of turning an uninhabited island nearby into a paradise on earth had no doubt been Yukari's suggestion; Aso, while horrified by the inanity of it, must have helped her out. How else could the vegetables and fruits growing on Battery No. 6 be explained? Moreover, the boy wasn't naked; they were rags by now, but he was clothed. The bare essentials for survival must have been prepared at the outset and brought to the island.

Where, then, was Yukari, the boy's mother? Probably dead and buried. If she were alive, she'd have to be somewhere other than Battery No. 6. In any case, she wasn't a living inhabitant of the island. Assuming Aso hadn't lied about absolutely everything, Yukari had become pregnant that summer nine years ago—and given birth the following year. That made the boy eight years old. If he'd been living with his mother for the whole time, he'd know how to speak. Instead he must have lost his mother when he was around five, and forgotten, during the solitary years that followed, even the little he'd learned from her. Whether Yukari had died on Battery No. 6 or abandoned the child and escaped alone would be clear if and when they dug up the mound under the wooden tablets. Kensuke's hunch was that Yukari rested in peace under that mound of earth.

The satisfied expression on Aso's face as he lay at death's door... At long last, Kensuke understood. Aso had smiled to himself for secretly having disseminated his seed here on earth. The force that aided the strange seedling from afar didn't work for plants alone. Kensuke was looking at the proof.

Sensing that Kensuke was staring at him, the boy met his gaze. Almost no expression appeared on the boy's face as he turned it back toward Battery No. 6 shrinking in the distance.

THE HOLD

1

There is an observation platform shaped like a five-needle pine at the tip of Cape Futtsu. A climb to the top reveals a panoramic view that encompasses Yokosuka and Cape Kannon. Hiroyuki Inagaki had brought his son with him to the observation platform for the first time in a while.

The tide was visibly rapid between Breakwater No. 1 and Breakwater No. 2. A sandbar extended like an arc from the promontory in front, falling only a little short of Breakwater No. 1. Shortly after the war, you could cross over as far as Breakwater No. 1 in a jeep at low tide, but these days that was no longer possible. A mere row of dots, the sandbar was now barely visible above the water, making the crossing extremely difficult even on foot. As a child, Hiroyuki had heard how someone had tried to walk across only to become stranded when the tide shifted. The unfortunate man was said to have been washed away by the current, and his body was never recovered.

It was a windy Saturday afternoon in early summer. For some time now, Hiroyuki had been staring intently at the rapid current between the two breakwaters. From their position on the observation platform, the ships looked as small as peas on the water. Indeed, that very stretch of sea was where he worked. Hiroyuki was a fisherman. He fished for Futtsu conger eels between the breakwaters for twenty-five days a month.

He'd inherited the job from his father fifteen years ago. During that time, the face of Tokyo Bay had changed dramatically. The sandbar that stretched out to sea now pointed much further to the north than before. Landfills had been created and the seabed dredged to widen the sea-lanes. These changes wrought by man had disrupted the balanced rhythm of the tides, resulting in sand being washed away and the sandbar being eroded at its south end.

For all the changes that had taken place, however, Hiroyuki did not feel particularly concerned. As long as his catch brought in the monthly target of no less than one million yen, he could have cared less how much the face of Tokyo Bay changed. He wanted to slap down that million yen on the table in front of his wife every month. As long as he did that, she had no reason to complain.

"Okay, let's be off."

Hiroyuki playfully pushed his son's head down. Katsumi was a very quiet and withdrawn child. He made no response and continued to gaze wistfully toward the Miura Peninsula. But the moment he saw his father going down the stairs, he chased after him in a hurry.

There was a man selling roasted corn on the cob in a stall at the bottom of the stairway.

"Want some?"

Not waiting for his son to answer, Hiroyuki bought a cob from the vendor whom he seemed to know.

"Have you seen the wife round here?" he asked as he took his change.

The vendor only laughed and shook his head.

Hiroyuki handed his son the corn and beckoned with his soy sauce-stained hand to follow after him:

"Come."

Katsumi didn't really want the corn, but knew that refusing something offered by his father would invite his wrath. His father might even strike him. Katsumi took the corn without a word and spied his father's expression to gauge his mood. He began to nibble at the cob and tagged along behind his father. His mother had strictly forbidden him to eat snacks between meals. His father, however, would buy Katsumi sweets and candy, not out of carelessness but in willful defiance of his wife's wishes. Every time this happened, Katsumi felt himself to be in an impossible position. He would earn a tongue-lashing from his mother if he ignored her but would get his ears boxed if he refused what his father offered. The worse part of it was that his father always bought him things he didn't want.

Katsumi dawdled several yards behind his father as they walked along the beach on the north side of the cape. The cape jutted out into the sea and divided the waves into the raging and the calm. Rough waves broke on the southern shore, while gentler waves washed the northern side of the cape. The calmer shore was host to hordes of four-wheel-drive vehicles from Tokyo. The drivers and passengers of these cars that lined the shore had come to spend an enjoyable Saturday afternoon by the sea. Young people sped about on jet-skis in the water, while on the beach families barbecued fish, the adults drinking beer. Every corner of the beach teemed with summer fun and resounded with happy peals of laughter.

Hiroyuki stopped walking and looked around. His son now lagged more than thirty feet behind him. The boy shambled unsteadily this way and that, eating the piece of corn with a plain expression of disgust. As he watched, Hiroyuki was overwhelmed by a surge of irritation.

Unaware of his father's annoyance, Katsumi was watching a jet-ski speeding over the water and spraying a shower of seawater in its wake. Yet this was no look of envy; Katsumi was terrified of water. He would always find some excuse not to take part in school swimming lessons. He was also averse to taking baths. This was no doubt the reason why he could hardly swim, even though he was already eleven years old. As far as his father was concerned, the inability to swim was tantamount to betrayal in the son of a fisherman.

Hiroyuki bellowed out his son's name. The roaring engines of the jet-skis drowned out his voice, however, as the riders sped around in circles. Still looking out to the sea, Katsumi dawdled along the beach, kicking up sand. Hiroyuki shouted his name again and started walking toward his son. As a shadow loomed over him, Katsumi became aware of his father's presence. He flinched instinctively. He thought he was in for a beating.

"Give it here!" roared his father.

He took the corn from his son and finished it off.

"Now that's the way to eat corn. Got that, lad?"

He tossed the corncob away and wiped his mouth with the back of his hand.

Hiroyuki was startled by a shriek from down by his side. Katsumi was holding his stomach and groaning in pain. At first, Hiroyuki couldn't tell what was the matter.

"We're sorry!"

The apology came from a father and his son as they came running up. They had their hands stuffed into baseball gloves.

Hiroyuki looked down and saw a ball at his son's feet.

The boy and his father had been playing catch in front of the nearby pine grove and the ball must have been overthrown, hitting Katsumi in the ribs.

The two approached Hiroyuki and Katsumi, both bowing apologetically. "Sorry! Are you all right?"

"Can't you be more damned careful?" yelled Hiroyuki, throwing the ball back in their direction.

Katsumi was still squatting down on the sand. Hiroyuki took his hand, pulled him to his feet, and started examining the side of his chest where the ball had struck. He found nothing much wrong, just a faint red bruise under his T-shirt.

"It's nothing at all. You'll be okay." Patting his son reassuringly on the ribs, Hiroyuki pronounced a clean bill of health.

Katsumi began to walk, but his pace was even slower than before. He still held his side, his face distorted in an exaggerated look of misery. He shortly began to drag his feet, his tongue dangling from a half-open mouth, and he let out deep sighs. This served to irritate Hiroyuki badly enough that he felt the need to take his anger out on someone or something.

The boy and his father whose ball had struck Katsumi had returned to the area by the pine grove to resume their game of catch. Both wore matching polo shirts of a well-known brand, and both reeked of the city from head to toe. The little boy was about Katsumi's age and extraordinarily agile for a kid from the city.

Picking them as the target to vent his anger on, he strode over to where they were playing and called to them in a thick, menacing voice.

"Say, you two over there!"

They stopped playing catch and turned to face Hiroyuki with anxious expressions that only fueled the flames of his resentment. The timid, nervous look in their eyes strengthened his resolve to vent his spleen on them to his heart's content.

He stopped within a few paces of them and growled, "I want your name and address."

"Huh?" The father looked at once puzzled and contemptuous.

"My boy says it hurts so much he can't walk. What you gonna do if he's broken a rib or something?" Hiroyuki held out his left arm and pointed behind him to where his son was; only, his son wasn't there.

Katsumi had pretended it had hurt more than it did, to get a little sympathy from his father. Yet when he realized that he had only incited his father's wrath, his throat parched with fear. On this particular occasion, his father's anger just happened to not be directed at him. Nonetheless, Katsumi was terrified. As his father walked away, his back radiated malevolence. Left to run its natural course, it could well develop into violence. Katsumi wanted to avoid such a scene at all costs. What terrified him more than calling his father's wrath upon himself was seeing him beat up others. It was particularly horrifying when the victim was his mother. At such times he could hardly breathe.

It was not until he felt Katsumi tugging his hand that Hiroyuki realized that his son was standing by his right side.

"Dad," the boy appealed in a trembling voice. He had

apparently been calling for some time now, but his father had been too wound up to notice.

Hiroyuki saw that his excuse for a fight was being snatched from under his nose. "What," he said, forcefully shaking off his son's hand.

"I'm all right. I'm fine..."

Katsumi tugged at his father's hand again, trying to get him to step back. He was telling his father to let things be and just go home, to stop taking his anger out on other people.

"You're fine? Then what was that face back there?"

Hiroyuki's anger had found a different target. Their gloved hands now dangling at their side, the boy and the father who'd been playing catch remained motionless, waiting to see which way things would go. The muzzle of Hiroyuki's anger was now directed at someone else. Their anxious looks revealed that they still saw this as no reason to feel relieved.

"I'm sorry, Dad," Katsumi apologized to his father, his face creasing up, on the verge of tears.

"Fool, don't apologize so easy!" Hiroyuki's hand rose.

The moment his father's eyes changed color rarely escaped Katsumi. Immediately before an eruption of anger, his father's eyes would go from black to white, with the black part suddenly rolling up. Katsumi instinctively squeezed his eyes shut and covered his head with his hands.

When hitting his son failed to assuage his anger, Hiroyuki started kicking him around on the sand.

His tear-sodden face thick with sand, the boy kept on apologizing, "I'm sorry, Dad. I'm sorry." Where had his son learned to beg for mercy in such a craven, pathetic, sniveling way? It was enough to drive Hiroyuki insane with anger.

The eruption did not last long. Hiroyuki suddenly reined in his hands and reached out to pull the boy up to his feet. It wasn't that he was concerned that others were looking at them. It was simply that a passing storm had convulsed his frame and blown itself out in an instant. Once the storm had passed, he didn't even remember what had caused his anger in the first place. It had been a ludicrous sequence: baseball hits son in ribs, son exhibits a painful expression, father sets out to get even with the culprits who threw the ball, son suddenly claims there's nothing wrong, hence father gives son something real to cry about. Hiroyuki was at a loss to describe the absurdity of it in words. He slowly shook his bowed head and muttered to himself.

...I'm beginning to be like pop.

His son sobbing convulsively before him reminded him of himself at that age. He had been exactly the same. As the one wielding angry fists now, he'd become the spitting image of his father. Realizing this made him no more capable of altering what he had become. Knowing where the violence in his veins originated didn't help him resist the impulse. The mass of emotion just surged up to shake him.

He lifted his gaze to discover that the father and son who had been playing catch were gone. The city types that filled the beach always had the fanciest equipment. The ball and gloves had certainly been nothing more than just another fancy possession. Having lost their interest in playing catch, they must have returned to their car to find other fancy things to play with.

He lightly cuffed his son's head as they made their way

along the beach towards the park. Though they had more time to spare than they knew what to do with, he felt strangely tense, almost afraid.

"Stupid bitch!" he said out loud.

His wife's absence was at the root of his uncontrollable vexation. Every aspect of the scenery struck him as detestable. Normally so pleasant, the sound of the waves now jarred his nerves.

"Where can that stupid bitch be?"

Most Futtsu fishermen did not work on Saturdays because the market was closed on Sundays. It was their only day off. He had awoken that morning on his day off to find his wife gone.

Being his day off, he got up several hours later than usual. It was shortly before nine o'clock when the parching thirst of a hangover disrupted his sleep. He rolled over and shouted for water. No matter how many times he shouted, there was no reply.

He got out of bed, and as he made his way to the kitchen, he noticed that the house was somehow different than usual. Normally, at this time, his wife would be sitting on the sofa in the living room watching television after having finished her morning household chores. His breakfast would have been there on the table, the dishes and pots all washed and stacked to dry near the sink, the laundry done and the house cleaned. That's how it was every Saturday morning.

Yet this morning, wherever he looked was untidy. Dirty dishes were stacked high in the sink, dirty clothing stuffed in the laundry basket.

"Nanako!"

Calling his wife's name, he made his way upstairs and looked into the children's room. His wife was not there either.

Hiroyuki had no choice but to prepare his own breakfast from whatever he found in the refrigerator. He then waited for his son to return from school and took him out on a stroll during which he might look for his wife.

As they crossed the park, Hiroyuki tried to remember what had happened the night before. He recalled drinking more than usual since he wouldn't be working today. But he felt he hadn't even stayed up that late. Before workdays, Hiroyuki made it a rule to go to bed before nine o'clock; he had to get up very early, at half past two. But he just couldn't remember what time he'd gone to bed the night before. His wife would have gone to bed at the same time. They always slept next to each other, spreading their futons out on the tatami of a six-mat room. Hiroyuki only had to turn to one side to see his wife's face as she slept. He did remember seeing his wife's face last night. She'd been fast asleep, her breathing inaudible, and her face had been lit up in the light of the lamp near her pillow. Hiroyuki had observed his wife's face as it was illuminated by the weak source of light.

Suddenly, his head was throbbing with splitting pain. He ran over to the water fountain where he drank and lightly padded his head with his hand. When he tried to think, a black force repelled him. Always hazy, always just out of reach... What had happened the night before? His efforts to remember proved futile.

Hiroyuki washed his face in the gushing spray of water.

"Let's try the Fishermen's Co-op."

He turned the water off and turned his drenched face toward his son.

Katsumi nodded, but he was suffering an attack of anxiety that he couldn't begin to describe. It was the dread that his mother might never return.

2

There was rarely much traffic on the road that ran from east to west by the fishing port. The boats left on the vacant plot of land accented the aura of desolation that pervaded the port on the fishermen's day off. There were a few stalls selling shellfish, but the place was too far off the way for the sightseers clamming at low tide.

The roots of the trees lining the sidewalk were overgrown with grass. Hiroyuki did not hesitate to walk on the road instead. He was conscious that his son was deliberately negotiating each clump of grass so as not to step off the sidewalk.

"The fool," Hiroyuki thought to himself.

The boy's mother had told him never to step off the sidewalk. The sight of his son unconditionally obeying his mother to the last word galled Hiroyuki to no end.

A broker's shop selling marine products stood before the Fishermen's Cooperative Association. As Hiroyuki looked into the back of the shop, a hefty woman came out, wiping her hands on her apron. He acknowledged her with a nod of his head.

"Don't suppose you've seen the wife at all?"

The tone of his question suggested that he was puzzled by his wife's absence.

"No...at least not today."

Not being on particularly friendly terms with the shopkeeper, he felt little disposed to prolong the conversation. Once she got the bit between her teeth, this fishwife would keep callers all day with her prattle. Hiroyuki beat a hasty retreat into an alley just outside the shop.

As they wandered here and there along the coast, through the park, and around the Fishermen's Co-op, Hiroyuki approached countless people with the same question.

"I don't suppose you've seen the wife, have you?"

He would repeat the question whenever he spotted a familiar face. It was unlike Hiroyuki to be the first to speak, to be so spontaneous with his greetings. He was known as an unsociable character. He couldn't understand why he was behaving in this manner. His behavior mystified himself. It was as though he were trying to impress upon all of them that he was walking around searching for his wife.

Hiroyuki's home was on a corner two blocks down the road from the fishwife's shop. The house occupied almost the entire plot it was built on. His boat, the *Hamakatsu*, was moored near the western extremity of the port, making it but a few minutes' walk from his house. Two years ago, they had enlarged their house. Since that time, they had used the older, original part of the building for storage. Hiroyuki had been born and raised in the part of the house that now housed his fishing tackle. During his entire thirty-three years, he had never lived anywhere else.

"I'm home!"

He was through the front door and into the house now, but still no one answered. Hiroyuki had expected to see his wife's all-too-familiar face pop out and greet him, dispelling his misgivings. The silence disillusioned him all too quickly.

"So she's not back yet."

He clicked his tongue and strode across the living room, throwing open one of the sliding screens to the Japanese-style room beyond.

His daughter Haruna and his father Shozo were sitting on the floor at the low table facing each other. They were both eating jam buns. Although Shozo was only fifty-five years of age, his emaciated form and white hair suggested a man of over eighty.

Shozo had almost lost his life at sea. That was twenty years ago. He'd taken his boat out of the harbor in calm weather, but the wind had changed suddenly and the boat was being buffeted mercilessly by tail waves generated by southerly winds. His face was hurled against the edge of the boat and he was thrown overboard. Luckily, he was saved, but the accident served to trigger the gradual onset of senile dementia, impairing his perception, memory, and speech. For the past few years, his life had become a monotonous cycle of eating, excreting, and sleeping. It was not clear whether his condition was due to the accident or whether the accident had only served to call forth the symptoms of an innate disposition. Hiroyuki and the other members of his family guessed that it had probably been innate. There were other grounds for suspecting that this was the case. Their daughter Haruna, now approaching her seventh birthday, had begun to show symptoms of aphasia or some similar disorder.

She'd always been able to learn and interact normally, but for the past three months she couldn't speak properly and was making moaning sounds instead. For about a month, she still seemed to have a mental image of things she wanted to say and was simply having a hard time enunciating them.

Then one day, she abruptly gave up trying to speak at all. Haruna had always been an odd child and had been experiencing difficulties at school. Since losing her ability to speak, she'd stopped attending school altogether. Whenever they had time on their hands, she and her grandfather would sit together devouring jam buns. All you had to do was give her a jam bun to keep her occupied. The family soon discovered that a great deal of trouble could be avoided by simply stocking up on jam buns and giving her more than she could eat. Hiroyuki was gradually losing the vitality, motivation, whatever else it took to set his family right.

As he observed his daughter and his father, sitting opposite each other eating jam buns in silence, the sight depressed him anew. How irritating it was not to be able to ask either of them whether his wife had returned while he had been out. Irritation was not the word; he was beginning to feel as if two dark walls were closing in on him from above and below to crush the life out of him. One he had given life; the other had given him life. Now he was trapped between the two.

He closed the sliding panel, unable to watch them any longer. Hiroyuki was partially resigned to suffering some kind of brain impairment himself in the future, but this was one reality he naturally preferred not to contemplate.

...Just where on earth has she gone?

Hiroyuki folded his arms on his chest, baffled.

As five o'clock approached, his irritation was aggravated by hunger. He felt an overpowering resentment at his wife for having left the family to fend for themselves. With no one to take out his rage on, it only grew and grew.

The one possibility he could think of was that she had

suddenly left him. Hiroyuki himself had felt tempted to leave home and desert his family. His emotions rose to an explosive level as he imagined himself saying it: "Leave, you bitch, if that's what you want. But before you do, make sure you kill the kids and the old man."

He relived in that instant his own hunger for affection as a child and wiped tears from his face with the back of his hand, which clutched a can of beer.

He suddenly remembered the bankbook that was kept in the drawer of the kitchen cupboard. Upon locating the bankbook, he flipped through the pages, but found nothing unusual. No large sums of money had been withdrawn lately. If his wife had indeed left him, she had done so on an impulse.

In that case, she'd just as likely be back as fast as she'd left. She'd succumbed momentarily to temptation, that was all.

Feeling somewhat better, he decided to go out. He knew a bar called *Marié* where he could get something to eat.

"Have some of those jam buns," he told his son, put on a pair of sandals, and went out.

Hiroyuki made his way along the road by the fishing port toward the park. The gray water in the enclosed harbor was tinged with the crimson of the cloudy dusk sky. There was neither wind nor waves, and the boats moored along the wharf stood motionless side by side. Hiroyuki looked where his own boat was moored.

Even from where he was standing, he could clearly see the name of his boat, *Hamakatsu*, on the hull. He halted. It felt like his heart was in his mouth and he didn't know why.

His pulse began to race; the blackest fear welled up from some pinprick in his heart and spread through his body. He swallowed hard. A low-pitched drone seemed to fill his inner ear.

Hiroyuki had no idea what was causing the attack. He looked towards the harbor. As soon as he spotted his own boat, he felt his chest constrict. No one knew that boat better than he did, he had used it for years. He had spent more time on that boat than at home. What could be bothering him? His forgetfulness had been pronounced of late. He sometimes couldn't recall events from the day before.

Maybe there was something he'd left undone at work, something on the boat that needed servicing, some piece of tackle that needed to be put away. He tried to think if there was anything like that he might have forgotten, but his mind remained blank.

He looked ahead and saw the red neon sign, *Marié*, on the left. Though desperate for answers, he went inside and closed the door behind him.

"Hi stranger!" The bar's madam beamed at him as he walked through the door. He was generous with his money, and the bar valued his patronage.

The moment Hiroyuki heard the madam's voice, the anxiety that had been eating away at him simply vanished.

3

As always, Hiroyuki woke up a little before three o'clock in the morning. He woke up instinctively and had not need-ed the prodding of an alarm clock for years now. Of course, there was no precise time laid down to go fishing. He fished for conger eels all alone. The earlier he set out, the earlier he could return. The sooner he got back, the sooner he could start drinking. He sat cross-legged on the futon and gazed into space. The rest of the family was asleep. His wife would have normally been sleeping on the futon next to his, but she was not there. When she was around, she got in the way; when she wasn't around, there were extra chores for him to do.

…Where on earth is she?

He had absolutely no idea how to go about searching for his missing wife. The only thing he could do was to go out fishing as usual and wait for his wife to return. He cursed and slammed his pillow against the tatami matting.

"Someone prepare my breakfast!"

His yell reverberated through the entire house, but there was no reply. They were all asleep in their own rooms: his son and daughter upstairs, his father in the Japanese-style room behind the living room. Not that any of them gave the impression of being alive at all even when they were awake.

Hiroyuki did not budge—not because he was averse to making his own breakfast, but because it just didn't feel right. On this particular morning, he was unable to motivate him-self to go fishing. The only justifiable reason for not going out would have been poor weather. He did for a moment find himself wishing he could stay home thanks to some storm.

He'd rarely wished for bad weather before. In fact, Hiroyuki often went out on rough days when other fishermen took the day off. He was well-known in the Futtsu fishing community for his nerve. That was why the *Hamakatsu* boasted catches that far surpassed those of other boats. Hiroyuki was not engaged in fishing only for the money; he got a thrill from tracking conger eels as they moved from place to place, using his instincts to net bumper catches. Not only that, he enjoyed boasting to others about his successful hauls. It was as if he had no other way to prove his worth as a human being.

Hiroyuki heaved himself up. Even in the closed room, he could sense the conditions out in the open air. The weather was nowhere near as bad as to warrant calling off the day's fishing. Not feeling like it was no justification, but slacking off. And there was one more reason why he could not simply stay home that day. He felt he *had* to set out to sea, that day more than any other. His feelings were contradictory: he did not feel like going, but he felt he had to go.

He pulled open the shutters. It was still pitch-dark outside. It was the time of the year when the days were longest. In another hour the eastern skies would drain their darkness.

Two days earlier, Hiroyuki had netted a very creditable catch. Even his dragnet had caught many fry of conger eel. Another such profitable day awaited him. He tried to spur himself on with such positive thoughts.

He dressed in his usual style: a jacket over a T-shirt, the bottoms of his jogging pants tucked into rubber boots. His clothing that day was different in but one respect. He wore a different hat. He replaced his usual hunting cap with a straw hat given the growing heat of summer. Thus clad and with a sack of frozen sardines slung over his shoulder, he crossed the foot-wide plank that linked the wharf with the stern of his boat.

For conger eel fishing, there was no set time for boats to leave the harbor. Some boats would go out at about the same time as Hiroyuki, while others set off as he returned to the harbor at around two in the afternoon.

The sputtering of engines starting up began to break the predawn silence of the harbor. Hiroyuki started his generator and joined the others in banishing the silence that had reigned. He then lit up the deck of the *Hamakatsu* with a searchlight. There was one job that remained to be done before he left. It involved throwing sardines into the tubes used to catch the conger eels. The synthetic resin tubes measured about six inches in diameter and were a little over two feet in length. A couple hundred of these tubes were stacked on the left side of the foredeck. Hiroyuki began the process of putting a sardine in each tube and stuffing them with a cap fitted with rubber flaps. The eels would be enticed into the tubes by the smell of sardine. The rubber flaps at the mouth of each tube were arranged to trap the catch inside once it entered the tube. The two hundred tubes were attached with rope to a cable that stretched about three miles. This was the most common method of fishing for conger eels, and it involved letting the cable out at a uniform speed and allowing the tubes to sink to the seabed. Then all you had to do was wait, and later lift the tubes. Some of them would be empty, but more often than not a tube would contain more than one eel, sometimes as many as ten.

Since the rubber flaps prevented the conger eels from escaping, they would squirm around in the dark slippery tube. Hiroyuki was definitely not one for metaphors, but he thought the slippery squirming interior of the tube and the struggling eel resembled nothing so much as sexual intercourse. What pitiful creatures men were to be lured by a scent into a trap from which they could not escape! It was Hiroyuki's own story, too. He'd fallen into a trap set by a woman, when he was just twenty-two, that period of life when he was most set on having a good time. Trapped, unable to escape, he had set up home and started a family. The woman had become pregnant with his son Katsumi, and the inevitable obligation, marriage, had followed. He had not married for love. The love he had thought would bloom in time never did. Nothing changed. If he were asked whether he felt any affection for his wife, or children, he would have had to shake his head. It had all transpired beyond his control. Hiroyuki had never once liked another human being.

By the time he finished loading the tubes, the eastern sky was already light. Hiroyuki sat down on the cover of the ship's well for a smoke. As he smoked, he gazed at the movement of clouds above Mt. Kano. Upon waking he would first look at the dawn sky, then later, before leaving the harbor, check the clouds over the surrounding mountains. Fishermen always turned to the mountains for clues as to how the weather would turn out that day, whether it was likely to be windy or rainy. Any fisherman who did not know how to accurately read the winds and skies in and around the fishing grounds risked losing his life at sea.

The sky immediately above was more or less clear, although fine cloud cover could be seen in the direction of Mt. Kano and Mt. Nokogiri. Moreover, the mountains themselves appeared to be capped in lower clouds. The few patches of cloud in the sky right above him were drifting inland, indicating to Hiroyuki that southerly winds were already blowing inshore. It was very likely that these would be full gusts before the morning was out. Hiroyuki's instincts, honed over many years, told him that things didn't look good.

The sky told him that even if he did leave the harbor, he was not likely to get very far out. He would have to check the conditions out at sea and make a speedy retreat back to the harbor if the winds got too strong.

Today, Hiroyuki was going to fish off the south side of Breakwater No. 2. The debris floating in Tokyo Bay was said to make a round tour of the bay before washing up either on the north beach of Cape Futtsu or at the tip of the Miura Peninsula. Debris floating south of the line between Cape Kannon and Cape Futtsu, however, could flow out into the open sea instead of ever being washed ashore. That day, Hiroyuki wanted to fish in an area south of that line. There was no special reason for this hankering, he simply felt compelled to make his way as far as that patch of ocean.

Some ashes from the cigarette in his mouth fell onto his knee. He brushed them off with his hand and they scattered on the well cover. The cover was painted a dull green, but the paint was peeling off in many places. That was the first time Hiroyuki noticed that he was sitting atop the boat's well, and suddenly every downy hair on his body stood on end. A chill ran from his buttocks up his spine and a massive shiver rippled across his body.

Its top sticking up at roughly the center of the boat, the well was about as deep as the height of an average man and measured about six feet by nine. Its central location was ideal for a tank of its kind, for it was here that the boat's bottom was deepest. The boat's well was intended to hold the conger eels after a catch. When not in use, however, the well was covered by two planks to prevent accidents. Something unearthly ascended into the air from that covered hold filled with seawater. Even a veteran of the sea like Hiroyuki was affected enough by the eerieness that he jumped to his feet without thinking.

As he stood he caught sight of a black crevice between his legs. The planks had parted slightly. Hiroyuki dealt a light kick to force them back together and closed up the crack. As he did so, his body was shaking.

The wind grew stronger, and the boat rocked with a chopping motion, causing seawater in the well to splash inside the tank. The sound was a little different than usual, as if the water was splashing against something else.

Hiroyuki looked up at the sky again. The clouds were scudding faster. The southerlies were promising to whip up strong. But that wasn't enough reason to pack up and go home. Before the wind got any stronger, Hiroyuki had to get some work done.

Jumping back onto the wharf, Hiroyuki untied the boat's mooring rope and carried the loose end back onboard with him. The boat gradually began to move away from the quay under its own inertia.

4

Hiroyuki turned off the engine of the *Hamakatsu*. Once all two hundred tubes were thrown into the sea, it was only a question of waiting two hours until the conger eels got caught in the traps. Having cast the line, it was time for a short break, for a meal. Around eight o'clock, he was in the habit of eating a second breakfast.

The shadows of the tankers plying the Uraga Waterway bore down heavily on Hiroyuki's boat. Thanks to a fractional difference in course, there was no risk of collision. Compared to the massive tankers, the six-ton *Hamakatsu* looked like a mere speck of flotsam. Small as the boat was, there was a fair amount of space in the cabin, making it quite possible to spend the night should the need arise.

As Hiroyuki relaxed and ate his rice ball in the cabin, he began to feel uneasy about the instability of the boat. As he had predicted, the southerly winds had grown stronger and were causing the boat to rock violently. The sky that had appeared clear enough during the morning was now covered entirely with dark threatening clouds speeding across the sky-light. It was really the kind of weather that warranted calling off the trip and returning to port. Finding that he had almost no appetite, Hiroyuki left the cabin and threw his half-eaten rice ball into the sea.

His stomach was heaving, but not from nausea. It was a complex conspiracy of tension and fear. To be sure, the way the clouds were moving was disconcerting, but that did not seem to be the source of his anxiety. He couldn't stop thinking about that well. Hiroyuki rested his hand on the cabin door and looked down at the well by his feet. Although he remembered having kicked the cover planks closely together, he could see that the black crack had reappeared. He could hear the sound of water splashing at the bottom of the tank. Though it contained not a single eel, something was surely in there. Whenever the boat pitched violently, whatever it was could be heard thudding against the side.

Hiroyuki steeled himself before thrusting his hand in the gap between the planks. A hideous stench arose from the tank, and Hiroyuki pressed the towel around his neck against his nose. Still determined to look in, he moved the wooden panels further apart.

An angled shaft of light penetrated the darkness of the well to reveal a human foot. The seawater at the bottom of the well was lapping against the sole of a pale foot. Hiroyuki poked his head inside to peer deeper into the well. There were the hips...on up to the back...and pale, pudgy shoulders. And with every rock of the boat, a head thudded again and again against the wall of the tank. The body of a woman floated facedown at the bottom of the well. Though he could not see her face, Hiroyuki knew immediately who it was.

"Nanako..." he called to his wife, "so this is where you were."

No sooner had the words left his mouth than it all flashed back in his mind's eye as plain as day. He relived the sensation of his hands gripping her neck. He saw his wife's face desperately gasping for air. He could not make out what she was saying. Yet her torrent of abuse was seared into his brain.

Hiroyuki and his wife had had a violent quarrel the evening before last.

Hiroyuki had come home dead drunk and started to watch television with his mouth hanging half-open. His wife charged into the room and confronted him:

"Just look at you! Just look at that sloppy face of yours!" She brought a hand mirror and thrust it in front of his face. "Just take a look at yourself!"

Sure enough, the face looking back at him from the mirror was a sorry one. His mouth still hung half-open, even as he looked in the mirror. Not only was he drooling, but the crumbs of a snack he had eaten back at the bar stuck to the corners of his mouth. There it was, his face, ugly and worn-out. It was a face that looked older than his years. He was disgusted with himself. His wife's taunts hit their mark. She was right, and for that reason, he felt infuriated. What right had she to complain when she was receiving upwards of a million yen every month?

The mirror flashed for a moment, reflecting the fluorescent light. The flash seemed to urge action.

Slapping the mirror out of her hand, Hiroyuki roared at her, his articulation thick with the effects of drink.

"How dare you!"

Noting the change in the color of his glaring eyes, she steeled herself and looked away. The sight of her husband gearing up for an episode of violence was terrifying enough. She bit back the rest of her taunts, holding her resentment in check.

Yet, with that "How dare you?" barely out of his mouth,

Hiroyuki slumped down helplessly, his cheek against the surface of the tatami matting, his breath sputtering. Nanako stared at her husband for a while in his slumped, powerless condition. Her gaze betrayed contempt, like she was witnessing the dying moments of some monster. Suddenly, she began spitting out the words she had held back. Inside his head, befuddled as it was with drink, Hiroyuki registered her taunts, rebutting each one silently. He would not engage in a battle of words in which he was bound to lose.

He couldn't imagine what the bitch had to complain about. Him, stupid? Look at who was talking, daft bitch! How she went on in that superior whine about having made the top ten of her class! It made him sick. A fisherman didn't need to be an Einstein. He only earned such good wages because he had the strength and instincts of a man. And what was all that about genes? Who was passing on what to who? Both the kids? So what? Oh, now he saw what the bitch was getting at, it was all his fault that their girl had aphasia. His high-handedness was to blame? How the bitch went on and on with the gibberish!

It wasn't the first time he'd heard it. It was the same old quarrel repeated night after night, the same tired old taunts and complaints every time. Not only would she complain about having to look after her senile father-in-law and aphasic daughter, she would also accuse him of physical abuse and not caring for his family in the least. She claimed that she felt she was locked up in a prison cell. She bitterly lamented how deeply she hated her existence, how she couldn't take it anymore. He had but a single reply to all her complaints: month after month, he never brought home less than a million yen.

She had declared that she intended to leave him. He reacted with derision. Did she have anywhere to go? Who would have her? Had she forgotten how he'd taken her in and fed her? More than anything, how did she think she could make a living? She was incompetent and she'd end up dying in a ditch somewhere.

"I'm leaving" was just another tired old line paraded out again and again until it had completely lost any value it may once have had as a threat. She kept saying she would leave him, but she never even tried. She didn't have parents she could depend on, and she worried about her kids' future and her own job prospects.

But then Nanako said something she had never, ever said before. Exhausted from unleashing her torrent of grievances, she seemed almost to have shrunk. Her strength drained from her shoulders, she muttered as if to herself, "It'd be awful if he turned out like you."

This last remark pierced Hiroyuki's heart like a barbed fishing hook. What she meant was clear enough in light of her previous taunts. If she did leave him and desert the children, their motherless son would grow up and turn out like Hiroyuki. That was what Nanako saw as "awful."

It had been twenty years now since Hiroyuki's father had almost drowned at sea. Hiroyuki's mother had disappeared around the same time. He'd lost his mother when he was about Katsumi's age. His mother had deserted her family, running off with a younger man... At least, that was the account given him by his father. At the time, however, his father's senility had already been kicking in, making it difficult to gauge how much of what he said was true. For all that, there was no reason to believe that his mother had left for any other reason. As far as Hiroyuki could remember, his mother and father had done nothing but fight. It certainly seemed quite plausible that his mother, unable to endure his father's violence any longer, just left him and disappeared.

Hiroyuki had taken the news of having been abandoned by his mother without displaying any emotion, or so he believed. He could not remember having received much, if any, affection from his mother, and his only value had seemed to lie in deflecting his father's violence from her. As he grew older, however, the fact that his mother deserted him began to turn increasingly into a feeling that he was an unwanted presence in the world. Hiroyuki grew up feeling constantly resentful, and his self-confidence was always so fragile that it could be shattered with a single blow.

Perhaps that was why he'd gone to pieces that evening. Without understanding the cause of the blaze raging in him, Hiroyuki got to his feet, hit his head on a chest of drawers, and tottered across the room, coming down on top of his wife. It was as though flames erupted from every pore of his body. He was never one to waste time on words, but this assault was unlike previous ones, and his wife probably sensed what was coming. She did not attempt to cry out, but simply closed her eyes as if in resignation, and placed her hands on her husband's, which gripped her neck. It almost seemed as though she wanted him to squeeze harder, and Hiroyuki straddled her as she lay there, bringing the full weight of his body on his hands. When he gently removed them, Nanako was dead.

Hiroyuki got to his feet and for some reason switched off the fluorescent light. He turned on the small bedside lamp instead, shining it on his wife's face. She looked to be asleep. She was now released from her prison cell. She even looked content.

He strained his ears. There was not a sound to be heard. His father, his son, and his daughter were all asleep upstairs. The silence was so complete that he almost felt he could hear their breathing as they slept.

He already knew how to dispose of his wife's body. He would throw it into the sea. If he sank the body in the sea south of Breakwater No. 2, it would never be found.

He wrapped his wife's body in a fine nylon net and carried her over his shoulder onto his boat. He then dumped the body in the boat's well, there to stay until he could permanently dispose of it. That was all he could do then. The rest could wait until the day after next, when he'd sink the body while out fishing. Persuading himself thus, he put the planks back on the hold and went home.

He drank a glass or two of sake and went to sleep, and something happened in his mind that was very much like throwing his wife's body down a well and putting a lid on it. His brain cells confined the memory of his deed to its deepest recesses and capped it with a lid—one that was destined to be reopened soon enough.

5

...What a thing to have gone and done.

Two planks of wood formed the cover of the well. Hiroyuki removed one and stood it on the deck. He looked up at the sky, then sank down exhausted on the deck. The pit of his stomach began to heave. He deeply regretted what he'd done. Yet, his deed had been exposed to the light of day and there was no more escaping into oblivion.

"So! Why don't you get going?" his wife's still corpse seemed to provoke him with the reality. It seemed to be suppressing a smirk as it swayed back and forth.

What to do? First, he had to get down into the well with some rope, tie it to his wife's corpse, and haul her out of the well. He would then attach weights to the body and sink it. Having lain in seawater for a day and a half in the early summer heat, the corpse emitted an unearthly stench. The smell had smoldered in the confined space of the tank, shooting up like a flame through the opening of the removed plank. It occurred to Hiroyuki that leaping into a fire to retrieve a body would have been easier.

Having to get rid of the body was his wife's punishment for him. Hiroyuki cursed his own deed. But the task could not be avoided.

He tied a towel over his mouth and nose, knotting it firmly behind his head. He tied the end of some rope to the winch, while taking the other end in his hand. He peered into the well, as if he hadn't done enough of that already, and caught sight of his wife's blanched foot. The skin was puffed

123

up and had begun to peel.

The boat rocked violently. Hiroyuki put his hands on the edge of the well for support. He had almost fallen in.

The current was getting faster. As he scanned the sea around him, he noticed that there was not a single fishing boat in sight; they must have all scuttled back to harbor.

Everyone agreed that the waves in Tokyo Bay were terrifying. Waves came in two types, rollers and choppers, and the complex indentations of Tokyo Bay's coastline was perfectly configured to generate choppers. Waves were even now rushing in at random angles and breaking into white spray. If Hiroyuki wasn't careful, a chopper could smash into the deck from an unexpected angle and flood the boat with water.

Leaving the rope for the time being, Hiroyuki dropped anchor to set the boat against the wind. The boat could capsize if the waves came at its hull.

It was then that it hit him that he hadn't a second to waste. He was in for serious trouble if he didn't dump the body and get out of there soon.

A chopper breaking hard by spurred him to action.

With his hands on either side of the well, he lowered himself down to the bottom. Trying to avoid looking at the body as much as possible, he felt around for his wife's ankles. The best way to do the job seemed to be to bind the legs together with rope and haul it out upside down. Perhaps he could get it over with without having to look at her face.

Every time the boat pitched unexpectedly, Hiroyuki staggered and his wife's legs would slip from his grasp. He cursed aloud and clamped the end of the rope between his teeth. In that split second, his entire body was jarred by an awful premonition. An uncanny shudder ran through the length and breadth of the boat, and it pitched once like never before and started to list. From that point on, everything unfolded in slow motion. Slowly, ever so slowly, the opening of the well, which until then had been above him, rolled down to his side, throwing the other plank off with a thud. Soon his only source of daylight, the opening, was completely submerged in the sea and Hiroyuki's world went pitch dark.

The seawater flooded in at his feet, reached his waist and then his chest in no time, and forced his body up, up.

...She's capsized.

Before the word "capsized" could come to his mind, his body had grasped the situation and braced for death. He was too panicked even to breathe. In that state, he struggled up to reach air and rammed his head against the bottom of the boat. The water began to stop flowing in, leaving a single head's breadth of air. Thrusting his face up into that pitch-dark sliver, Hiroyuki coughed violently. He must have swallowed a large amount of seawater.

His heart literally shrank in his chest. He was dead for sure unless he managed to control his panic. His brain raced in a frantic search for some way to save himself... Yes. That was it. He'd fill his lungs to capacity, dive down to find the opening of the well, and swim out.

He tried to remain calm. There was still plenty of air left. There was no need to lose his head. No good would come of a frantic exit. Straying too far from the boat meant certain death.

He suddenly remembered. What happened to that rope he'd been holding just a few moments ago? The other end of the rope had been wound round the winch on the deck. The boat had capsized just as he was trying to bind his wife's legs with the rope. He would not drift away from the boat as long as he held on to the rope and pulled himself back along it.

No matter how much he groped around in the water for the rope, his fingertips were unable to locate it. It was taking too long. He resigned himself to swim out without the guidance of the rope. He took several deep breaths to fill his lungs. The more he tried to inhale the air trapped in that cramped, dark space, the more suffocated he felt. His panic was making him hyperventilate. Hiroyuki was no longer sure he could make it, when ten feet was all he needed to dive at most.

With all his remaining strength, he forced his head under the water and lunged downwards. In an instant, he saw a three-foot-square opening cut out in the darkness beneath him. A faint light filtered through from below. The opening of the well was right in front of him. "Nothing to it," he thought as he placed his hands on the edge of the opening and thrust his head through. He thrust out his chest, and then his waist, and right when his body formed a V shape, Hiroyuki felt something pull at his foot. Though the upper part of his body was now outside the well, his legs refused to follow. He was fast losing what breath he had. He gathered his remaining strength and tried to yank his foot free. To no avail. There was no choice but to go back. Any more hesitation, and he'd die like that in a V shape.

As much as he hated to, he pulled back the upper half of his body and came up where he had been before. His head emerged from the water with such force that he bumped it hard on the floor of the boat. A bolt of searing pain shot through him. The sliver of air had shrunk in size; the boat was slowly sinking. Now, to get any air at all, Hiroyuki had to bend his head and thrust just his nose and mouth out of the water.

He bent his leg and groped around with his hand to find out what had caught. A moment before, he could have sworn that his foot was tangled up in rope. Yet, now, his hand detected nothing there at all. Maybe something had decided to hold his foot...

But this was no time for speculation. Filling his lungs with what little air remained at the top, he lunged down headfirst once more.

No sooner had he thrust his head downward than a spectral human form drifted toward the hazy opening. Its hair fanned out around the head. As though to block the exit, the wife's corpse had wandered out from the side, and it danced like a dark shadow in the faint light from below.

The sight made Hiroyuki gulp seawater. Terrified by his wife's movement, which seemed willful, he used up all the air in his lungs.

...Exit's blocked.

There was nothing to do but surface again.

This time, he had almost to lick the bottom of the boat to get any air. He let out a silent scream. The smell of fuel, which must have leaked from the engine, assailed his nostrils.

It was all up with him, all over.

He pissed himself, and started crying. Above, the boat floor. Below, the sea. The only exit was occupied by his wife. Hiroyuki had no space left to live.

He was like a conger eel caught in a trap. His wife's corpse was the rubber flap at the opening of the eel tube. With arms and legs akimbo, she clung with grim tenacity to the opening to prevent his passage.

Hiroyuki didn't have the strength left to laugh at the irony. A man who'd trapped countless conger eels in dark tubes was now snared himself and waiting for death.

With the pounding of the waves, the roar should have been a lot more thunderous, but it was strangely calm all around. Death was approaching with a steady tread. There was no escaping it.

As he thought of his imminent death, a notion popped into his mind. Twenty years ago, around when his mother disappeared, Hiroyuki's father had narrowly escaped death. Hiroyuki had never doubted his father's story. But now, with death staring him in the face, he understood the truth. Just as Hiroyuki had done, his father had killed his wife and used his fishing as an alibi for disposing the body out at sea. His father's mental troubles had nothing to do with having hit his head. His terrible deed had slowly driven him mad.

The same blood ran in his veins, and the past was repeating itself. Even if Hiroyuki were to return home alive and somehow manage to bring up his son single-handedly, Katsumi would no doubt end up doing exactly the same thing. Where to sever the awful chain?

In death. All he had to do was die. With the death of both his parents, his son would grow up in a new environment. The thought made it a little easier for Hiroyuki. Perhaps he could meet death with composure.

Then he heard two sounds coming from above, with a

brief interval between them. There it was again, two sounds. It was not the waves striking the boat; it sounded more artificial.

At first he listened vacantly. But when he fathomed the meaning of the sound that was penetrating his brain, he became alert and thrust his face upwards. There was still a little air left. A few more knocks came from the exterior of the keel.

His body reacted reflexively, his right hand clenching into a fist and banging against the bottom. As if in response, two sounds from above. And now Hiroyuki, thumping the bottom twice. From above, another answer of two knocks.

He was saved!

Just when he'd given up hope of ever getting out alive, he was given a second chance. Hiroyuki had witnessed a similar scene a few years ago. A rescue boat from the Maritime Safety Agency was rushing to the aid of a fishing vessel that had capsized as a result of poor handling. Hiroyuki, who'd been fishing, interrupted his work to pull alongside and watch. The rescue squad used the same procedure to check if anyone had been trapped in the cabin. They straddled the keel of the overturned boat and knocked on its bottom, reassuring any survivors that help was on the way; they would send down their divers if anyone responded. The divers took an extra regulator down with them to insert in the mouth of the survivor. Other fishing boats had also gathered around to watch the operation, and when the trapped fisherman emerged safely from the sinking boat, there was some wild cheering.

The sounds he now heard raining down from above were to let him know that the Maritime Safety Agency had come to his rescue. Hiroyuki had lost all sense of time. He wondered how long ago the boat had capsized. It was just conceivable that a patrol boat had discovered him by chance.

Hiroyuki roared with joy at his good fortune. He had been granted a new lease on life; he'd be able to breathe real air once more.

He thrust his face under the water and looked down. He expected to see his wife blocking the opening, but she wasn't there. She had vanished. Perhaps a wave had caught her and washed her out of the well. She was probably sinking deep just then. Hiroyuki tried hard to believe that this was the case. Without his wife's body, no criminal charge could be proved against him.

Just when everything had looked so desperate, his fortune had suddenly changed for the better. Almost as soon as his wife's body had disappeared, effectively disposing of itself, the rescue team had found him. Hiroyuki could not wait for the divers to come get him.

Suddenly, his body was hugged by powerful arms. They were here!

He could hear no voices, but he felt the reassuring words in his stomach: "You're all right now."

Hiroyuki felt for the diver's arm and clung to him. The diver put his arm around Hiroyuki's shoulder and inserted a regulator snugly into his mouth. Holding the mouthpiece tightly between his teeth, he drew in air. It had the aroma of a highland plateau; never had air tasted so sweet. Determined to never let go of it, he bit deeper into the mouthpiece, sucking in the air over and over again.

He was ecstatic. Once back in the land of the living, he

would be able to love them all, his son, his daughter, even his senile father. The shell that encased him was cracking and breaking off like the lie it had always been. He was sorry not everything could be the same again. He was going to beg for his wife's forgiveness. He had no idea how to apologize to the dead. His desire to do so, however, was genuine.

Hiroyuki had taken it for granted that the diver would escort him in a downward dive. But he felt himself suddenly floating up instead. In an instant, he was gazing at the keel of the *Hamakatsu*, which was now barely afloat. Resembling nothing more permanent than a leaf on the water, the boat looked as if it would go under at any moment. The patrol boat made its way towards them. People jostled about on the deck; they all seemed to be shouting things, but Hiroyuki couldn't hear their voices.

He could see all around him, all of the sea and the sky. Bursting through the clouds, shafts of light poured down onto the crests of waves as they broke and spewed their foam. Catching the light, the spray scintillated like jewels hurled in every direction. This was the sea he had known from childhood. Cape Futtsu stretched straight toward him. The wind and waves were strong. Never had he seen the sea so sublime, it shimmered. A sense of relief enveloped him, and his body felt lighter and lighter.

A phrase he'd never once uttered in his life came to him now: *All clear!*

He spoke the words and they felt good. He spoke them once more.

The patrol ship retrieved the two bodies simultaneously.

It was obvious that one was that of a woman who'd been dead for two or three days. The other was that of a man who'd just breathed his last. What this meant would be understood in due course.

What they would never understand, however, was why the man had died with the woman's cadaver locked in his embrace. He certainly didn't look like he'd clutched at straw in panic-stricken desperation. Far from anguished, the man's expression was serene. Something else that troubled the rescue team was that the woman's right thumb was plunged down to its base in the man's mouth. How on earth could the dead woman insert her thumb into the man's mouth? Nonetheless, that was how it looked to those who saw the corpses.

The man must have bitten down hard on the thumb, for his jaws refused to unclamp even after the recovered bodies had been laid on the deck of the patrol boat. When they pried his mouth open and removed the thumb, they found that it'd nearly come off. They tried giving the man artificial respiration to see if he could be revived. It was useless. He showed no signs of returning to life. He was dead. They could have saved him if they'd reached him just a few minutes earlier.

The man's serene expression, however, soothed the rescuers' feelings. It wasn't easy to bite down so fiercely and at the same time wear such a serene expression. But this man had accomplished the contradiction.

DREAM CRUISE

Masayuki Enoyoshi sat against the mast with his feet stretched out on the bow hatch. In this sloppiest of postures, he seemed to be deliberately facing away from the cockpit. It was not possible to sit on the bow hatch when the main and jib sails were set; anyone sitting there would obstruct the sail whenever the boat changed direction. At that particular moment, however, the small yacht, twenty-five feet long, was motoring out into Tokyo Bay along a sea-lane. Bordered on both sides by landfills, the sea-lane was like a little bay within a larger one. All the yacht's sails were down. Yachts were prohibited from crossing this patch of sea with their sails set. Any yacht being powered by its sails was likely to obstruct the heavy maritime traffic that plied this part of the bay.

Enoyoshi guessed what the Ushijimas, the couple who owned the boat, were up to. They were going to use this time with the sails down to talk to him. Still inexperienced, Ushijima was far from proficient at using the sails to steer the yacht. It'd been annoying just to watch. Apparently unable to gauge the direction of the wind, Ushijima kept fussing about in the cockpit working the sails in and out with an uncertain look on his face. The way he glanced windward and shook his head, it was obvious the yacht wasn't sailing how he wanted it to. Enoyoshi had felt more uneasy watching Ushijima's expression than from the lurching of the boat and had wondered whether they'd make it safely back to the marina.

Yet Ushijima it was who had his hand on the tiller now in the cockpit just behind Enoyoshi. When it came to steering with the nine-horsepower outboard motor, the helmsman was finding it easy enough to maneuver the yacht. Leaving a trail of white foam in its wake, the yacht silently made its

way between the landfill that served as the central breakwater and the pier of the Ariake Ferry. A trip around the tip of
Wakasu Marine Park and slightly up the Ara River brought
you back to the Dream Island Marina. With renewed confidence in his ability to handle the boat, Ushijima self-con-
sciously placed a foot up on the bench and struck a pose at the
tiller. Ushijima's wife Minako did not appear on deck. She
was probably in the cabin down below looking for something
to drink. Enoyoshi did not miss her talkative presence. He
was only too grateful for the peaceful interlude.

Enoyoshi glanced at his watch. It was a little before six
in the evening. This mini-cruise was only intended to provide
a superficial sampling of the crannies of Tokyo Bay and was
due to return to the Dream Island Marina by evening.

The sun was setting on the western horizon. If this were
the open sea, they would have beheld the majestic sight of an
evening sun quenching itself on an unobstructed horizon.
Here the view was not all that different from what you could
get from the pier, but the inexperienced skipper had neither
the skill nor the courage to get the boat out into the open sea.
A cluster of super-high-rises under construction in the sec-
ondary coastal development area rose in the western sky like
a clump of bamboo shoots springing from the buried nutrients
of the landfill.

A thin evening mist began to envelop the black, steel-
framed skeletons of the unfinished skyscrapers silhouetted
against a crimson background. Although one would not have
expected construction to be in progress on a Sunday, thunderous booms could be heard. It was difficult to determine exactly where these sounds were coming from, but each massive

reverberation only served to exacerbate Enoyoshi's feelings of unease. Though he could not pinpoint the source of his anxiety, it was there all the same. The booms echoing up from the seabed to the bottom of the boat reached Enoyoshi's very guts.

Emerging from the cabin, Minako pointed excitedly in the direction opposite the sunset. "Say, look over there!" she chirped with affected youthful gaiety.

At that moment, the yacht, named *MINAKO* after the woman, was about to pass the tip of Wakasu Marine Park. The instant the boat shifted course, Disneyland immediately came into view. It was just that time of evening and lights were beginning to come on in the distance. What Minako was urging the men to look at with her Betty Boop squeak was Disneyland and the lights from the hotels that lined the nearby coast. The girlish tone had little childish innocence about it, conveying more of a selfish insistence that the others get involved. Enoyoshi reacted with nothing more than a quick glance and otherwise resolved to ignore her.

But she called over to him, "What are you doing musing over there, come get some beer!"

Clasping the mast, Enoyoshi turned to look at her. She stood holding up a can of beer.

Enoyoshi made a noncommittal grunt and wondered what to do. He felt pathetic that he couldn't just say no. So, should he refuse to have anything to do with her inane chatter by staying put in his sanctuary, or should he get his hands on a beer and pay the price of enduring her "sales talk"? There was no denying his thirst, and beer was appealing.

With one hand still on the mast and the other on the

boom, he crawled towards the cockpit to take the beer offered by Minako.

"Thank you. It's just what I needed."

He bobbed his head in appreciation, roughly popped the pull tab open, then gulped down the beer. It was chilled and tasted delicious. Detecting contentment on Enoyoshi's face, Minako ventured, "Well? Don't you think it's just marvelous?"

The moment he heard her start, the beer seemed to lose some of its savor. How many times had he had to endure this spiel that day? Her tone suggested that she was not so much asking for an opinion as forcing him to accept her own. He made another noncommittal grunt in response.

In an attempt to change the subject, he vainly wracked his brain for another topic. The three of them on the yacht had precious little in common to talk about. This was the third time that Enoyoshi had met Ushijima. As for Minako, he had only met her that morning.

Ushijima, who'd been quiet, chimed in, "You can do it. It's all yours for the taking."

Enoyoshi didn't reply. If only they set the sails again. That would shut them up. They wouldn't have the leisure to harass him if they had to trim the jib sail and main sail. They'd be flailing about in utter confusion. But while they cruised the calm waters of the evening sea using the outboard motor, it was all too easy for Ushijima to stand there beer in hand minding just the tiller.

Enoyoshi had met Ushijima at a high school reunion in July, two months ago. It hadn't been a class reunion but rather a grand reunion of all the old boys. Hundreds of them attended the annual event. In the ten years since Enoyoshi graduated he'd never once attended a reunion. That year, he happened to have the weekend free and decided to go for a change. Disappointed not to find as many old classmates as he'd expected, Enoyoshi milled around the room searching for familiar faces. In the process he made small talk with Ushijima and they ended up exchanging business cards. Ushijima had graduated seven years before Enoyoshi and his card said *Ministry of Agriculture, Forestry, and Fisheries*. A month later, Ushijima asked Enoyoshi out for a drink and proposed the current outing.

Now that he thought about it, Enoyoshi should have suspected Ushijima's motives and been altogether more circumspect. In the past, there'd been acquaintances who'd contacted him out of the blue, asking to meet up for old times' sake, only to approach him then with some dubious scheme. It now seemed only natural that, graduates of the same school or not, the act of inviting a stranger involved an ulterior motive. If they were still fellow students, that would have been one thing. In the adult world, however, any relationship usually revolved around an eye to some sort of gain.

"First picture whatever it is that you desire, that you want to have."

Ushijima's face was close by and the voice came from right behind Enoyoshi's ears. The dim light of dusk revealed the lines of age etched on Ushijima's brow. Whenever Ushijima looked down, his thinning hair also became apparent. Enoyoshi felt that the man, who'd initially appeared young for his age, had suddenly gained many years.

"What is it that you want in life?"

It was clear that the answer Ushijima was seeking was something that required a fortune to buy, like a yacht or a Mercedes. Enoyoshi chose a different sort of thing. He could have picked anything, so long as it couldn't be bought.

"Now that you mention it, I suppose I'd like a child."

Enoyoshi wasn't married, nor was he even remotely engaged. He was single and had told so to Ushijima.

The couple exchanged surprised glances.

"Are you married?" asked Minako in wide-eyed puzzlement. As she turned toward her husband, her look turned fierce, conveying annoyance at having been misinformed.

Ushijima, nettled, peered at Enoyoshi. "I thought you said you were single?"

"Sure, I'm single. But I'm living with this girl, and if I could get her in the family way, that's all it'd take to get her to marry me."

It was a lie. There was no woman in his life. Pious a lie as it was, he began to loathe himself. His inability to just say no to anyone was pathetic and made him feel like some kid who was never going to grow up. All he could do was be inconsistent in the hope that the other would realize that he wasn't interested.

His wish wasn't granted, and Minako began to address the lie. "Suppose you did have a child and it led to marriage. You'll need money. There'll be the cost of the wedding and you'll have to find somewhere to live. And your child, of course. Do you realize how much it costs to raise kids?"

The Ushijimas were childless, but this didn't make them feel any less qualified to lecture Enoyoshi. They insisted that the salary earned from an ordinary company job wasn't enough to raise a family. Always struggling to make ends meet, he'd never be able to realize his own dreams...

The Ushijimas were trying to get him interested in a pyramid-type sales scheme funded by foreign capital. Enoyoshi was well aware that the organization in question was not involved in anything illegal. The concept of cutting costs through non-store retailing and handing the margin to the salespeople was not a bad one. The salespeople belonged to different echelons of a pyramidal hierarchy—the higher the level, the greater the performance bonus. The Ushijimas were apparently on the third rung from the bottom and were eager to move up. To do so, they had to recruit salespeople by hook or by crook. Persuading new blood to sell the products manufactured by the company, training the rookies to become great sales reps, was the only way to improve their ranks. A car salesman no doubt familiar with marketing techniques, Enoyoshi would be a great catch for the Ushijimas. In fact, the products manufactured by the company included a car-care line.

Rising in rank meant making more money, enough to buy an apartment in just one year. The Ushijimas claimed they were making double what they made as civil servants from the pyramid scheme. Otherwise, they wouldn't have the yacht. The yacht was an absolutely indispensable tool for their recruitment efforts. Once they were out at sea, they could hammer their victim with their recruitment pitch without worrying about the victim escaping. The yacht also served as proof that the scheme could indeed make your dreams come true. For the Ushijimas, yachting was like holding one of those home parties where the host peddled some product.

"Imagining it is key. Imagine it long enough and hard enough and it will come true."

Ushijima argued his case fervently, but Enoyoshi would have none of it. The world that Ushijima was painting held no interest at all for Enoyoshi. He wasn't indifferent to making money, but he simply wasn't ready to pursue it at the price of wrecking relationships. He could indeed imagine where it would all lead if he went after ever-increasing sales bonuses. He'd find himself in a sort of religious cult, a clique of similarly minded fanatics with one goal and one ideal, and it would be impossible to break away.

The Ushijimas reacted with clear displeasure and irritation. They spoke disapprovingly of Enoyoshi's lack of imagination, calling him a fool, even hinting that he was an inferior human being. With their vaunted imagination, they predicted that Enoyoshi would live and die as a pathetic man working all life long just to eke out a living, without worthwhile dreams.

Enoyoshi could not even be bothered to argue with them. Of course, spending his entire life as a mere salesman was a distinct possibility. It would have been pointless to tell them that the idea didn't really upset him. It would have been tedious. All Enoyoshi wanted was to get off the yacht as soon as possible. He'd had enough of not having solid ground beneath him and being aboard someone else's yacht. He loathed the craven subservience that the unaccustomed setting was inducing in him.

The yacht was moving steadily northward about a hundred yards east of the Wakasu Golf Links, which stretched north to south on a slender tract of land. It was only another mile and a half to the Ara River Bay Bridge, and beyond it was the entrance to the Dream Island Marina. He wouldn't have to put up with them much longer now. Once off the yacht, he would never have anything to do with them again.

His prayers for haste notwithstanding, the engine of the *MINAKO* sputtered and came to a stop. So strangely that Ushijima stopped in mid-sentence and gulped. He looked over at the outboard motor.

"Odd, very odd."

Enoyoshi glanced unconsciously at his watch. 6:27 p.m., that was when the yacht came to a standstill. A Keio line train was crossing the iron bridge ahead of them, making a distinctive sound. The light from the train windows formed a stream of white in the evening sky above the mouth of the river. Lights were lit in almost every building that lined the bay. The yacht had stopped just as the black surface of the sea began to glimmer with the reflections of these lights.

The area where the yacht had stopped ruled out the possibility of having run aground. They were several hundred yards west of the sandbar known as Sanmaizu that extended due south of the Kasai Coastal Park near the mouth of the former Edo River. Iron poles marked such shallow stretches of water to indicate the hazard. At night the tips of these poles were illuminated. There was little risk of accidentally running aground on sandbars unless there were strong winds or a dense fog. The Dream Island Marina staff had warned them repeatedly about the shallows outside the entrance, and for all his faults as a sailor, Ushijima had been steering the yacht with particular attention to avoiding the shallows.

"The engine's stopped, hasn't it?" Enoyoshi noted incuriously, making no move to get up from his bench.

With a dubious look, Ushijima unscrewed the cap on the gasoline tank and peered in to check that it wasn't empty. He gingerly pulled the hand starter. The engine started immediately. The Ushijimas looked relieved, but only for a brief while. As soon as the skipper shifted into forward gear, the engine sputtered and died once more.

Now, instead of trying to restart the engine, Ushijima tilted up the drive unit out of the water.

"What is this?" Ushima exclaimed wildly, making Enoyoshi spring up. All three of them looked at the propeller.

In the evening darkness, soaked with seawater, the thing looked almost black. Ushijima reached toward the drive unit and retrieved, from in between the trim tab and the propeller, a child's blue canvas shoe. It had probably been floating nearby when the laces got tangled in the shaft and the whole shoe ended up being wound in to the propeller.

It was one of those Disney products, with a Mickey Mouse motif. Ushijima turned the shoe upside down to check the size. It was small and probably belonged to a young boy just several years old.

Shrugging his shoulders, Ushijima handed the shoe to Enoyoshi and made a face. His attitude suggested that he wanted Enoyoshi to get rid of it one way or another. With all kinds of objects floating in the sea, it wasn't strange to find a child's shoe. Yet, Ushijima seemed to find the thing somewhat sinister and seemed even afraid of it. After handing the shoe to Enoyoshi, he used a towel to wipe the palm of his right hand meticulously.

Ushijima prodded with a look, and Enoyoshi was about to throw the shoe back into the sea when he noticed a name on the heel. *Kazuhiro*, it said in black marker pen.

"Little Kazuhiro," Enoyoshi muttered to himself.

"Just throw it away, okay?" Ushijima commanded rather menacingly.

Rather than hurl it away, Enoyoshi set it on the surface like a little boat and gave the heel a gentle shove.

The virtually brand-new left shoe bobbed unsteadily as it floated away. The current in this area was pretty swift, close as it was to the mouth of the River Ara. The shoe floated south and soon melted into the blackness of the sea. Enoyoshi pictured a little boy hopping about on his right foot.

Ushijima lowered the drive unit back into the water and started the engine. They'd removed the shoe that had caused the engine trouble; they ought to be ready to go. Enoyoshi's watch read 6:35. They'd lost five minutes but it looked like they'd return on schedule at seven.

"Let's be off," said Ushijima, putting the boat into forward gear. This time the engine didn't stall and churned steadily.

The feeling they got in the next few moments was hard to describe in words. A gurgling sound could be heard from behind the drive unit and there was a rush of tiny bubbles to the surface. It was clear that the propeller was turning to drive the boat forward. Yet the yacht was not moving. It felt like being in a dream, or rather, a nightmare, where no matter how hard you try to run away from the monster, your feet can't get traction and only your heart speeds off. All three aboard felt more or less like that. Although the hull and deck of the yacht lay between them and the water below, it was as if their own feet had become entangled in some piece of rope that floated up from the seabed.

Enoyoshi and Ushijima remained absolutely speechless, while Minako nervously kept standing up and sitting down on the bench. She demanded in a strident tone that verged on a scream, "What's up? Why aren't we moving?"

Ushijima fiddled with the gears and tried putting the engine in reverse. The yacht refused to move in either direction.

"Could you try leaning over port?" asked Ushijima.

As requested, Enoyoshi and Minako leaned overboard the left side of the vessel. As it tipped, Ushijima put the engine into forward gear, to no avail. They tried motoring forward with the weight on starboard, then backwards weighted on starboard, and finally backwards weighted on port, but the yacht refused to budge, as though it'd taken root.

Ushijima switched off the engine. Minako started to say something, but he waved her silent.

"Hold it, will you?" Saying so, he plunged in thought, probably sifting through his limited experience regarding what to do to get an immobilized yacht moving. Enoyoshi had been longing to return to the marina and be rid of the couple, but given the situation, he had no intention of rushing Ushijima. The man's expression was not just serious, but grave. Recruiting for a sales scheme must have been the last thing on his mind just then.

"Right," Ushijima said as if to rally himself, and stood up. He announced the next step they needed to take. "Let's take a sounding."

Ushijima opened a foot locker and pulled out an anchor tied to a piece of rope. He gradually lowered the anchor into the water. When it had sunk a few dozen feet into the water, Ushijima stopped feeding out the rope and was still for about seconds. Then he heaved a big sigh and began pulling the rope back up. There was no problem with the water depth. The yacht hadn't stopped because its long keel was stuck in some sandbank. They had not run aground, it was certain now.

"Weird, isn't it?" expressed Enoyoshi. There was nothing else to be said about the situation. The unease of having such a precarious footing was something he'd never had to experience on land.

Returning the rope and anchor to the locker, Ushijima banged it shut and sat down on top of it. He clearly wasn't in any mood to talk. Minako turned on the cabin and navigating lights and opened the hatch. The light from the cabin made the clean white surface of the cockpit gleam as though it was coated in fluorescent paint.

The sense of crisis that Enoyoshi was beginning to feel was probably mild compared to what the Ushijimas must have been going through. After all, Enoyoshi was not crew, just a guest on the yacht, and as such he was not responsible for what was happening. It would have been another matter entirely if they'd been stranded far out at sea with no land in sight. As it was, they were a mere hundred yards or so east of Wakasu Golf Links, whose lights were clearly visible. On the north and the east, too, land was not far away. The shoreline appeared as a belt of light and a murmur of evening activity blended with the puttering of car exhaust.

Meanwhile, the Ushijimas became more morose with every passing minute. Ushijima looked dumbfounded about the yacht having come to a standstill, while Minako, manifestly resenting her husband for his incompetence, snorted and sighed loudly to pressure him to get the thing moving again. The whole situation was a painful slap in the face for Minako, who'd been raving to Enoyoshi about the joys of having a yacht, who'd been trying to entice him to join her in relishing a clearly superior level of life. *Well? Don't you think it's just marvelous?* It was like seeing your pet do something totally stupid when you've bragged about its clever tricks and invited people over for a little show.

Quite apart from feeling anxious about his footing, Enoyoshi was getting quite curious as to how Ushijima meant to get them out of the fix.

Clueless though he was, Enoyoshi offered a theory. "Maybe some rope got tangled around the keel?"

Ushijima raised his face and nodded rather eagerly. "That's just what I was thinking. It could have caught on a fixed net or something."

"Is this where they set nets?"

Ushijima shook his head. "Actually, no. This is a shipping lane."

"So..."

"Some clump of rope, from a fixed net or something like that, could've drifted over and caught on the keel."

It was obvious even to Enoyoshi that if that was the problem, the other end of the rope was still embedded securely on the sea floor. Such a coincidence seemed too far-fetched. He had to force back a smile as he envisaged a piece of rope forming a noose and rising up from the seabed to ensnare the keel of the yacht the way a cowboy would lasso a steer.

"In that case, what are we going to do?" the yacht's namesake broke in. Contorting her thick lips, she glared at her husband. Enoyoshi somehow couldn't get on with that jowly face of hers. Her vanity showed in the contours of her face and her make-up. It was probably she who'd first dabbled in the sales scheme, then sucked in her husband. She probably goaded him on as his sales partner.

"Get the rope off the keel, I suppose."

Enoyoshi could imagine with ease what Ushijima had to do now. It was quite simple. Dive down under the yacht, feel for the rope, and get if off the keel. Yet the mere sight of those black waters below was enough to give him the jitters. With the sun now completely set under the horizon, the always dark water of the bay appeared even blacker now, reflecting the inky night sky. The very thought of holding his breath and diving into the murky depths was enough to choke him.

The boat was not equipped with a mask or an underwater light, and Ushijima would have to grope around in the dark to get the job done. Even if he had a mask, there would be near zero visibility in the sludgy waters of Tokyo Bay.

But Ushijima stayed silent, unmoving. Pensively biting his lower lip, he shot laden glances at Enoyoshi, who did not wonder why Ushijima wasn't showing any sign of making a move when what needed to be done was clear. Enoyoshi understood. Ushijima didn't want to go. He wanted Enoyoshi to go, but instead of asking, he was silently hoping Enoyoshi would offer to go.

...Slim chance.

Enoyoshi had absolutely no intention of obliging him. To communicate this to Ushijima, he got to his feet and turned his back on him gloweringly. He was under no obligation whatsoever to work for the benefit of *MINAKO*, let alone risk his life.

"Enoyoshi." Just as he was heading toward the cabin, Ushijima called him back.

Enoyoshi turned to see that Ushijima was unbuttoning his shirt. The skipper appeared to have decided that there was nothing to do but handle the job himself. "Well, good," Enoyoshi remarked inwardly.

Winding a rope around himself several times and tying it in a bowline knot, Ushijima handed the loose end to Enoyoshi.

"I'm counting on you," said Ushijima, giving Enoyoshi a slap on the shoulder.

"You're in safe hands," Enoyoshi assured him, gripping the rope tightly for his host to see.

Ushijima entered the water feet first and lowered himself up to the shoulders. With his hands on the rim at the stern, he bent and stretched his arms as if chinning himself up on an iron bar, and regulated his breathing. It was still early September, so the water could not be that cold. As he bobbed up and down in the water, Ushijima's face appeared gray in the light from the cabin. His reluctance to just go ahead and do the job was painfully evident from his expression. Yet, in the next instant, Ushijima thrust himself up out of the water, held his breath, and plunged down under the surface.

A yacht's keel is a board that protrudes straight down into the water from the center of the hull. The keel of

MINAKO was three feet wide and four feet long. Hence, Ushijima's dive, if it could be called a dive, involved nothing more than a descent of several feet at most. The length of rope that needed to be extended was negligible. Even so, Enoyoshi hurled out a couple of dozen feet out into the sea so that Ushijima would have plenty to spare if he needed it.

Half a minute later, Ushijima plopped his head out of the water. He tried to get a grip on the yacht but failed, and treaded water with just his head above the surface.

"How's it look?"

Ushijima shook his head vigorously in response. His face looked even grayer than before. Most probably, on his first dive, all he could do was locate the keel itself.

Ushijima regulated his breathing in preparation for a second attempt. He hadn't been down there a minute before Enoyoshi felt a bump at his feet, and the hull reverberated in a way that suggested that Ushijima was struggling down there. The sensation from the length of the rope conveyed the same. Ushijima had to be there right underneath, but Enoyoshi felt a pang of anxiety and tried pulling in some rope.

Just then, his hands registered a violent jolt, and the rope pulled taut as if some enormous fish had caught on the other end. As he tried to maintain hold of the rope, Enoyoshi was pulled halfway over the side of the yacht.

"Please, give me a hand," he summoned Minako, who rose from the bench and came over to his side. As a precaution, he had her hold the end of the rope while he pulled with all his might. Enoyoshi's arms felt Ushijima's full weight. He had a bad feeling. Maybe there'd been some accident.

Just a few feet from the yacht, Ushijima's head burst up

through the surface. Though he was treading water, he didn't seem to be gaining any buoyancy. His body was arching back, and he looked like he might go under.

"Hold on!"

With this shout of encouragement, Enoyoshi pulled even harder on the rope to lift Ushijima up. Ushijima was trying to say something, but no words came from his mouth. Perhaps it was a silent scream of terror. It was dreadful, his expression slackening the next moment as he began to sink, his thinning hair fanning out on the surface of the water like seaweed. Enoyoshi pulled with every ounce of strength he had, for he felt sure that Ushijima was about to drown.

It was impossible to pull him straight up the side of the yacht. Going around to the stern, Enoyoshi grasped Ushijima under the arms and heaved him up toward the cockpit. Ushijima was now bent double with his abdomen against the rim of the stern. When his cheek brushed against the deck, he vomited. From his mouth, in intermittent bursts, came not only the seawater he had swallowed during the dive, but also the remains of the sandwiches and beer he'd had for lunch. His whole body convulsed with each violent upchuck. His feet were still dragging in the water. Minako yelped and sprang aside; even as she let out screams, she ran to the cabin to get a towel.

Trying to heave himself aboard, Ushijima frantically crawled forward. When he'd pulled his legs out of the water, he rolled over faceup, tried to take a breath, and started coughing violently.

Enoyoshi was not sure how to assist someone who had nearly drowned. All he could do was ask over and over again if Ushijima was "okay." Slinging the towel that Minako had given him over his shoulder, he began to rub Ushijima's back. His head thrust over the side, Ushijima kept retching though nothing was coming out of him except tears and saliva. Still, he would not stop. Urged by violent convulsions, he continued to turn his stomach inside out.

Enoyoshi decided that Ushijima would be better off lying down on the bed in the cabin. Offering Ushijima the support of his shoulder, he started to walk him to the cabin. It became clear after only one or two steps that Ushijima was completely powerless from the knees down. It was not so much that the strength had left his legs, it was as though he'd actually lost his legs from the knees down. After finally managing to get Ushijima on the cabin bed, Enoyoshi covered him with the bath towel, a tracksuit jacket, and anything warm he could find. Ushijima's shaking showed no signs of abating; if anything, it was getting worse by the minute. From time to time, his pale lips uttered a dreadful moan that resembled the howling of a wild beast. The change in Ushijima's appearance was so dramatic that all Enoyoshi and Minako could do was stand in stupefied silence by the bedside.

At first, Enoyoshi had imagined that Ushijima might have suffered something like the following. In need of fresh air, he tries to make his way straight up to the surface. But, running out of air halfway up, he swallows seawater and panics. Perhaps his lifeline has caught on the keel. At any rate he panics and starts to drown. The terror of groping around in the dark sea was indescribable and the slightest mishap could bring on panic.

But the total look of horror on Ushijima's face simply

defied the imagination. His eyes stared blankly into space, his gaze probably registering nothing at all, and his auditory and olfactory senses didn't appear to be working either. All his organs of perception were still under the spell of whatever trauma he'd experienced.

Enoyoshi asked Minako whether they had anything stronger than beer. She retrieved half a bottle of red wine and an alumite drinking mug from under the galley.

"This might not be strong enough to bring him around," said Enoyoshi, sitting Ushijima up and trying to pour some wine into his mouth. At first Ushijima seemed able to swallow only a few drops, but gradually his throat began to move more briskly, and in no time he'd drunk two cups of wine. His eyes began to show some semblance of life. The tremors that had shaken his body were subsiding and his breathing was growing calm.

Enoyoshi decided to start by asking Ushijima whether he'd accomplished what he'd set out to do, that is, remove the rope wrapped around the keel.

"Mr. Ushijima, did you get it done?"

Ushijima shook his head vigorously.

"So the rope's still tangled on the keel."

This time, Ushijima shook his head even more violently than before. He reacted in exactly the same way when Enoyoshi repeated himself. Ushijima shook his head when he was asked if the job was done. He likewise shook his head to deny that any rope remained caught on the keel. If he wasn't simply delirious, then there was only one rational conclusion. What had brought the yacht to a halt had yet to be removed from the keel—and it wasn't rope. Something other than rope had caused the yacht to stop. As Enoyoshi thought this through, the boat lurched suddenly, twice. It didn't feel like a wave, but rather, some force that was working on one point of the boat to attempt to pull it down.

Enoyoshi's anxiety instantly turned into fear. This may have been his first time on a yacht, but as a boy he'd enjoyed many a thrilling tale about the mysteries of the sea. Even the most orthodox of tales about phantom ships had sent a good chill down his spine. The entire crew of an enormous sailing ship would disappear without a trace, everything just as they had left it. What happened aboard the ship? The stories simply posed the question and never told you why the entire crew simply vanished off the ship. They impressed strongly upon readers that the sea itself was a mystery, that it was a space where the world of the living and the world of the dead were commingled.

Enoyoshi looked around fretfully. Where was the lifeline to land—the radio? Search as he may, he couldn't spot anything of the sort.

"Where's the yacht's radio?" Enoyoshi asked Minako. She in turn looked at Ushijima and listlessly rubbed her prostrate husband's shoulders. She was trying to get her husband to answer.

Enoyoshi repeated the question, and Ushijima's dull gaze glided sideways.

"There is no radio?" rephrased Enoyoshi.

This time Ushijima nodded. So there was no radio set aboard. As near as they were to land, they couldn't call for help. With a radio, they could contact Dream Island Marine Services and get them to send a tug. A tow from a tugboat with a high-power diesel engine would surely unmoor them. But there was no radio.

His throat dry from the tension, Enoyoshi poured some wine into the mug that Ushijima had used, and downed the whole thing in a gulp. Ushijima was the only man on board with any sailing experience, but the trauma had rendered him useless. Minako just clung to her husband and made no attempt to take the initiative. Enoyoshi, who'd blithely assumed that he was only a guest, felt a terrible weight on his shoulders now.

He kept glancing at his watch, swallowing nervously again and again. It was already eight o'clock. He shuddered to think that they might have to spend the night out at sea. The next day, Monday, he had an important deal to make. He'd had enough. He just wanted to go home to his apartment and lie down on the familiar bed. If only he could...

No sooner had the thought occurred to him than he made his way up to the cockpit and scanned the area to the west. A concrete embankment ran north to south along the perimeter of Wakasu Marine Park, and lined up parallel to the embankment on his side were numerous tetrapods whose boot-shaped ends protruded out of the sea.

If he clambered up over the tetrapod blocks, it would be easy to jump onto the embankment. Enoyoshi estimated that it was no more than a hundred yards from the yacht to the tetrapods. Even allowing for error in his reckoning due to darkness, it was a short distance that Enoyoshi could swim comfortably. His heart began to beat fast. Sink or swim. It was worth a try. It was still quite an adventure to swim in Tokyo Bay at night. He felt his short-lived resolve wither as he gazed down at the waters of the nighttime sea.

The cabin hatch opened and Ushijima came crawling up. He was more intent on moving his lips than his body, as if impatient to tell Enoyoshi something. Enoyoshi extended his hand to help him sit on the bench, but Ushijima just lay on the cockpit floor.

"How do you feel?"

Moving about by himself was certainly a sign that Ushijima was recovering, physically at least. But what he did next was to shudder and croak, "This boat isn't going anywhere." His tone made him sound like a stubborn old man.

"Why not?"

"I touched, with this hand." He held up a palm.

"Touched what?"

"The hands."

...Ushijima's hand had touched hands?

Enoyoshi began wishing that he'd never asked. There were millions of scary tales about dead spirits pulling at the legs of swimmers, but if Ushijima was trying to tell him some yarn about a hand emerging from the seabed to take hold of their keel, that was too far-fetched even to be a joke.

After a moment of silence, Ushijima opened his mouth again. "A child is stronger than you'd think," he said.

Enoyoshi couldn't reply. What was he to say to that? Perhaps the shock had been too great and Ushijima had gone mad.

"Child?" There was nothing but to repeat the word.

"There's a child clinging to the keel."

At this, Enoyoshi held his breath. The picture of a child's drowned body clinging to the keel formed in his mind.

"You know those hugging dolls they had years ago that you could put on your arm? Reminded me of them, except the face was all bloated like a balloon, you see," Ushijima said with some feeling.

Calm down, Enoyoshi reprimanded himself. No good would come of letting into his mind a monster born of another's imagination. Enoyoshi had to go over the facts carefully. What had caused the creature to form in Ushijima's mind?

"Was the child you saw a boy?"

"Mm-hmm," Ushijima replied and nodded. Enoyoshi was on the right track.

"Six years old or thereabouts?"

Ushijima thought for a while and then nodded. Enoyoshi was convinced now that he'd guessed right. Images don't usually spring up from nowhere. In this case, without a doubt, the boy's shoe that had got caught in the propeller provided the grounds, as it were, of Ushijima's imagination.

Enoyoshi tried to trace the steps in Ushijima's psychological process in the sequence in which they had occurred. The catalyst to the chain of associations had been the Mickey Mouse shoe, which must have been lingering somewhere in the back of Ushijima's mind when he attempted the dive. Where had the boy dropped his left shoe? The bridge? The embankment? Or perhaps the boy had drowned and just one of his shoes had come off in the water? If so, the boy's body would indeed be floating around in the sea somewhere.

Ushijima, who'd dived and started groping around on the bottom of the yacht with both his eyes tightly shut, must have touched something slimy clinging to the keel, maybe seaweed, that conjured up the feel of the skin of a drowned boy. Instantly, an image had flashed in Ushijima's mind. In the first place, he could never have seen anything in that sludge at night. Ushijima hadn't seen whatever he'd seen with his eyes. He had seen with his mind's eye an illusion formed by his famous imagination. A drowned little boy clinging to the keel, his face bloated like a balloon, eyes sunken deep into mushy flesh, the tip of a pale tongue sticking out from his mouth... A drowned boy's body clinging tightly to the keel like a hugging doll and immobilizing the yacht...

At this point, Enoyoshi felt sure he knew what Ushijima's answer to his next question would be.

"The boy you saw, he was missing one of his shoes, right?" he asked. Ushijima would surely nod. They'd found only the left shoe wedged in the propeller.

Knowing the answer, Enoyoshi studied Ushijima's reaction. But Ushijima narrowed his eyes, peered up at the sky, and shook his head to say no.

"He had shoes on both feet?"

This time Ushijima's reply was direct: "The boy had bare feet." There was no trace of hesitation or uncertainty in Ushijima's voice, and that was what baffled Enoyoshi.

In any case, he could not just sit there doing nothing. It occurred to him that they should try to restart the engine once more and get the yacht moving. Finding that the cuff of his shirt got in the way when he tried to tug the hand-starter, he decided to remove his shirt rather than simply roll up the sleeve and began to unbutton. Ushijima lay at Enoyoshi's feet, his posture unchanged. From under the open hatch, Minako caught sight of Enoyoshi taking off his shirt and called to him with a note of relief in her voice.

"So you've decided to dive at last."

No doubt she'd misinterpreted Enoyoshi's removing his shirt. He hadn't the slightest intention of diving under the yacht, and her remark annoyed him. The way she'd said it, she seemed to assume it was his duty as a man to dive and remove the obstacle. Enoyoshi felt no obligation whatsoever to rescue the yacht for her.

Starting the engine, Enoyoshi tried putting it in forward and reverse alternately, but the yacht remained motionless. It was futile. Irritated by his powerlessness, still resentful of Minako's gross remark, Enoyoshi was beginning to feel quite angry. He also felt annoyed by how passive he'd been. He ought to show them he could kiss goodbye to their yacht if he wanted. He'd show them he had the freedom.

His withered resolve began to rear its head once more. Come to think of it, there was no other way of getting off the ship. The simplest and most effective thing to do was to swim to shore, telephone Marine Services, and have them dispatch a tugboat.

Enoyoshi took a large plastic sack from an accessory case under the galley and began stuffing his clothes and shoes inside. Making sure there was some air in the bag too, he tightly knotted the opening.

At first, Minako had been staring rudely at him as he removed his clothes, but the bizarreness of his behavior struck her all of a sudden and she began to look worried.

"Say, just what is it you're up to over there?"

Enoyoshi tied the sack to his right thigh, sandwiched it between both legs, and stood up on top of the bench.

Minako reached toward him, but sooner than her fingertips could brush against his body, Enoyoshi had plunged into
the sea. Instead of swimming straight away, he began to tread
water, adjusting the plastic sack between his legs. As he
looked towards the yacht, the Ushijimas poked their faces
over the side like a couple of puppies peering out of a cardboard box. Minako looked like she was whining but Enoyoshi
couldn't hear her exact words as he bobbed up and down in
the sea.

"You'll be all right, I'll call Marine Services for you."

He tried hollering this, but he wasn't sure if they'd heard
him. Minako still seemed to be wailing. It'd only be an hour's
wait for the tugboat. But until it arrived, they'd have to savor
the fact that hell lay just a plank's breadth under that "marvelous" world of theirs that they so loved to force on others.

Turning round, he began to swim using only his arms,
the buoyant plastic sack gripped between his legs. He'd prac-
ticed the crawl countless times with a polystyrene board
between his legs and could complete twenty lengths that way
in a twenty-five-meter pool. Be brave, he told himself. Yet
stamina wasn't the issue. His attention was concentrated on
the bottom side of his abdomen and legs. If, at that instant, a
slimy thing brushed up against his stomach... His heart
quailed at the thought. Why wouldn't the little boy release
his embrace of the keel and come after him? Surely, if Enoyoshi opened his eyes underwater, he would see that little
boy's bloated face right there. The hideous visions kept coming, disrupting his stroke. He was wasting a lot of his
strength, and his fatigue grew greater with every stroke and
his stomach was heaving into his mouth. As the nausea came,

he sensed that his life was in danger. Panic equaled death. The night sky was cloudless and the moon shone brightly as he pressed ahead in the water. Yet the lights of Wakasu Marine Park did not appear any closer. It was maddening how ineffective he was in closing the distance to the embankment.

Enoyoshi forced himself to take a break, ceasing his strokes and turning over to float on his back. Making sure his nose and mouth were clear of the water, he took deliberate breaths to fill his lungs with air. He tried to fend off the nightmarish visions by picturing the yet-unseen nude of the woman he'd recently started to date. Imagining tangible particulars was the only way to elude the darker fantasies.

Raising his head from the water, he saw that he was now quite a distance from the yacht. A look to the shore confirmed how much closer it was than the yacht. He reckoned that he'd completed two thirds of the distance. The strength returned to his limbs. The shore that he'd thought so far away was actually right there within reach. One last spurt and he'd reach land. Enoyoshi rolled over and began churning the water with vigorous strokes.

It wasn't until he clambered up the tetrapod blocks in front of the embankment and his body was completely out of the sea that Enoyoshi felt alive again. The lower portion of the tetrapod was submerged in water, but at the top it was dry and the grainy feel of its surface heartened him. Looking out to sea, he saw the *MINAKO* in exactly the same position, its mast helplessly swaying from side to side.

From below the interlocking tetrapods surged the sound of breaking waves. If he fell through a gap he'd be in some serious trouble. Judging it wise to get over to the embankment on all fours, he crouched, and caught sight of a tiny shoe wedged in a crevice in the intermeshing blocks.

There it was, where he could touch it. In the faint glow of the night-lights, it looked black, probably from being waterlogged. Enoyoshi brought his face closer to it. The tip was wedged tight into the gap and the whole shoe had probably come off the owner for that reason. The wearer must have been playing atop the tetrapods and tripped. The upper canvas bore a Mickey Mouse motif, and a closer look revealed that it was a right shoe. The name written on the heel in black felt pen was legible even in the dim light. *Kazuhiro*. There could be no mistake. This shoe and the other they'd found on the yacht's propeller formed a pair.

Enoyoshi looked up. It amazed him how calm he was. Calmly, he observed to himself, "With the right shoe here, no wonder the boy's barefoot."

Glancing out, he saw the yacht rocking violently on the perfectly placid surface. Enoyoshi thought he glimpsed the figure of a child with bare feet hugging the keel, playing.

A D R I F T

1

Like a white cascade, the squall swept over the *Wakashio VII*, a deep-sea fishing boat with a hold full of tuna. Once having passed, the squall swept over the sea in a southerly direction. The rainbow that formed in its wake appeared to be a triumphal arch welcoming the boat back to its home port. A few hours earlier, they had passed through the sea off the Ogasawara Islands, and a short journey further north would bring into sight the profile of Torishima Island. Heading further north, they would reach the island of Hachiojima. Kazuo Shiraishi had a growing sense of relief, as if they were already back in Japan.

As Kazuo stood on bridge watch, it gradually sank into him that the yearlong voyage was finally drawing to a close. This was his third such voyage. Yet his heart felt fuller than it had upon returning from his first. This was no doubt due to the period of extended idleness that awaited him before the next voyage.

Upon returning from his second voyage seven years ago, Kazuo took up work in a fisheries warehouse as a cargo superintendent in charge of grading tuna fish. His memories of that second voyage were not pleasant; he had become particularly annoyed by the ugly mood that prevailed among the crew. He consequently applied, though not in so many words, for a job on land.

Despite being qualified as an engineer, he continued to cling to his land-based job at Wakashio Fisheries for the next five years, persistently rejecting any possibility of returning to sea.

Then two years ago, while driving the firm's van to Tokyo, he became stuck in heavy traffic. He was overcome by the claustrophobia of being surrounded on all sides by trucks. In that instant he realized that he really didn't belong on land after all. He belonged at sea with its unimpeded vistas. To describe how the sun set at sea, Kazuo would often form a circle with his arms, although such a gesture could never truly capture the actual grandeur of a sunset at sea. Whenever, stuck in congested traffic, he happened to recall a seascape, the beauty of the scene felt all the more poignant. How deep was the calm silence at sea compared to the deafening din of traffic! Thus awakened to the lure of the sea as if for the first time, Kazuo resolved that it was time to set out on a third voyage, and promptly contacted the company to this end.

As the ship's assistant engineer, Kazuo had been satisfied with this voyage. With a respectable career under his belt, he was regarded by everyone aboard as a full-fledged seaman. No one treated him like some green cabin boy as they had on his last trip, and there had been no feuding factions aboard the boat this time. Having successfully completed its mission in the South Pacific, the *Wakashio VII* now had its refrigerated hold full to the brim with large southern bluefin tuna. Moreover, they'd encountered no conditions during the voyage severe enough to be considered life-threatening. All in all, the voyage had gone off as planned. The entire mission would have been perfect had it not been for an incident in which two crewmembers were swept overboard off the coast of New Zealand. Miraculously, one of these men was rescued, a feat that caught the attention of the newspapers. Sadly, the reporters focused exclusively on the dramatic sea rescue, totally ignoring the fact that another man had lost his life in the incident. While saddened by the death of a crewmate, the ship hands were also overjoyed that another, earlier given up for dead, had been returned to them. What should have been seen as a tragic event strangely gave rise to the jolly mood of a carnival. Perhaps this was because the lost crewmember hadn't been very popular.

The triumphal arc of the rainbow appeared just two or three days before they were to reach the Japanese mainland. As Kazuo stood at watch on the bridge, a smile came unnoticed to his face. The voyage had garnered a huge catch. He stood to make a pretty penny. Thinking how he'd spend this money, he couldn't help but grin.

Just one of the ways he could spend the money was to cover the costs of his wedding. Kazuo had turned twenty-seven during the voyage and was seriously considering marrying a girl back home. During the voyage he had finally decided to formally propose to this girl upon his return. As for any future deep-sea fishing voyages, the two of them would have to discuss it first and decide if that was what they both wanted. If she opposed any future trips, he'd listen. As Kazuo thought things through, he realized that this could be his last voyage. That this might be his last homecoming made the moment on the bridge all the more emotional for him.

As the clouds that fueled a squall fell behind in the distance, shafts of summer sunlight began streaming down through the clouds ahead, forming patches of light and dark on the face of the sea like so many spotlights. It was three in the afternoon. Ahead to port could be seen the profile of a boat that resembled a yacht as it slid from a dark area into a patch of light. After straining his eyes in that direction, Kazuo used his pair of binoculars to make sure. It was in fact a small oceangoing cruiser. Although the vessel seemed to have emerged from a gap in the clouds themselves, it was heading directly toward them on the portside as though to cross paths with the *Wakashio VII*, which was running on autopilot. Kazuo gave five consecutive blasts of the steam whistle. In addition to indicating alarm about the cruiser's direction, they were meant as a warning. After sounding the whistle, Kazuo peered through the binoculars again. The cruiser was traveling with its sails down. There was no sign of anyone onboard. There should have been someone standing watch on a boat of that kind, no matter what the circumstances. Without someone to keep watch, there was always the risk of a collision.

Kazuo sounded the whistle again, while observing the cruiser through his binoculars. Nobody appeared on deck. He wondered if their whole crew was fast asleep in the cabin. He certainly couldn't think of any other way to explain the total absence of anyone on deck. Looking suspiciously like a phantom ship, the cruiser bore down on a collision course with the *Wakashio VII*.

Kazuo lost no time in calling Captain Takagi and informing him of the situation. The captain silently scrutinized the cruiser with unaided eyes as Kazuo waited.

"Odd, very odd," muttered Captain Takagi at last before putting the ship's engine in neutral. With the engine idling, the boat continued to drift forward for a while under its own momentum, before it finally came to rest. The hull of the cruiser was by now right below the deck of *Wakashio VII*. Closer inspection revealed that what they had taken for a small cruiser was actually a luxury yacht about forty feet in length. Its deck was white and the rest of the hull a regal maroon, with double lines running along the side. They could see a diving platform mounted on the beautifully curved stern. It was obvious at a glance that the yacht's owner was extremely wealthy.

Seamen assembled on deck in twos and threes along the portside. From there they called down to the yacht.

"Anyone down there?"

The repeated shouts of the men brought no response from the yacht. Not a single face emerged from the cabin below. A forty footer of this type would normally be manned by four or five crewmembers at the very least.

"What should we do?"

Boatswain Shibasaki turned to the captain for instructions, a scowl on his face. It was clear he just wanted to forget this matter and head on full-speed ahead toward their home port of Misaki.

"Well, we can't pretend we haven't seen it."

Captain Takagi then unfolded his arms and ordered the junior seamen to lower a boat. The yacht could have been in an accident, and he couldn't just ignore her and forge ahead. It was the duty of all seamen worthy of the name to come to the aid of ships in distress.

A rope from the *Wakashio VII* was tied firmly to the bow cleat of the yacht. Once they'd prevented the vessel from drifting away, a seaman boarded the yacht. He quickly surveyed the cabin quarters before shouting back.

"There's no one here!"

"Double-check the berths and bunks!"

With this command from the captain, the scout went back down into the cabin, before returning a minute or so later.

"There's not a soul aboard, Captain!" Then he added in a lower voice, with less confidence, "There's something weird about this…"

But this was drowned out by the captain's roar: "Give me her registration number!"

The man read off the number that appeared on either side of the yacht: "KN2 – 1785, sir!" The KN indicated that the boat was registered in Kanagawa Prefecture.

"Got that. Stand by and await further instructions!"

Returning to the bridge, the captain placed a call via the Inmarsat phone to the Third Maritime Safety Division headquartered in Yokohama to report a deserted ship adrift at 29 degrees north by 141 degrees east. Asked for a detailed description of the boat as it was discovered, Captain Takagi gave a frank account of what he'd just seen.

"Any persons adrift in the sea around the vessel?"

"Negative."

"Any objects adrift near the boat?"

"Negative."

"Any suspicious cluster of fish or fowl?"

"Negative."

Every question could only be met with the same answer, "Negative." The yacht simply lay afloat on calm waters with its sails down.

The Third Maritime Safety Division contacted its air rescue team at Haneda, where arrangements were made to immediately dispatch an aircraft to that stretch of sea. During the two to three hours it would take the plane to reach the ship, the *Wakashio VII* was obliged to remain on location and to keep an eye on the deserted yacht.

The nineteen crewmembers of the *Wakashio VII* reacted in one of two ways to this turn of events: some groaned about being held back when they were so close to Japan; others wondered about this intriguing yacht that had appeared out of nowhere. Kazuo belonged to the latter group. He'd always dreamed of sailing the ocean someday aboard a luxury yacht just like this one. The sudden appearance of the yacht some-how presaged the fulfillment of his dream. He felt a strong urge to board her.

They waited two and a half hours before they heard the roar of an approaching aircraft, the one dispatched by the Maritime Safety Agency.

The aircraft circled high above the *Wakashio VII* several times, searching for any evidence of people set adrift. The plane scoured the area no more than thirty minutes and head-ed back to its home base.

What course of action to take next was discussed in a second telephone conversation between the *Wakashio VII* and the Third Maritime Safety Division. Any obligation the fishing vessel may have had toward the abandoned ship was fulfilled by notifying the Maritime Safety Agency. Although the agency had dispatched an aircraft to confirm the report, the *Wakashio VII* had kept the yacht under surveillance the whole time. There could be no justification for compelling them to do any more than they'd already done.

Still, as a practical matter, they couldn't just leave the yacht and go. Who knew where it might drift unattended? A patrol boat from the Maritime Safety Agency would have a difficult time relocating the deserted boat. Naturally, the agency requested that the *Wakashio VII* stay put and keep an eye on the yacht until a patrol boat arrived.

Captain Takagi thought for a moment before responding to the agency's mildly worded request. It would be all too easy to refuse. They did not want to tarry any longer. If, by any chance, they ended up being detained for a few days with the home port so close, the crewmembers would turn rebellious. Takagi's prime concern as captain was precisely how best to keep his men's irritation and discontent under control.

On the other hand, there was that blot in his copybook about the two men who'd been swept overboard off the coast of New Zealand. Although one had been rescued, the other had lost his life. That had been an accident pure and simple, but the captain knew that the Maritime Safety Agency would launch an inquiry immediately upon their return. Volunteering to aid the agency with the present case was surely the wise thing to do; it would buy the kind of goodwill that might stand them in good stead later.

Captain Takagi came up with a compromise. "How about if we towed the yacht part of the way back?"

The compromise would permit the *Wakashio VII* to continue her northward journey, with the yacht in tow, while maintaining contact with the patrol boat heading down south from Shimoda. The vessels would rendezvous at a point where the *Wakashio VII* could relinquish its load. With a yacht in tow, they would be forced to reduce speed to around five or six knots, but that was far preferable to waiting idly for the patrol boat to arrive.

The Maritime Safety Agency accepted Captain Takagi's proposal, whereupon it fell to the *Wakashio VII* to tow the yacht.

No sooner had the decision been made than Kazuo appealed to the captain, "Shouldn't someone man the yacht just in case?"

It would surely be of help if a seaman aboard the boat in tow handled any unforeseen problems, making fine adjustments as necessary, provided the yacht's equipment functioned normally. It would eliminate the need to lower a boat every time a problem arose.

"You like her, don't you?" Takagi had read his mind.

"Yes, sir."

"Well go ahead then."

The captain gave him a walkie-talkie, which would easily work over the distance and was much handier than using the radio.

It was decided that Kazuo should man the yacht all alone. Why no one else had even bothered to volunteer puzzled him. Excepting crew who had to go on watch, there was surely no work to be done on a ship on the final leg of its journey home. How comfortable it would be, he imagined, to sleep in the cabin of the cruiser, rather than on a bunk in a cabin shared with four men! He saw himself sprawling out in a double berth all to himself.

As Kazuo boarded the yacht, the veteran seaman Ueda handed him a supply of food and water. The average age of the crew of *Wakashio VII* was thirty-seven, with Kazuo being the youngest at twenty-seven, and Ueda the oldest at fifty-seven. This survivor of many a crisis at sea wrinkled his creased face further and muttered, "Won't see a ghost ship every day."

The words gave Kazuo pause. Ghost ship... Was that how the other crewmembers felt about the yacht?

Kazuo finally understood why the other crewmembers were giving him curious looks. It explained why no one else wanted to board the yacht; they didn't see it as a luxury yacht but as some hideous thing from hell.

It was only as Ueda's boat drew away that Kazuo experienced his first doubts.

Come to think of it, what had happened to the crew of the cruiser?

...Swept overboard.

Kazuo had assumed that they'd fallen into the sea because of an accident. Perhaps some crew had been swept overboard by a huge broadside wave and the rest had plunged into the sea in a vain attempt to rescue their mates. Since the lifeboat was still in place and showed no signs of having been used, they couldn't have taken it to escape some crisis aboard. Kazuo had been under the impression that his crewmates thought more or less the same, but now, it occurred to him that perhaps the yacht had been deserted for some other reason. It gave him the chills, rather too late.

Ueda's boat safely tucked back, *Wakashio VII* slowly began to pull away, causing the towrope connecting it to the yacht to snap tight. The luxury boat started to glide along in the calm waters. With an air of regret, Kazuo stood for a while on deck and stared at the stern of the *Wakashio VII*. The ship wasn't leaving him behind, it was just fifty yards or so ahead.

The rope was tied to the bow cleat. If he felt in need of even a casual chat, he could always use the walkie-talkie. He had nothing to worry about.

The evening sun was setting into the western horizon. Somehow, its scarlet hue that evening seemed to set it apart from all other sunsets he'd seen. He couldn't put the difference in words, but he thought of the color of blood.

Kazuo was due to spend the night all alone in the cruiser's cabin. He was far from excited, and two cold shivers ran through his body.

2

Once the sun had set, Kazuo went down into the cabin and sank back in a plush sofa adorned in Gobelin fabric, thrusting his feet out on the table before him. He felt for all the world as if he owned the yacht. The large sofa in the main cabin could easily accommodate ten people. It suddenly occurred to him to determine how many crewmembers could sleep aboard the cruiser. There were berths for six people: two in the fore, two in the main cabin, and two aft. There were extra pipe berths for another two people, thus revealing that the yacht was designed to comfortably accommodate up to eight people. He swiftly surveyed the surroundings to decide which berth to occupy that night. He chose the captain's room in the aft of the boat. The room was spacious and equipped with a queen-sized bed, just the kind he could sprawl out in to his heart's content. Although it was still too early to retire, he tried lying on the bed just to see how it felt. His back pressed tightly against the surface of the berth, Kazuo gazed up absently. Lying there, his skin felt the vibrations of the lower hull as it sliced through the waves. He was truly thankful for the calm weather. Rough seas would no doubt roll a boat like this, to his dismay.

As he lounged at perfect ease in these relaxing surroundings, he began thinking about sex for the first time in quite a while. Yet the welling urge was short-lived. Before he knew it, he was sitting up straining his ears. He was sure that he had heard a noise, something that sounded like a human voice. It seemed to have come from the main cabin. Yet there was no one on this boat except him.

Kazuo went back to the main cabin and looked around suspiciously. Under the galley was a refrigerator, and from behind it came an electric hum. Kazuo felt a surge of relief; the strange sound had been nothing more than this. Opening the refrigerator door, Kazuo found several bottles of white wine left there to cool. One bottle was open and its content partly consumed. He decided to take a new bottle, uncorked it, and drank the wine straight from the bottle. He couldn't be bothered to use a glass.

It had been many years since he had tasted chilled white wine. Aboard the fishing vessel, there had been nothing as sophisticated as white wine in the way of liquor. The men almost always drank a strong brand of *shochu* gin. This was no doubt why the wine had for him a special savor.

He drank half the bottle, accompanied by a pleasant sensation of tipsiness radiating from his stomach throughout his body. Kazuo felt relaxed, very relaxed.

...What on earth had happened on this boat?

It was a question that surfaced time and time again in his mind. Until now, Kazuo had never in his life been aboard such a fine cruiser. Thus, it was difficult for him to imagine what kind of accident could have beset such a craft. He was not even in a position to judge whether it was realistic to conceive that the entire crew had been swept overboard simultaneously. Would that be in fact just too much of a coincidence?

...*Phantom ship*

The words came to mind every time he tried to think.

Kazuo recalled a phantom ship he'd read about as a boy. There are few people who have never heard of the *Marie*

Celeste, a phantom ship case that occurred well over a century ago. An English sailing ship discovered her floating adrift in the Atlantic. The ship's movements appeared odd, so the crew of the English ship boarded her to investigate. They could find no trace of the captain, his family, or the seven crewmembers who should have been aboard. It appeared that they had been about to enjoy a meal: coffee cups, bread, eggs, and utensils had been set out on the table. Moreover, the ship still had ample stocks of food and water. Apart from a torn sail, the ship was perfectly seaworthy. People had evidently been in the cabins shortly before the English boarded. There was also ample evidence that the passengers had been enjoying their journey. Nonetheless, the humans aboard the ship, and only they, had disappeared from the ship like smoke. Although the *Marie Celeste* was discovered back in 1872, a credible explanation hasn't been provided to this day.

As a child, Kazuo had tried to solve the mystery. There could have been, he imagined back then, a quarrel. During the course of the fighting, they'd all been thrown overboard somehow, leaving the ship deserted. Or there could have been an outbreak of the plague, with some of the crew making a desperate escape by lifeboat with all but the barest of provisions. But, tragically, the lifeboat had capsized. It was all too easy for a child to come up with such theories, but they did not explain the very real aura of daily routines that had remained so strongly in the air. There had been no sign of any disturbance or trauma to support the theory of a quarrel or plague. The orderly way the table had been set for a meal ruled out such scenarios. Always raising more questions than he could answer, Kazuo had given up the chase in frustration.

Just as on the *Marie Celeste,* this cruiser's cabins were in perfect order. Although no meal was out on the table, the boat had an ample supply of drinking water and fuel. It was also in perfect condition. The interior of the cabins had been kept meticulously tidy, suggesting a penchant for cleanliness on the owner's part.

There had been no lack of space on the boat. It had been occupied by a family of four, whose belongings were packed neatly in the lockers.

According to the boat's log, the cruiser's home port was the Bayside Marina, which it had left six days earlier. The log bore a detailed account of each stage of the voyage, coming to an abrupt end on the fourth day. In other words, just two days earlier, some serious incident had occurred on the boat. As far as Kazuo was concerned, all the relevant information regarding the circumstances of the yacht had been uncovered during their initial investigation and relayed to the Maritime Safety Agency. But he hadn't read the log yet.

Taking the logbook from the chart table, Kazuo moved to the sofa, where he sat down and drained the wine remaining in the bottle.

The leather cover of the logbook bore the name of the boat's owner: *Takayuki Yoshikuni, Captain.* Kazuo started to read it from the beginning; the log began on the day of the boat's departure.

July 21, Friday. Fine weather.

Dead calm in Tokyo Bay, but backwash from maritime traffic sometimes causes us to roll unexpectedly. Son and daughter have just started summer vacation, our traditional summer cruise gets under way. Children over the moon, but my wife refuses to get into the spirit of things. Accustomed to more genteel surroundings, she prefers to be waited on hand and foot. She finds life on an oceangoing cruiser rather difficult. After all, the obligatory midnight watch will not be to everyone's liking. Being averse to sunburn, she insists on wearing an enormous straw hat whenever on deck. Not quite what one expects on a yacht.

Conversely, both my kids are turning into first-class yachtsmen. Takahisa did good by me, winning in the Snipe class of the All-Japan High School Yachting Championships. Yoko may still be in elementary school, but she did very well, too, placing third overall in the Open Regatta, Hobby class. Even if only four yachts participated!

Both kids couldn't be better crewmembers. I really don't know what I would do without them. My wife will not pull her own weight, but if the kids manage to cover for her, I believe we will enjoy a fair open-sea cruise.

We will therefore sail longer than we first intended. This will now be a ten-day cruise, around the island of Torishima and back. Perhaps we can get as far south as the Ogasawara Islands? No. That will be next year's treat...

Reading the log up to this point, Kazuo already had a clear picture of the owner and his family. With a son in high school and a daughter in elementary, the owner and his wife had to be in their forties. The son belonged to a high school yachting club. The daughter, probably a fifth- or sixth-grader, was also crazy about sailing. Then there was the wife, who, being of genteel upbringing, did not enjoy life at sea. From what the log suggested, they were not only well-off but the very image of a happy family. Kazuo couldn't tell what the father did for a living, but he certainly didn't seem like a regular salaried employee if he could get ten consecutive days off work at this time of year and, of course, afford the upkeep of a luxury yacht. He had to be either the owner of his company or a successfully self-employed man.

As Kazuo read on, his envy subsided. The owner's unabashed love for his wife and children made it difficult for him to feel resentful toward the family and its privileged circumstances. The log, in fact, was invigorating to read and put Kazuo in a sunny mood. Here was the kind of family you never saw in the seaside fishing community where he'd grown up. His parents had fought constantly like alley cats, and they'd been too poor to afford a car, let alone a luxury yacht. As the second of four children, Kazuo had never been pushed by his parents to excel in either sports or studies; nor could he recall being praised by them, ever. His family had never spent so much as a single night away together on vacation. The life portrayed in the log reflected so many ideal family virtues, not one of which his own family had evidenced. Perhaps, it was just that this family was too perfect.

But by the third day out of port, the idyllic voyage was seeing signs of trouble, if that wasn't an overdramatic way of putting it. The father was beginning to get bad vibes about something and it was communicated in the pages of his log.

July 23, Sunday. Cloudy, occasional rain.
...
...It may have been a coincidence, but I'm not sure. I do

feel uneasy about this sort of thing when we're out at sea. I wish she hadn't mentioned the dream at all.

When Yoko described the dream she'd had last night, my wife gasped and fell silent. She reacts badly to things of this nature. She must have had the same dream.

Although I can't be sure, I think I had the same dream too. I can't be more precise because I simply have no clear recollection of it. Perhaps, as Yoko recounted her dream, I came to feel that I'd also had the dream. I simply can't say.

Nothing could be as appalling as seeing your family, your dearest loved ones, drown in the sea before your very eyes and finding yourself unable to lift a single finger to save them. If that weren't bad enough, the sensation of having pushed them over yourself lingers in yours hands. Why, why? I cannot understand. It's the last dream anyone would want to have! Maybe the dream was born of fear. The terror of losing loved ones becomes so obsessive that you come to glimpse the worst possible scenario. Let that stand as the interpretation. Enough! I'd rather not think about it again...

It was clear to Kazuo what the writer was saying. A discussion of the previous night's dreams revealed that every member of the family had had the exact same dream the night before. Each had pushed the others into the sea with their own hands.

The log then went on at length to describe how smoothly the voyage was going. The writer was attempting to dispel the uncanny dream with a forced tone of cheerfulness, and Kazuo just skimmed these pages.

July 24, Monday. Fair, N wind 3-4 m, Temp. 30°C
   ...

   Yoko made another strange remark today. She has a
habit of doing this and it's beginning to annoy me. She seems
convinced that she has some strange powers. Such nonsense
must be the fad at school. She was probably scaring her
classmates with that kind of talk at the school outing before
summer vacation. The scene isn't all that difficult to imagine. I know Yoko shared a room with three others. When it
got dark, the silly girl must have told them, "There's someone else in this room." Hinting that there was a fifth "presence" managed to scare the others. And so now she's trying
the same trick on us. It's the kind of thing she would do.
   Listen, Yoko. There are only the four of us on this boat.
There is no fifth presence here or anything of the kind. Last
year, when I brought one of my friends along, you didn't like
it, did you? You said you had nothing against him but that it
tired you having to be on your best behavior all the time. So
I planned this cruise for us to be all by ourselves, just the four
of us. Have you got that? The only ones here on this boat are
the four of us, the family. Just as you wanted...

   Although there was no exact indication of when this
entry was made, it was probably at night. After all, the log
came to an abrupt end with the following few sentences.

...Tomorrow morning we'll enter the waters south of Torishima and begin our cruise around the island. We must
thank God for this excellent weather and calm voyage. ? I
just heard someone scream. Takahisa is now on watch. He

probably saw a shark's fin cutting through the water. Such a sight is certainly not comforting, especially in the moonlight. Now that I think about it, today at dusk...

At this point, something no doubt caught the writer's attention, for the sentence wasn't finished. He must have abandoned the log to go investigate.

As the captain was making this entry, his son stood on watch, while his wife and daughter were probably asleep. The log recorded what the daughter had said earlier that day. Yoko had apparently tried to persuade her father that there was some other "presence" aboard the cruiser. Her father had dismissed her concerns as childish nonsense and later chided her in the log. The daughter seemed to be fond of making remarks that hinted of the occult.

Closing the leather covers of the log, Kazuo threw it onto the table. According to the entries, something had happened on July 24th—two nights ago. The four of them had either vanished that night or been swept overboard the next morning, though the details of this weren't clear. Two things bothered Kazuo now that he'd read the log. The first was that the entire family of four had apparently had the same dream at the same time. The second was that the presence of someone other than the family members had been sensed by at least one passenger. Otherwise, the log spoke of nothing unusual. It seemed a faithful description of a smooth voyage.

Kazuo took a second bottle of wine from the refrigerator. He needed to get a little more drunk if he wanted to sleep that night.

3

Kazuo was aware that he was dreaming. But not waking up, he remained crouched atop a large rock surrounded by the sea, crushing the crabs at his feet with a fist-sized stone. The more crabs he crushed, the more came clambering out of the water to try to crawl up Kazuo's feet. As he brought down the stone, he felt, first, the hard shell resist before it cracked and splintered, and next a mushy sensation. The top of the large rock was so littered with smushed crabs that hardly an inch of the surface was visible. Like an obsessed man, Kazuo continued to exterminate the crabs. He sensed a gaze burning into his back and wondered whether it was his conscious self staring at his dreaming self. But no, the gaze embodied a powerful will intent on senseless slaughter, and it gave Kazuo no choice but to wield the stone.

Soon there were no more crabs left alive on the rock, but the urge to continue killing did not abate. Where could Kazuo find the life on which to vent his murderous rage? The feeling of being watched grew stronger, and the gaze was urging him on. Obligingly, Kazuo raised the stone high over his head and smashed it down on his feet. The dull thud of tearing flesh and splintering bone reverberated upwards through him. Although he felt no pain, he suffered the horrible anguish of knowing that he was rending his own flesh. He kept smashing at his feet with the stone until the bones were pulverized, and the torment finally shook him awake.

His eyes now opened and fixed on the ceiling, Kazuo gasped and held his breath. The scene of the dream receded into thin air together with the putrid smell of dead crabs, and the features of the real world, the rocking of the boat and the lapping of the waves, came into focus. Kazuo sensed that something was different. He hadn't been roused from his sleep just by the terror of a nightmare; his seaman's instinct that something was amiss had also stirred him. Instantly forgetting the dream, he concentrated every nerve in his body on the motion of the boat. It seemed subtly different from when he'd fallen asleep.

Getting up, he went to the cabin and tried to calm his breathing. Telling himself to relax, he glanced at his watch, which read 12:30 a.m. He'd only been asleep three hours. His heart was pounding violently. He was getting the feeling that the boat wasn't plying water.

It was but five steps up from the cabin to the cockpit. A tall man, Kazuo dashed up stooping, opened the hatch, and made his way out.

Although he was quite sure that he'd turned on the navigating lights before retiring, he found out differently. The expansive teak deck was illuminated only by the moon and stars above. The stern of the *Wakashio VII*, which should have been visible straight ahead, wasn't there.

"Of all the..."

Unable to believe his eyes, he vainly scanned in every direction. There was no sign of any boat. The line that separated the sky and the sea was now a deep dark thing that also engulfed the cruiser. Kazuo stood all alone in the midnight ocean. An acidic taste came surging into his mouth.

Kazuo crawled towards the bow to check the bow cleat that secured the rope from the *Wakashio VII*. The rope was gone. It had apparently come undone from the bow cleat. Kazuo swallowed in alarm. This was absolutely impossible; no amateur had tied the knot; veteran seamen were all masters of rope-work. The rope had been bound to the cleat with a cleat knot and wound around twice for good measure. It simply couldn't have come undone on its own. He'd checked several times after the yacht had gone into tow. Could someone with a grudge against Kazuo have contrived a slipping knot? That seemed unlikely, but then, who on earth could have untied it when there was no one else on the boat but himself? Could he have done it himself? It was a hazy idea. Kazuo held out his palms and stared at them. He vaguely remembered seeing himself from afar untying the knot under some sort of compulsion. Another scene from the dream?

What he'd read in the log flashed into his mind.

...There's someone else on this boat.

It was something more concrete than a hunch. He was being watched. Something was skulking somewhere on the boat and following his every movement closely. Jumping back, he glanced around in all directions and screamed. He could shout as loud as he wanted, but there was no boat in sight and it was useless. He had no time to waste. He had to make contact with the *Wakashio VII* immediately. Returning to the cabin, he grabbed the walkie-talkie and pressed the SPEAK button.

"Come in, please come in."

There was no response. If the rope had come loose as far back as a few hours ago, then the *Wakashio* was out of transmission range. He tried to get through repeatedly, but the handset remained silent. The walkie-talkie was useless.

Undaunted, he kept shouting into the thing until his voice was hoarse. "Come in, please come in!"

Kazuo strained his ears. He thought he'd heard something, some faint noise coming from the remote depths of the walkie-talkie. An instant before the buzzing could form into words, Kazuo had instinctively thrown the walkie-talkie at the floor to smash it. It was too late, the buzzing had conveyed the words to his brain.

"Crush the life out of them."

That was what it sounded like. It was a dark, damp voice, like some message from the seabed deep below. Kazuo was now in a state of near-panic, on the verge of a fit of hysteria.

He responded with a shower of abuse, and, rallying himself by making as much noise as possible, he managed to make his way to the radio set.

Don't let it get to you, he chastised himself. It's just your nerves. Hurry and contact the *Wakashio*!

He was unsure about how to operate the set. He felt that by fiddling with it long enough, he'd eventually get through. But when he turned on the switch, the radio refused to come alive. Examining the rear of the set, he realized that the battery connection cord had been severed, probably to prevent anyone from using the set.

Incredible. No means of communication. Relax, relax...

If he lost his head, he was bound to make mistakes. It was imperative that he think through things calmly. There was no need to rush. Whatever was going on, the seaman on watch aboard the *Wakashio VII* was bound to notice that the yacht was no longer in tow. They probably knew already. They were sure to retrace their course and could be there on the horizon by now.

Kazuo thrust his head from the cockpit and gazed in a northerly direction. No signs of the ship. He strained his ears in vain for the familiar old blast of her steam whistle.

It then occurred to Kazuo that they hadn't noticed yet. After all, seamen on watch were more often than not preoccupied with the foreview, seldom paying attention to what was behind the ship. They happened to be towing a boat on that particular occasion, but old habits died hard. No one could have possibly imagined that the rope would work itself loose in the first place. To make matters worse, the yacht's navigating lights had been off all the time. They might not notice until morning that the boat in tow was missing.

There were still a few hours to sunrise. Yet those few hours seemed like an eternity. Kazuo was not at all sure that he could hold out that long against the indescribable presence that pervaded the boat. Like most seamen, Kazuo tended to be superstitious. Venturing out to sea, nature's untrammeled domain, you often encounter phenomena that are beyond the pale of human understanding. You stand a far greater chance of experiencing the paranormal at sea than on land.

There was no longer any room for doubt. The boat's owner and his family had disappeared through no accident; some mysterious force had worked upon them. What they'd dreamed, they'd gone and done. Goaded by a malevolent force... And it was trying to control Kazuo now.

"Please help me," prayed Kazuo. Though he worshipped no god, there seemed to be no other way to stave off his fear.

There had to be some explanation. Kazuo tried to think as logically as he could. Thinking, and acting, could distract him if nothing else.

...Was the boat always cursed? No, something happened on this voyage. When?

Kazuo retrieved the boat's log and began turning the pages. During the night of the 23rd, all members of the family had the same dream. On the following day, the daughter, Yoko, sensed the presence of someone else on the boat. This meant that they must have picked up whatever it was on or before the 23rd. "Picked up"? The words came to him just like that. But indeed, they'd picked up something nefarious. Didn't the log say something of the sort? Kazuo seemed to remember a passage that he'd merely skimmed. The incident had seemed insignificant to the father, who'd barely mentioned it in the log, and so the reader hadn't given it much attention either.

Kazuo hurriedly turned the pages in search of the section. He was sure there'd been something of the sort.

"Here it is!" The entry was dated July 23rd and appeared to have been made at around noon.

...

Yoko has this annoying habit of picking up any shell she finds. She found something very odd this time. Strange that it should have been drifting in the ocean. It's a bottle containing some kind of shell, resembling a bivalve. The shell is about the size of a human hand and much larger than the neck of the bottle, but there it is inside the corked bottle. I wonder how anyone could have gotten the shell into it without damaging the bottle. Surely the thing can't have grown to that size in the bottle? Perish the thought!

I told her to throw the thing away, but she ignored me and hid it somewhere where Daddy can't find it. She's clearly afraid I'll toss it overboard if ever I find it. But Daddy isn't so cruel as to throw away any of her treasures, even that shell. I wonder why Yoko doesn't find the shell "creepy". The shell's pattern looks like an eye. If you hold the bottle up and take a close look, it's really quite frightening, the way it seems to be staring back at you.

Those are EYES if ever I saw one. Normally the inside of a half-open shell is a lustrous pearly color. But this shell has a fleshy mound bulging out on each side. It's altogether different from the thin muscle that pulls the halves together; it looks like flesh, with scarlet capillaries on the surface. The lens and gelatinous cornea are a cloudy brown, with the overall shape of the eye slightly warped. They resemble the eyes of a rotting tuna and seem to exude malevolence. An uncanny gaze I must say. We really should get rid of the thing! Treasure or not, I can't stand it. Where could the silly girl have hidden it?...

Sometime around midday on the 23rd, Yoko had found a bottle and picked it out of the sea. The bottle contained a shell resembling a bivalve. What was more, the shell bore a pattern that looked exactly like the eye.

...This is it. The source of the curse.

The problem was where the daughter had concealed the shell. He had to find it and find it fast. And then what? Return it back to the sea, of course.

Since the couple had been sleeping in the aft berth, the children must have been using the fore berth. Ever conscious of what was behind him, Kazuo began to go through the contents of the locker.

His consciousness seemed to skip, and the next thing he knew, he was staring at his hand, which was on the locker door, as though none of this really concerned him. His hand seemed to be an organ separate from his own body. When the hand moved slightly, he felt the urge to crush it. He wanted to destroy every animate object, every living thing. A gaze that bore down on him from God knew where told him to.

Throwing his head back with a growl of defiance, he fought the murderous urge. If he didn't hurry, it would get the better of him. Losing the battle meant doing to himself what he'd done in his dream.

He didn't stop at the fore berth; in the main cabin, in the aft berth, he searched every nook and cranny that could hide anything. Yet he found nothing like a shell in a bottle.

"Where could the damned kid have hidden it?!"

Taking his anger out on the boat's furnishings, Kazuo turned the whole place upside down.

Before he knew it, his elbow was bleeding. He had apparently struck it on the corner of the table during his rampage. Could he have done it on purpose? He simply couldn't say. He couldn't even recall, beyond a haze, what he'd been doing a few seconds ago. Touching the lukewarm, viscous stuff with his left hand, confirming the color of blood, he panicked and went on another mad rampage. He no longer knew whether he was searching for the bottle or just trying to maim himself. He cut his shin on the shard of a broken wine bottle, and soon slipped in the blood, landing forcefully on his buttocks.

Yet, for all his fervor, his search was in vain.

...I can't stay here.

It occurred to him to escape. It could just make things worse for him, but he hadn't the leisure to think about it. Chanting "can't stay here" like some magic charm, he found a flashlight and made his way out on deck. There was nothing but sea on all sides. He had to resist the urge to jump overboard.

...Gotta escape!

Shining the flashlight over the deck ahead as he moved, he searched for the lifeboat stowed at the rear of the cockpit. Upon boarding the cruiser, they'd confirmed that the lifeboat was still there.

Praying, he opened the locker, and there to his immense relief he found what he was after. This was the only chance he had left. The Maritime Safety Agency was bound to dispatch another aircraft in the morning. The lifeboat was brightly colored so as to be clearly visible from the air. They would find him sure enough. It also had a stock of several flares. Placing the container holding the boat at the edge of the deck, Kazuo pulled the tag as directed in the instruction manual. The lifeboat emitted a quiet hiss and began inflating. Securing it with a thin rope, he lowered it into the sea. Before climbing into it, he looked around one last time. He caught sight of three waterproof bags marked SUPPLY SACK in the container. The owner must have specially prepared them to supplement the emergency supplies that came with the lifeboat. Guessing that they contained water and food, Kazuo tossed all three bags into the lifeboat and jumped in after them.

It was probably because there hadn't been much wave

action that the whole thing had gone smoothly. Just six feet in diameter, the circular boat was labeled as being good for six people, but it was cramped enough even for one.

Kazuo cast off the mooring rope, and the lifeboat rocked unsteadily away from the yacht. He was surprised to find no relief in watching the yacht steadily recede into the distance. He could only rationalize to himself that it was the anxiety of being in such a frail craft as the rubber float. As he thrust his legs out in front of him, he felt the motion of the sea on his rump through the bottom. Compared to the cruiser, this boat was like a leaf.

More than a hundred feet had opened up between Kazuo and the yacht. The sensation of being watched should have been gone by now. Yet, far from fading, it seemed to have grown in intensity. His adrenaline level was rocketing, but now he had nowhere to escape. Off the lifeboat there was nothing for him but death.

He watched as an irrevocable distance opened up between him and the yacht. Just as she disappeared out of sight into the darkness, his mind seemed to jump the rails. His perceptions became so clouded that he was no longer capable of understanding what exactly was happening. Countless people were conversing in his head at once. The incoherent din sounded like the roar that dominates the floor of the stock exchange. Eventually the voices merged into one and prodded him from behind. Kazuo thrust his hands into the sea and scooped up seawater to bathe his aching temples. Leaning out over the side, he sunk his face into the seawater and peered down below. A dark, fathomless vortex was spiraling at the bottom of the nighttime sea. Gazing into it, Kazuo was nearly sucked in.

He never did notice. Kazuo never did find out where the daughter had hidden the small glass bottle. She'd tucked it away in a SUPPLY SACK. Tossed onto the lifeboat, it now sat snugly between the rubber bottom and the side tubing. In the silver sack, among packs of water and cans of food, the eyes kept quiet.

WATERCOLORS

1

Early in the evening on a late summer day, the bridge over Shibaura Canal was swaying in the wind. On either side of the canal, old buildings rubbed shoulders with new ones in a higgledy-piggledy array, and strong gusts of wind blew in through the spaces between them. Looking south from midbridge, the third building was stained black with what looked like streaks of soot on its rear and side walls. Whether the black streaks were grime accumulated over many long years or an artificial design was hard to say.

Until two summers ago, the building housed a discotheque called *Mephisto* on its third, fourth, and fifth floors. Each floor had a separate entrance, and customers could enter the disco through their entrance of choice, depending on how the spirit moved them at the time. The higher the floor, the more extreme the music, fashion, and interior design. Dancers on the fifth floor were mostly half-naked women clad in black bondage gear. Unable to join their ecstatic coterie, most men contented themselves with viewing them from the side.

In those days, you didn't have to go far in this neighborhood before you caught sight of women trussed up in bondage fashion. They used to walk the streets outside in the garb they danced in. When they had to take the train, they draped a coat or cape over themselves to conceal their exposed flesh.

Women clad in what amounted to nothing more than underwear vanished with the bursting of Japan's "bubble economy." Just where did they all go? The whereabouts of at least one of these women is known. Her name is Noriko Kikuchi and she has drifted back to this neighborhood. Her frenetic dancing experience at *Mephisto* had taught her the joys of self-expression. She thus became an actress with a small theatrical troupe, and it was in such a guise that she returned to the same building that once dominated the times.

Tokyo is home to countless small theatrical troupes. Although there are an estimated three thousand, the fact is that it is virtually impossible to ascertain the exact figure. Many groups will assemble and disperse for a single production, resulting in a different total emerging with every reckoning.

Many of these small troupes are nothing more than groups of like-minded individuals who get together now and then to offer performances to small audiences of less than three hundred per run. Yet some will on occasion make it to such venerable venues as Kinokuniya Hall and the Honda Theater. The provisional goal of people involved in these groups is to perform at such noted playhouses.

The theatrical company that Noriko belonged to appeared set to attain that goal. Called *Kairin Maru*, which made it sound like a fishing boat, the troupe was on its way up, having attracted an audience of more than fifteen hundred to its last production. Mustering an audience of over twenty hundred on their next run, they believed, was their ticket to Kinokuniya Hall. Members of the troupe had all pinned their hopes on Manager-Director Kenzo Kiyohara, a man of superhuman energy. If the troupe managed to get bigger, it would catch the eye of the mass media, making it more likely that the actors would get the kind of break they sought. The future of the troupe members thus lay in the capable hands of Kiyohara.

The playhouse that Kiyohara had chosen for the performance of their next play was that building wedged between the Shibaura Canal and the First Metropolitan Expressway—the building that had been the home of *Mephisto* until the year before last. The lighting, acoustic, and other equipment had all been left behind, making it not an altogether incongruous setting for a playhouse. After the disco had gone out of business, the owner of the building had been hard-pressed even to rent the premises out as a venue for local community events. It had never hosted anything like a full-scale drama production. The decision to stage that particular play must have involved a fair amount of risk; some leading members of the troupe had vigorously opposed the choice. Yet their misgivings transformed into fervent enthusiasm upon seeing the script. They appreciated the multi-layered composition of the play, the way the stage settings would use the building's structure to impressive effect. As every member of the troupe agreed, difficult though it would be to pull off, it was a challenge well worth taking on.

Kiyohara was constantly striking out in new and original directions. He believed that the scenario for a play should change according to the contours of a playhouse, and with it the performances. Any troupe's rendering was likely to become somewhat stereotypical after a dozen or so performances. What set performances by *Kairin Maru* apart was that the troupe managed to avoid this pitfall. This was mainly due to Kiyohara's constant pursuit of freshness. Yet the theater is always a chancy business; it is impossible to gauge how something will go until the night of the performance. Kiyohara and the members of his troupe were brimming with both anxiety and expectation as the opening performance drew near. If all went according to plan, the path to Kinokuniya Hall would be theirs to walk. Conversely, if the performance went off badly, their collective goal was likely to remain tantalizingly beyond reach for some time to come.

2

The third floor of the building was roughly parallel to the Metropolitan Expressway. Every time a truck drove past, the building would vibrate. The roar of traffic did penetrate the building and could be heard by the audience, but not enough to distract attention from the performance.

As director, Kiyohara always sat among the audience, scrutinizing the stage from their perspective. He would mercilessly point out any mistakes he noted in the performance to cast members once the curtain came down. Accused cast members would have to rethink their roles and make proper adjustments by the next day. Thus, their theatrical production underwent a transformation even after opening night, right through to the final performance. A play honed to perfection over two months of rehearsal would often be turned upside down after the first performance. It was Kiyohara's practice to use feedback from the audience to refine the production.

As he briefly scanned the audience gathered to watch the first performance, he noticed that there were no empty seats in the house. The floor space once used for the disco was flat, and seating had to be provided by stacking boards to form tiers, which involved a great deal of exertion. The effort was more than rewarded, however, when spectators filled the seating to capacity. If the audience continued to pour in as they were doing on this opening night, the troupe should easily exceed their target of twenty hundred over the fifteen scheduled performances. Kiyohara looked away from the stage and drew a long breath of relief.

A telephone was ringing onstage. The young woman played by Noriko Kikuchi reached to answer it.

She wore a running outfit with a scarf wrapped around her head, the kind of look she'd never have permitted herself back in her disco days. Before her outstretched hand could lift the receiver, she heard a man's voice behind her and started to turn around. That very instant, Kiyohara noticed something that had definitely not been there in rehearsal: Noriko and the actor behind her seemed to lose their concentration. Noriko brought her hand up to her cheek, and glanced up toward some point on the ceiling. Reacting to this, the actor behind her also looked up at the ceiling. Kiyohara, shocked, almost stood up from his seat. Water was dripping from the ceiling. Drops of water were dripping down, wetting Noriko's cheek. This accident had diverted the actors' concentration from their roles.

Yuichi Kamiya in the sound effects booth was pissed off. Having voiced to Kiyohara a difference of opinion, he'd been replaced at the last minute. He was still unhappy about being relegated to the non-acting staff. On the face of it, he had voluntarily stepped down from the role and the part was given to a junior actor who'd been his understudy. But that was only the story put forth to cover his dismissal. Everyone in the troupe knew the truth. Kamiya was simply the latest proof that going against Kiyohara, autocratic director-manager, meant losing your part.

To have rehearsed for all of two months to perfect a role only to see the effort go to waste was the worst thing that could happen to an actor. Once relegated to the non-acting staff, you no longer had a ticket quota to fill and you also got paid, though a mere pittance. Comforting himself that by losing the part he was at least better off financially, Kamiya tried to come to terms with the blow. But now, in the sound effects box, he was thoroughly fed up with just sitting there at loose ends as a mixing assistant.

Kamiya gazed lethargically out from the booth, which was up behind where the audience sat. Set higher than the surroundings, sound effects commanded a good view of the stage and the audience. He could thus see Kiyohara's back as he sat there in the audience. Well over six feet tall and with the broad chest of a wrestler, Kiyohara had long, bleached hair that he tied back at the nape of his neck. Even in the dim stage lighting, Kamiya had been able to pick out Kiyohara instantly. As he looked down at the man, Kamiya's gaze began to radiate hatred—hatred for the man who'd snatched away his part, who'd left his self-respect in tatters. Yet Kamiya was unlikely to break away from the man's spell.

What Kamiya felt toward Kiyohara were the dual emotions of hatred and awe. Had he been able to dismiss Kiyohara's talent as a director, Kamiya would have left the troupe long ago. Kiyohara's overbearing and inhuman attitude was more than intolerable. Kamiya stayed with him because he possessed an almost tangible talent.

The disgraced actor had joined the *Kairin Maru* five years ago, soon after it formed. All the current troupe members recognized him as a mainstay member of the group. Were he to leave the troupe and join another company, he would have to start all over again from scratch as a lowly trainee. His reluctance to leave was even greater now that the *Kairin Maru* was just one step away from making its Kinokuniya Hall debut. Kiyohara may have bawled him out and taken his part, but there was little Kamiya could do but grin and bear it and anything else that came his way. But this did nothing to curb his resentment from mounting by the hour.

Reacting to an instruction from the mixing engineer sitting beside him, Kamiya pressed a switch in front of him. The telephone onstage began ringing. In response to the ringing, Noriko stopped what she was doing and went to answer the phone. She succeeded in conveying through her expression and gestures her character's mixed feelings of anxiety and hope. Kamiya was fascinated by the delicate nuance of her motions. She was a petite woman with a pale complexion and coquettish features. The running outfit she was wearing now concealed the contours of her body, but in the past she'd played roles that required her to undress onstage and reveal her splendidly proportioned physique.

Kamiya had never imagined that Noriko would develop into such a successful actress, though he was instrumental in getting her into *Kairin Maru*. Having met her at the disco *Mephisto*, he was the one who introduced her to Kiyohara. When *Mephisto* closed, Noriko found herself without a stage; recognizing her plight, Kamiya casually suggested to her that she might like his troupe. The invitation was really nothing more than a pick-up line he dropped to any girl he fancied. Little did he imagine then that in a mere two years she'd become the troupe's leading actress. He now regarded her with conflicting emotions, for she knew her own worth and asserted her importance in the company to the point of eclipsing him. There was a time when Kamiya seriously thought he was falling in love with Noriko. He hit the brakes when he learned that Kiyohara and Noriko were bound with more than platonic ties.

Kiyohara was not impartial in the way he handled members of the company. Some could give a poor performance without being criticized, while others would be yelled at after the best of performances. Kiyohara was a law unto himself, and no one else understood the distinctions he drew and the criteria he applied. It was obviously not simply a question of favoritism. But Noriko was special. During rehearsal he treated Noriko as someone special. That was not to say that he was easier on her. He was horrendously brutal.

Although tongue-lashings were dispensed universally, he had never directed physical violence toward any member of the company. There had been times, however, when he subjected Noriko to the most appalling outbursts of violence, as he screamed at her:

"Oh bitch, what the hell are you doing? You're no actress and never will be! Quit and save the profession a lot of grief! That's no good for God's sake! How many times do I have to tell you? Strip, you whore, it's all you're good for! Forget yourself now, you've got no place in the part!"

Not content with unleashing a hail of abuse, he would rush over to where she was, kick her legs out from under her, and slap her in the face. She'd fall to the floor, shed a silent tear or two, but never cry out loud. Fixing him with a determined look, she'd redo the scene, altering the nuance, and he'd shout that it was no good and knock her down again... So violent was the treatment that it pained the onlookers. Slow to catch on though Kamiya was, even he began to understand the nature of their relationship after seeing them go at this for six months. There was no way they could keep this up unless they were bound by carnal ties and strong bonds of trust. The violence that bound the two signaled the strength of a union both spiritual and carnal.

There was further proof. With the end of rehearsal, all resentment disappeared from between them and they'd engage in rapt conversation, the very image of peace and harmony. The woman who had just a moment ago been the victim of Kiyohara's cudgeling and kicking would now be falling about in entranced laughter at his remarks and hanging on his every word as he spouted his theories on the art of performance. Everyone knew what they were about, it was an unspoken understanding. The members of the company did not gossip about Kiyohara and Noriko because they understood and accepted their peculiar relationship.

Kiyohara had honed Noriko for that opening night's performance, and now she was showing the audience the result. It hadn't escaped the notice of Kamiya, either, that Noriko's expression had frozen for an instant. From the elevated position of the sound effects booth, the ceiling directly above the stage was not visible. Nonetheless, Noriko's gestures told Kamiya what was going on. He knew that water was dripping from the ceiling and that some drops had landed on her cheek.

3

Kamiya immediately caught sight of Kiyohara's hefty frame as he stooped up from his seat. Kiyohara cast a furtive glance behind him towards the sound effects booth. Despite the distance, Kamiya and Kiyohara's eyes met through the booth's glass partition. Unnoticed by other members of the audience, Kiyohara managed to communicate to Kamiya through deft gestures of his hand and facial expressions that something was wrong with the stage ceiling or thereabouts. Having noticed the problem already, Kamiya immediately understood what Kiyohara was trying to tell him and pointed to the ceiling. Seeing Kamiya's gesture, Kiyohara gave a big nod and slowly turned his face back toward the stage, still looking quite irritated. Kamiya was confident that he had correctly interpreted Kiyohara's gestured instruction.

Since the sound effects booth was closest to the floor above, Kamiya would be the natural choice to deal with a leak from the ceiling center stage. "Go up to the floor above, find the leak, and take care of it"—that must have been the meaning of Kiyohara's charade.

There was not a moment to lose. Every member of a small theatrical company, actor or not, must be prepared to assume lighting and stage duties. Kamiya recognized the seriousness of the situation. The hazards of water in such a place could not be underestimated. Wiring for the lights, though not visible to the audience, ran all about the stage. Should one of the connector sections become wet with water, everything on that circuit would short out. They could even be unlucky enough to have the whole stage plunge into darkness, wreaking havoc with the production.

Kamiya quickly exited the sound effects booth, only to stop dead in his tracks once out of the door. He didn't know how to reach the next floor. They had entered the building two days ago to prepare the stage sets, put up seating for the audience, and wire the lighting and acoustics. Although Kamiya had assisted in all of these operations, it had never once been necessary to go up to the next floor. He hadn't even seen the route up. The nearest door led to the outside of the building, with one passage leading to a fire escape. Kamiya opened the heavy iron door and ventured out onto one of the stairway landings. The moment he opened the door, he felt a blast of wind from the trucks driving nearby down the Metropolitan Expressway. It was like a different dimension. Traffic along the expressway a little after eight at night could slow to a congested halt one moment and resume at a high pitch just a few seconds later. Kamiya was amazed at how close the headlights streamed past. It seemed like he could reach out and actually touch the traffic. He'd been steeped in that alien dimension again, the one called the stage.

Adorned with colored lights, the Rainbow Bridge arched upwards over Tokyo Bay, with more of the aura of a Tokyo Tower than a bridge. The dark waters of the bay under the bridge were not visible from the fire escape landing, but the smell carried on the strong winds blowing off the bay.

Kamiya rushed up the fire escape to the next floor, where he tried the doorknob. Unlocked, the door yielded easily to his hand. It was pitch dark inside. The feeble light that came through the open door allowed him to just make out the vague contours of a corridor. Yet, to make his way along this corridor, he had to release the hand that was propping the door open. There had to be a light switch somewhere. As long as the power hadn't been shut off, the wall switch should still turn on the lights. Kamiya strained his eyes at a likely spot.

No sooner had he begun to move forward than he heard a heavy thud from behind as the door slammed shut, throwing him into complete darkness. He extended his hands and felt his way along the wall, nervously putting one foot in front of the other. There was little fear in his heart, however, so intent was he on getting the job done for his colleagues. Had he not been on such a mission, his progress would no doubt have been much more hesitant.

His hand felt something projecting from the wall, something that felt like plastic. Convinced that it was a light switch, Kamiya flicked it. There was a momentary pause before fluorescent lighting filled the corridor.

At the end of the long corridor, he could see an entrance that resembled a cave. He somehow remembered having seen something very much like it before. He was about to attribute this sensation to déjà vu when he realized that he had completely forgotten that this place had once been a disco. He muttered audibly as if to chastise himself for his foolishness. This was *Mephisto*, the disco he'd frequented, the one where he'd first met Noriko Kikuchi. No wonder he remembered seeing the entrance. What looked like the opening of a cave was in fact the entrance to a disco.

Where Kamiya was now standing had once been the cloakroom. He walked as far as the entrance and flicked another switch. This turned on the fluorescent lights inside the disco. The scene that confronted Kamiya was difficult to describe. The interior of a spaceship, a cavern, a fin de siècle underground arcade... There were extreme bumps on the walls, which were done in brilliant colors, unfaded in the least. The gaudy interior had looked so fantastic back then thanks to the colored lighting. In the white fluorescent glare, it suddenly looked inane.

Suspended from the slightly domed ceiling was a mirrored ball. The box seats in the corners were covered in dust. The small raised dancing platforms remained in the same configuration, but the room now lay in total silence. Kamiya only needed to close his eyes to recall the tumultuous uproar. Behind his eyelids, he could see Noriko as she danced frenetically there on the platform, her half-naked form pulsating to the beat of the music. Noriko never came with friends. She came to dance all by herself. He thought of the way she was then, and now, as she performed right there below him.

Kamiya shook himself out of his reverie. This was no time to wallow in sentiment. He reminded himself that he was here to find the source of the leak that scored a direct hit on Noriko. If he didn't solve the problem quickly, there was no knowing what chaos might ensue. The only places he could think of where water was likely to be used on this floor were the kitchen and the restrooms. Kamiya pictured to himself the layout of the floor below in an effort to work out what would be directly above the stage. He remembered the location of the restrooms opposite the dancing platforms. The restrooms were directly above the stage.

He quickly scanned where the kitchen had once been. Confirming that there were no leaks there, he made for the restrooms. The corridor leading to them was covered with a plush carpet, while the rest of the place was hard dance floor.

Kamiya assumed that a toilet was the source of the trouble even before opening the door; he could faintly hear water running somewhere in there. As he began to open the door, he felt a squelching sensation underfoot as water oozed out of the carpet. He was sure that the entire floor of the restroom was waterlogged, and he braced for what would greet his eyes upon opening the door.

It therefore came as no surprise that a pool of water a few inches deep covered the floor. Tiny ripples ran over the surface. Water was overflowing from a sink. The ripples were issuing from a point under the sink where water was dripping down.

Unconcerned that his shoes would get soaked, Kamiya made his way to the leaking sink. It was not of the washbasin type, but one of those deeper troughs provided to wash brushes and mops.

Kamiya bent over the sink, lowering his face to scrutinize it. The base of the tap was loose, and water spurted from the gap between the loose fixture and pipe. That alone could not have caused the problem; the sink would have drained the water away before it could collect and cause a leak. The problem was that the drainage pipe from the sink was clogged.

Kamiya wondered how he might reduce the volume of water flowing down from the sink. He wasn't sure if it would be more effective to fix the tap first and then unclog the drainage pipe, or the other way around. He tried pushing the tap down with his hand and twisting it back into place. Forcing it in this way was the worst thing he could have done, for the gap between the loose tap and pipe only widened. Unable to withstand the increased thrust of water, the tap was forced clean off.

"Shit!"

Now, instead of having a mere leak to deal with, Kamiya was faced with the prospect of a flood. A column of water as thick as the pipe struck the surface of water in the sink with a tremendous splashing sound, bringing water cascading onto the floor. On the spur of the moment, he thrust his finger into the mouth of the gushing pipe. The water pressure was too powerful; jets of water gushed out from between his finger and the side of the pipe, splashing his face and drenching the walls of the restroom.

"Damn!"

Kamiya abused the tap as if it were some defiant creature. The rent gaped wider and wider. The very thought of the damage this was wreaking on the stage made Kamiya freeze from head to foot in utter horror. He felt like running away and just leaving everything to take care of itself.

With the finger of one hand still stuffed in the pipe, Kamiya started groping for the drainpipe with his other hand. The only way he could resolve the situation was to remove whatever was clogging the drainage. He pushed his finger into the pipe and extracted the dirt that was jammed inside. Long, bleached strands of hair came out on his finger. So the culprit was hair! Hair washed into the pipe had clogged it, and prevented the water from draining away. Kamiya vigorously shook his hand to get rid of the hairy debris on his finger. Yet no matter how hard he shook his hand, he could not dislodge the strands. They clung to his finger and felt strangely alive.

Unconcerned, he continued inserting his finger into the drainpipe and extracting the clogged hair. No matter how many times he repeated the procedure, the water trapped in the sink showed no signs of going down. He paused to rest his hand. As he did so, he happened to turn and look down at his feet. He almost jumped with surprise. Covering the entire area of the floor, the hair removed from the pipe undulated in the water like so much seaweed floating in the sea. There was so much hair in the water that he couldn't see the color of the floor beneath. What amazed him was not only the sheer volume of hair, but also its color. The tangled mass was an indescribable mixture of hues: black, white, brown, red, pink, all merging to form a faintly disgusting blend. The overall effect was unpleasant enough that Kamiya tried to keep the hair off his feet by alternately standing on one leg and then the other.

In the end, he found it better to sit sideways on the edge of the sink, although the seat of his pants would get drenched. In this position he continued his efforts to unclog the drainpipe. He was unable to fathom why such an enormous amount of hair had come clogged from a sink that was intended for washing brushes, cloths, mops, and other cleaning gear. Although it defied his imagination to account for how such a thing had occurred in the first place, it was ultimately irrelevant. His only real concern was to deal with the situation somehow and divert the crisis at hand. Despite having lost his part at the last moment, Kamiya was fond enough of the company to not want to see it suffer a disaster. He simply had to do whatever he could to minimize any damage that this leak might cause to the troupe.

Had his efforts been rewarded? He suddenly heard a gurgling sound, accompanied by bubbles appearing in the middle of the sink, where a small vortex began to form. The water was draining through. Although he felt that he was making some progress, he did not relent. If anything, he redoubled his efforts to unclog the pipe. The tiny trickle of water that was now getting through was not likely to stop the leak. First he had to ensure that water was draining away in sufficient quantities, and after that he'd have to fix the broken tap. Only then would he feel that he'd dealt with the situation.

Having finally unclogged the drainpipe completely, he turned his attention to repairing the tap. He first paused to think how best to go about it. The water pressure was too great for him to effectively plug up the pipe. It occurred to him that his best bet would be to insert the tap into the pipe and bind it in place with wire or something of that sort.

He scanned the restroom for a suitable piece of rope or wire, and realized that he was in the ladies' room. Until now, he hadn't noticed that there was no row of urinals. The women's restroom was a realm he'd seldom penetrated, but this was no time for idle fantasizing. He opened the door of a broom cupboard at his side. There lining the shelves he found a stock of toilet paper. On the floor was a stack of buckets, along with a couple of mops. He was looking for something like a piece of string that was strong enough to secure the tap in place. He got down and crawled around in the cramped cupboard in search of some string. Beside the stacked buckets lay a coil of green tubing, which turned out to be a hose. It seemed a bit too thick and unwieldy for securing the tap.

When he pulled the hose, however, it felt much more elastic than expected. He decided that it might just prove sufficient for tying down the tap after all. He hauled the hose out of the broom cupboard.

The tap had sunk to the bottom of the water in the sink. He fished it out with his hand. It resembled the severed head of a dragon, with its mouth gaping. Opening the disattached tap, he pressed it into the mouth of the pipe and wrapped the hose around it several times, concluding with a tight knot. Checking to make sure that it was secured firmly in place, he slowly turned the tap off. The gush of water came to a halt. Not a single drop of water leaked from anywhere. The flow had been staunched.

Kamiya breathed a deep sigh of relief. Although it was hardly a creative achievement, he nonetheless felt a surge of accomplishment.

"If this were a performance..." He wondered just how he'd express this relief onstage. It'd be too silly and obvious to jump gleefully with joy. But a smile wouldn't do, either. If he looked in the mirror now, he'd probably see a man with a vacant expression. If anything, he'd still look agonized.

In fact, he ought to look in the mirror to see how his current state of mind was reflected on his face. He'd learn the most natural expression for a situation like this.

As he used two mops to soak the water off the floor, Kamiya made his way to the mirror. He looked closely into it, and a chill ran down his spine. He was momentarily unable to tell what was provoking the reaction. It was not so much his reasoning as his senses that had detected something unnatural. There couldn't possibly be anyone else in the women's restroom, here in the shell of a disco that had gone out of business two years ago. Yet something felt weird, didn't quite make sense.

He wondered how he failed to notice it until now. No doubt his mind had been so preoccupied that he'd seen but not registered it. Once he'd finished dealing with the leak, it must have started to rise to the fore of his consciousness.

In the mirror he saw the stall doors to five toilets. The doors of the two stalls to the left and the two to the right were open. Only the door of the stall in the middle was closed. The doors were designed to remain closed only when a stall was occupied.

...In other words.

Kamiya turned around and took a long hard look at the closed stall door. It seemed inconceivable that anyone could be in there.

All the lights were out when he'd reached this floor. The restroom had also been in complete darkness. Kamiya had had to turn the lights.

He was torn as to what he should do next. He didn't want to get involved in anything unusual. He'd already completed what he'd come here to do. He heard a voice telling him to return to his post on the double. All the while, his curiosity was becoming harder to resist. After all, inquisitiveness was a highly desirable quality in an actor. Wasn't Kiyohara always telling them that?

Kamiya moved a little closer and gave the door a poke with the end of the mop handle.

The door refused to yield.

He then tried giving the door a push with his hand. But the door wasn't stuck. It was locked from inside.

He was about to ask whether anyone was in, but thought

better of it. It seemed such a silly question, and if someone actually replied, he'd die of shock.

Reining in his curiosity, Kamiya gradually backed away from the door. He told himself that it was high time to get back to the sound effects booth.

Every time he moved his feet, the hair that he'd pulled from the drainpipe got tangled on his heels. He hadn't realized until now that the water flooding the restroom floor was forming a current. The water began to flow towards the closed stall door and into the space beyond.

The noise of a toilet being flushed came from the stall. As if drawn to the sound, the water covering the floor rushed into the stall, gurgling under the locked door.

Kamiya steadied himself, his frame now rigid from head to toe. Whoever it was inside the stall had just finished. Kamiya heard the metallic sound of the door being unlatched, and it began to open. Through the crack, he saw something black squirm—not just one, but innumerable black forms, squirming.

There was a tense hush. A sharp scream had brought Kamiya's consciousness back to reality somewhat. He'd been so deeply immersed in his acting that he'd forgotten why the collective gaze of an audience was upon him. He'd been breathing the very atmosphere of his own performance.

4

Within a month after *Kairin Maru* ended its run of *Watercolors*—the troupe's thirteenth production—all the reviews were in from the major theater magazines. In general, they were favorable, but some critics complained that the play's structure was simply too outré.

Let us quote some of the more important reviews.

From the November issue of *Monthly Play Guide*:

I'm still not quite sure how much of a conscious contrivance it was on the part of director Kenzo Kiyohara to incorporate the significance of that location. I have to admit being captivated by his unique technique of taking a device as the opening to a play.

The subject of the play is no doubt water, although water could not have been the original concept. The director himself would probably agree that he had to bring water into play to take advantage of the building's unique structure, famous in its day as the home of the disco Mephisto.

For all that, it is splendidly thought out. The action of the drama is played out on the third, fourth, and fifth floors of the building, with water flowing down from the upper floors to the lower, thereby providing a unifying vertical thread to the action. It must have taken a great deal of daring for the small theatrical company to handle such a large volume of water on the stage, especially in light of the ingenuity needed to drain it away successfully. Yet to take on such a seemingly unwelcome challenge as this is the hall-

mark of Kenzo Kiyohara.

The highlight of the piece was the performance of Kamiya, who fought a lone battle to bring under control a leak from the ceiling. In what amounted to a one-man show, his performance contained some very eerie moments. Still, one wonders why it had to be presented in the horror style. In this regard, the scene was rather puzzling...

From the October issue of *Stage Gallery*:

It is not a particularly new contrivance for actors to venture off the stage into the audience. Indeed, there are few, if any, independent companies that have not availed themselves to this device. Yet the device employed in this production by Kenzo Kiyohara is more complex. The disco known as Mephisto used to operate on three floors, each catering to clientele with different tastes. Each floor had its own turnstile for customers to gain admission through. Kiyohara has followed this system, staging different plays on each of the three floors—the third, fourth, and fifth. What serves to link each of these stages is the medium of water. Water will always fall downwards under the pull of gravity. Even in a concrete structure, water will find a way to leak down through the slightest crack. The effective use of water on its downward journey binds the three stages by a vertical link.

What makes Kiyohara the consummate businessman as well as showman is that he has priced the performance per floor. Those who watch the third-floor performance whet their appetites for the fourth-floor performance, which in turn spurs them to attend the fifth-floor performance. Thus, to grasp the significance of the man emerging from the flood-

ed restroom, one must watch the play on the fifth floor. In this manner, members of the audience are enticed to visit the playhouse three nights in a row.

From the winter issue of the quarterly *Performing Arts*:

One stage was almost turned into a swimming pool, with water spurting and gushing in all directions. Draining it all away afterwards must have presented the company with great difficulties. Yet the whole experience was well worth the effort. I found the scene with the multicolored hair undulating in the water quite overwhelming. Effective lighting techniques made the flesh tingle with the beauty and eeriness of it all.

The multicolored hair symbolizes the girls who once danced there. Although the hair does indicate a transition to the group-dancing scene, there can be no denying that the audience is provided with an insufficient explanation as to what is going on. The fourth-floor performance alone is not enough to enlighten them. However, the splendid contrast between the quiet of water and the massive blasts of the dancing scene denies the very need for an explanation. If the intent of this staging is beauty tout court, *this critic accepts that he has succumbed to the plan. All theorizing aside, I did find beauty in the morbidity of that world.*

FOREST UNDER THE SEA

Early winter, 1975

The soft soil underfoot had become hard bedrock before he knew it. Once out of the woods, he suddenly found himself atop a crag. With the rugged hardness of rock to reassure the soles of his feet, he made his way to the edge and peered over to find a sheer ledge dropping off no more than his own height. Here the woods abruptly ended, and below the drop extended a sloping strip of land covered by fallen leaves. Although there should have been something like a small stream winding its way down the eastern slopes of the mountain, no marsh was visible from this point onwards, nor was the sound of running water to be heard.

It felt like but a short while ago that the noonday sun, reflecting off the water, repeatedly caught the eye. Yet the stream vanished as if swallowed up by the earth.

There was little need to check the map. The underground water that welled up from this stretch of mountains fed a tributary of the River Tama, and upon swelling to much greater proportions, flowed into Tokyo Bay. Beneath the rock that felt so rugged to the soles of his feet ran the groundwater in streams formed of rainwater that had percolated through the hard rock. As Fumihiko Sugiyama thought of that crystal-clear water, something struck him as strangely incongruous. He lived in a high-rise condominium with a magnificent view of Tokyo Bay. He gazed upon the River Tama every day and could clearly remember the color of the water. The water was quite filthy and could only be described as a dirty blackish gray. He wondered how the unsullied, crystal-clear water flowing from the source could be transformed into such an

227

unsightly mess by the time it reached Tokyo Bay. As he stood atop the tiny crag, Sugiyama wondered how fascinating it would be to observe every subtle and detailed change in the color of the water as it flowed from the source to Tokyo Bay.

Sugiyama was about to jump down from the low crag when he found himself faltering. It was not that great a drop and could have been jumped easily. Yet he felt a surge of unease. The ground at the bottom of the small cliff was covered with leaves, which made for a strangely uncertain footing. Fallen leaves had frequently caused him to slip in the past while traversing mountainous terrain. Wet leaves stuck to the surface of rocks were a particular hazard because a hiker could easily slip and fall. Although the layers of leaf mold that lay under the leaves posed little problem, the leaves could also conceal a hollow in the rock or a tree root, which were often the cause of sprained ankles. Sugiyama was not concerned about spraining his ankle, however. He had visions of something like a bottomless dark pit lurking beneath the leaves. As he thought of the terrible consequences of jumping into something of that nature, he stepped back from the edge. Behind him could be heard the rustling of bushes being pushed aside. Suspecting that it wouldn't take Sakakibara much more than a minute to catch up, Sugiyama decided to wait for him on top of the ledge. Sakakibara was out of breath when he arrived to where Sugiyama stood. Sugiyama thrust his chin in the direction of the ledge to call Sakakibara's attention to what lay below. Sugiyama thought his expression would have sufficiently conveyed to Sakakibara his dilemma as to whether they should jump down. However, with a display of characteristic obtuseness, Sakakibara sprang off the edge without so much as checking his footing. He landed with a thud on the fallen leaves below. Due to the slight downward slope of the ground below, Sakakibara had landed on his rump. Sitting there with both arms extended behind to support himself, he pointed his jaw upwards and grinned at Sugiyama as if challenging him to stop wasting time and join him on the double. A man of hefty build and the antithesis of agility, Sakakibara was also a reckless character who had not infrequently provided Sugiyama with hair-raising moments in the past.

"Are you all right down there?" asked Sugiyama.

As if prompted by the question, Sakakibara started to rise to his feet, the sardonic smile still visible on his face. At that moment, however, his foot slipped on the leaves, dropping him down heavily again on his rump. Sugiyama laughed out loud. Preoccupied by something all of a sudden, Sakakibara crawled faceup to directly under the ledge and started to investigate the surroundings with a look of grave concern on this face.

"Say, look at this!"

He raised his hand aloft and signaled to Sugiyama to hurry and jump down. Gauging the steepness of the incline below, Sugiyama jumped and landed on his feet; he had managed to keep his balance and only needed one hand on the ground to steady himself. He turned to find Sakakibara now lying on his stomach, his face close to the bottom of the ledge. Right next to Sakakibara's rotund face gaped a dark hole similar in proportion to his friend's face. Crawling up to Sakakibara, Sugiyama peered into the hole.

"Could it be the entrance to a cave?"

Sugiyama's tone suggested that he was not so much asking Sakakibara as himself. He didn't want to get his hopes up, only to be dashed, so he suppressed the excitement he was beginning to feel. They had hiked the mountainside for half a day now and the only openings had been fissures in the rock, cracks hardly wide enough to insert his arm, let alone his body. Thus, trying not to get his hopes up, Sugiyama found himself believing that this aperture, too, was probably nothing more than the den of some animal.

With an earnest air, Sakakibara began brushing aside the leaves with his hands. At length, a soft, damp patch of earth was revealed, but Sakakibara continued working with his hands. There were signs of the air outside being drawn into the opening. Apparently, a current of air flowed through the inside of the cave. The opening was not small. Sugiyama's hopes began to rise slightly.

Impatiently lowering his backpack to the ground, he removed a collapsible shovel and began scooping away the dirt from the lower part of the opening. After digging away for less than ten minutes, he managed to sufficiently widen the opening for one man to crawl through. Both of them then took turns crawling halfway inside to examine the interior with a flashlight.

"We've done it! No doubt about it this time!" Sakakibara almost shrieked with excitement.

Sugiyama finally allowed himself to be convinced. Opposite the opening was an expanse of immeasurable proportions. Air rising up the mountainside was being drawn into the opening. If they listened carefully, they could hear the faint echo of water dripping somewhere in the depths of the darkness.

"Could be."

Although convinced that they had finally found what they were after, Sugiyama expressed a kind of reserved ambiguity; it was no simple matter to discover an underground cavern into which no man had ever set foot before.

Ever since his son had been born two and a half years ago, and especially now that his wife was expecting their second child, Sugiyama felt his appetite for adventure ebbing. He didn't find such a development totally unnatural; with two children to support, he was no longer able to throw caution to the wind in pursuit of adventure. He was almost resigned to never experiencing that ultimate adventure.

A young man just over thirty, Sugiyama was already seeing his youth slipping into shades of maturity, and this fact rankled him from time to time. Of late, he increasingly found himself releasing his grip on the accelerator on his motorbike, conscious of the risk of an accident, when he could go a lot faster and still remain within the speed limit. He'd only begun behaving this way after he'd gotten married and become a father. Such caution would have been unthinkable before. Intoxicated by the thrill, he would intuitively seek out danger and push his luck to the limits. During his teens and early twenties he'd lived for the thrill of living on edge between life and death.

However, his hunger for adventure had waned once he realized how little he would leave his wife and children if anything were to happen to him, given his meager savings and such. At thirty-one, there was no way he could be described as having had his fill of adventure—there were so many things left to do. It hadn't helped being stuck in the same old job at a newspaper-affiliated research firm for most of the past decade. Had he avoided getting mired in that kind of rut and been constantly alert and on the lookout for a better position, his footwork would no doubt have been more nimble now. At best, he had learned self-restraint; at worst, he'd become over-cautious. The challenge he now faced was whether to let the sight of the cave gaping in front of him be governed by an emotion of self-restraint or by daring initiative.

Sugiyama took the copy of the map from his backpack and entered a rough estimate of their current position. He also took a photograph of the surrounding landscape so they would be able to locate this place again in the future.

Not surprisingly unaware of Sugiyama's dilemma, Sakakibara was attempting to squeeze his hefty frame through the opening.

It was clear that he fully intended to enter the limestone grotto. They were wearing cotton overalls and had some caving equipment in their backpacks, although not the gear they would need on a serious spelunking mission.

Sugiyama tugged at Sakakibara's overalls and tried to pull him back.

"Don't you think we'd better leave that until later?"

Their journey around the mountainside on that particular day had been meant simply for discovering underground caves, not actual exploration. Sugiyama had tried to convey his concern that they had been lucky enough even to find a suitable cave, and that they should now be returning. Yet he did not have the physical strength to pull Sakakibara back.

Neither could there be any denying that he was also very intrigued as to what might be inside.

"There's no going back now!"

Sakakibara's tone was aggressive as he wriggled about to shake off Sugiyama's hand. Sugiyama angrily called to him and stood there tut-tutting in consternation. Yet he also felt something snap inside and found that he was reasoning with himself: *As long as we don't get trapped anywhere deep. As long as we just take a quick look inside. As long as we content ourselves with just that—nothing could possibly happen then.*

For ten meters or so into the cave, there was only enough room to crawl forward in single file. In the light of his headlamp, Sugiyama could see Sakakibara's rump ahead dancing side to side as he crawled forward after him. In fact, Sakakibara's rump blocked the whole tunnel, making it impossible to see ahead. Sugiyama couldn't imagine how a man of Sakakibara's build could ever have become a spelunker. Nor could he imagine whether it had been a good idea to invite Sakakibara on this mountain hike. There was something reckless about him, and recklessness could cost lives.

Sugiyama had known Sakakibara for no more than three years. He had met Sakakibara after joining the Pilot Caving Club in Hachioji. As a member of the Explorers' Club at college, Sugiyama had taken an active interest in both mountain climbing and marine sports, devoting his youthful energies to rock climbing and scuba diving. With increasingly less time and money to spend on adventure sports once he started working, he had focused on caving as a pursuit endowed with the dual aspects of both land and sea. Rock-climbing techniques were needed to traverse up and down shafts a hundred feet or more in length. Moreover, water was inevitably encountered in caves, given the nature of limestone caves, grottos carved out of limestone by the solvent action of running water. Hence, diving techniques were also required whenever a caving enthusiast wished to explore a current of crystal-clear water that was otherwise impassable. Sugiyama had no sooner taken up caving before he found himself hooked. There was no lack of spelunking sites in Japan, where numerous limestone plateaus could be found. Not only that, but in the mountains not too distant from central Tokyo lay virgin stalactite grottos that could only be described as halls of wonder. Not only was caving an inexpensive hobby, it was also one that fully sated his appetite for adventure.

The epitome of caving lies not in exploring grottos that have already been discovered by others, but in being the first to set foot on the virgin rock of an undiscovered cavern. There can be no sweeter taste for a spelunker than such a moment. It is said that anyone who has savored such a moment is destined to be forever addicted to caving.

As he crawled forward on his belly, Sugiyama couldn't help wondering if he was actually in an undiscovered cave. This would be the first time for him. He had been avidly studying the maps for months now. He was convinced that all the signs, whether the local geological features, topography, or sinuous course of the rivers, pointed to the presence of an undiscovered grotto in this locale. The previous evening, Sugiyama had been talking about this to Sakakibara on the phone. With the following day being a Sunday, their conversation had turned to arranging a casual mountain trek to search for caves.

They had set out early that morning, driving for about two hours and parking the car on the side of a woodland road. Several hours had already passed since they had left the car and began their trek into the mountains. They must have already walked three or four miles from the road. Not in his wildest dreams had Sugiyama imagined that a casual stroll like this would lead to the discovery of a cave. Sugiyama had agreed that, even if they should come across an opening, they would put off going underground until they could organize a fully equipped expedition with other members of the caving club. Sakakibara had humorously intoned the words "fully equipped expedition," as if to suggest with such a grand expression that the likelihood of their ever discovering a virgin grotto was less than zero.

They found themselves in a cavernous dome that was probably formed by a cave-in. Yet no matter how much they illuminated the ceiling with their lights, the beams lacked the power to reach the top, thus preventing an accurate assessment of how high the ceiling reached. It must have been at least a hundred feet above the floor of the cave. The cavern had opened up at the end of the narrow tunnel, and it was not until they stood that Sugiyama and Sakakibara became aware of its immense size. Upon realizing the vastness of the grotto, they were literally dumbfounded. Although prepared to encounter a dead-end, they now found themselves in an enormous subterranean cavern that surpassed their wildest dreams. Limestone results from the sedimentation of the remains of sea creatures. Therefore, this area of land was at some time in the distant past located at the bottom of the sea. Thrust up from the sea, the earth had become land, later to be covered by woodlands. Water erosion had then formed this gigantic cavern of majestic proportions. Sugiyama stared at the ceiling in blank amazement, not so much at the size of the cavern as at the incredible length of time that it must have taken to form. After an enthralled silence lasting almost a minute, both of them started to speak at once.

"Fantastic!"

There was no other way to describe it. Without a shadow of doubt, they had discovered one of the largest subterranean limestone caverns ever found in the Kanto region. Little could they have imagined that such a massive chamber existed under the mountains where they had been hiking just moments before. Excitement welled from deep inside to suffuse every pore.

"It's moments like this that make you realize you'll never quit caving, right?" Intoxicated by their good fortune, Sakakibara whistled a cracked tune as he scanned inside the cavern with his flashlight.

His whistling struck Sugiyama as annoying; it sounded out of place. Usually indifferent to Sakakibara's discordant whistling, Sugiyama now found that it rankled his nerves so much that he was unable to ignore it.

Suddenly Sugiyama felt apprehensive. There was always the risk that, negotiating a constricted passage into an expansive cavern, a spelunker would forget the route taken to get there. Sugiyama took out his compass, took a reading, then entered the direction on his diagram. Yet no sooner had he jotted it down than it occurred to him that he was being quite silly. After all, such precautions were only necessary when you intended to go down much deeper. It was far too hazardous for just two people to enter a newly discovered cave with such inadequate equipment. They should be calling it a day and making their way back.

Nevertheless, Sakakibara had made his way to the edge of the cavern and was shining his flashlight down in search of a route to pursue. He was still whistling. The sound reverberated eerily through the stalactite-girded arena.

"Say, Sakakibara, let's be getting back," Sugiyama called out to his partner, who had his shoulders hunched as he peered frantically at the floor.

Sakakibara finally stopped whistling. "Come look at this. There's a shaft!" Paying no attention to what Sugiyama had just said, Sakakibara stood there with a triumphant air. He looked even less inclined to leave than before.

On hearing the word "shaft," Sugiyama's resolve swayed, for he was renowned among the members of the Pilot Caving Club for having the best shaft-scaling skills. Sakakibara and the others were no match.

Thinking he might as well have a look to gauge the value of the find, he casually made his way over to where Sakakibara was shining his flashlight. In the vast bell-shaped cavern where they found themselves, there appeared little else that promised to lead them any further than the shaft where Sakakibara was directing his flashlight. Hanging down like curtains, the walls of the cavern merged up here and there with stalagmites that extended up from the floor of the cavern. There may well once have been a passageway leading somewhere off the edge of the cavern, but it had undoubtedly been blocked off by debris from the cave-in.

Making his way to the edge of the shaft where Sakakibara eagerly awaited him, Sugiyama peered down. The shaft slanted slightly rather than descend at a perpendicular. He could also see that the furthest extremity formed a gentle curve. As shafts went, it was not that deep, and could be negotiated well enough without ropes and a ladder.

Sugiyama had the chills. He was unable to tell whether it came from fear or excitement, although the tingling sensation in his veins suggested more thrill than chill.

"Well, are you game?" Sakakibara whispered with a grin, as if he'd read Sugiyama's mind.

Looking back, Sugiyama once again confirmed their route as far as the shaft, and tried to persuade himself that this was definitely the last move. Once he had managed to reach the bottom of the shaft, he swore, there would be no stopping him making for home.

Entering the ring of light from Sakakibara's flashlight, Sugiyama pressed his back into the sloping surface and began his descent.

"What's it like down there?" asked Sakakibara once Sugiyama was almost halfway down.

Not responding to Sakakibara, Sugiyama had stopped and was straining his ears to listen. He could hear the faint sound of water dripping somewhere. He remembered hearing a similar sound at the mouth of the cave.

"I can hear water!"

No sooner had Sugiyama responded than Sakakibara thrust his hefty backside into the shaft.

"I'm there!"

Sakakibara started down after Sugiyama, and there was no stopping him.

The shaft bottomed out in a gentle curve, which led to another level chamber of pretty much the same shape as the one before. It was a much smaller, bell-shaped cavern. A thin film of water covered the slippery surface of the cavern walls. So closely did the watery membrane adhere to the walls of the cave that you had to touch it to confirm that it was there at all. Percolating in through crevices in the ceiling, the water slid silently down the walls of the cavern to vanish through the floor of the cave without forming a single pool. The spectacle enthralled Sugiyama as he illuminated the area with his flashlight. He felt a surge of joy to think that he was the first person on the face of the earth to have witnessed this sight. It was the kind of moment savored once in a lifetime, if at all. The power of the moment made Sugiyama forget the oath that he'd made to himself before entering the shaft. The fact that the descending water did not form pools but disappeared under the floor of the cavern suggested that there might be quite an extensive chamber below.

Sugiyama and Sakakibara began searching for a route to that chamber. All feelings of self-restraint now thrown to the wind, Sugiyama was oblivious to anything else. The bait was too tempting, and he was being lured farther down into the bowels of the earth.

In one spot, Sugiyama felt a slight draft of air. A subtle current of warm air came wafting up from some place.

Sugiyama called Sakakibara over and sounded him out. Sakakibara knit his brows, deep in thought. There was no doubt about it; he too could feel air blowing up from somewhere. Yet there was no shaft visible nearby from which the air could be coming.

Baffled as to where the source of the air could be, Sugiyama began moving slowly with the sensation of a faint draft on his skin. He then stood in a depression filled with piles of rubble. At his feet lay all kinds of rocks, both big and small. He used his light to survey the topography once again. The depression where he stood seemed to be shaped like a basin or circular crater. It occurred to Sugiyama that this may have been a sinkhole filled up by a cave-in. If so, all they had to do was remove the stones to uncover a shaft below.

Both men began quickly shifting the stones, and eventually exposed quite a large boulder. They could feel a more substantial blast of air coming through gaps under this rock. Without a doubt, this was the boulder that was blocking the entrance to the shaft.

Sugiyama and Sakakibara both tried to push the boulder to one side. It tilted to reveal part of a circular opening to the shaft underneath. Releasing their grip on the boulder would result in the boulder falling back to cover up the shaft. Thus, they redoubled their efforts with one more powerful push. With the base of the boulder now facing sideways, they wedged a stone in a niche to secure the boulder in place. Now the entrance to the shaft was completely exposed. Whenever either man moved, stones at their feet would roll down into the opening, bouncing off the stalactites to create a sound that reverberated like thunder. Both men waited until all stones likely to fall had fallen and the commotion had died down. After all, they did not want stones falling on their heads as they descended the shaft.

Sugiyama made up his mind: there could be no turning back now that they had come this far. He resolved to see this through to the end.

Tying a rope round a rock, Sugiyama released the other end, and it fell towards the bottom of the shaft. Although he felt capable of scaling the shaft without a rope, he wanted to take every precaution to ensure a safe return.

"Wait here."

The tone of Sugiyama's command was calm, yet clearly a command. Although the two men were the same age, Sakakibara was Sugiyama's senior in terms of the number of years he had been a Pilot Caving Club member. It was thus with reluctance that Sakakibara nodded in compliance with what amounted to an order from a junior. Despite their relative positions at the club, Sugiyama far surpassed Sakakibara in terms of caving technique. Given the precariousness of the footing, one of them had to remain at the edge of the opening to make sure that the end of the rope remained in place, and Sakakibara was more suited to this task.

As Sugiyama lowered himself inside the shaft, he felt apprehensive once again. He wondered why, but simply attributed it to Sakakibara's annoying whistling. The man was looking down at him coolly now, all the while whistling some cracked tune. Sakakibara was all too relaxed, and this gave Sugiyama a nasty sense of foreboding.

Putting his foot on a small ledge, Sugiyama assumed a rest position. He began to contemplate the nasty premonition he had just had. This was supposed to be a virgin limestone grotto, one which no human had ever set foot in until now.

Yet an uninvited flash of intuition suggested to him that sometime in the distant past, someone had tried to access this shaft just as he was attempting to now. It was an impression that must have formed unconsciously from having glimpsed some evidence of a prior presence.

He brought his headlamp closer to a stalactite. The longer he inspected the wall, the more apparent became the bizarre pattern fashioned there. Daubed onto the contrasting ochre of the cave surface was dark-gray mud. He stretched out his hand to feel the surface. The pattern was clearly different from the cave surface. He wondered whether it was a motif that someone had intentionally fashioned there. No, he felt sure that wasn't the case. He concluded that it was more likely to have been a muddy stain on the back of someone who had passed through the shaft just as he was doing now. As this person had been passing through, the mud on his back must have rubbed off onto the limestone wall.

Sugiyama felt his energy rapidly ebbing away. The only reason he'd been tempted to this madcap adventure was the belief that no man had ever set foot in this grotto before. There was all the world of difference between being first and being second. Viewing this as a good a time as any, he called out to Sakakibara. As soon as he shouted, however, a hail of small stones struck him in the face. He immediately covered the top of his helmet with both hands for protection. Once the stones stopped falling, he looked up to see Sakakibara's blue overall-clad form bumbling about, and then enter and block the shaft.

"Say, Sakakibara!" he shouted even louder.

"Hang on! I'm coming down!"

Unable to contain himself, Sakakibara appeared to be lowering himself down the shaft, feet first.

"No, get out of there!"

Their ensuing argument over who was going down or up lasted but a few seconds. A sudden shower of small stones was immediately followed by a loud boom, a brief scream, and the horrible sound of crushing bone. Then, as quickly, the shower of stones subsided. The lower half of Sakakibara's body blocked the mouth of the shaft, preventing Sugiyama from appreciating the extent of the catastrophe that had just befallen him.

"What's happening up there?"

He voice began to quiver, for he already instinctively knew that something was very wrong. Sakakibara failed to respond, but a short moan percolated through the gloom instead.

Sugiyama made his way up until he could feel Sakakibara's feet on his head. He flashed his light up through the gap between Sakakibara's waist and the wall of the shaft. To his amazement, the space above the mouth of the shaft was no longer open; it was blocked by the boulder.

He was stupefied. He felt the blood drain from his head. As he braved the dizziness, he regretted that they hadn't properly secured the boulder. With every rockslide, the boulder had tilted under its own weight to fall back to its original position, encountering and crushing Sakakibara's head in the process. It was too cruel a punishment to be meted out to someone for simply having deserted his post. Yet Sugiyama could not suppress his desire to curse Sakakibara for his stupidity.

The beam of his flashlight caught the ghastly white of Sakakibara's jaw, under which the sinews of the neck were strained tight. His head was wedged between the side of the shaft and the edge of the boulder so that Sugiyama could not see the face from the nose up. For some time, Sugiyama just stared in blank disbelief. His legs trembled, and he felt nauseous.

"Are you okay?" He tried to say this, but the words would not come out of his parched mouth.

Yet the truth was only too obvious. No amount of talking would make any difference now. Down the strained neck ran thick rivers of blood. Sugiyama was on the point of reaching out for Sakakibara's foot to check for signs of life, when suddenly Sakakibara's body arched backwards and began to convulse. The movements were too unnaturally spasmodic to be anything but the throes of death. His eyes transfixed by the horrendous sight, Sugiyama shivered and tasted bile.

There could be no denying that his situation was desperate. It was like being trapped under a manhole capped with a one-ton manhole cover. Sugiyama was a trapped rat.

He felt he'd been there in the darkness much longer than just two days. He had spent the first few hours after being trapped floundering about trying to find a way out, wasting a good deal of time and energy. Now that he'd been there for a full forty-eight hours, he was huddled up almost motionless by the waterside, resigned to the fact that he had but two options, and only two options. The problem was which to choose. It had occurred to him that he could try pushing up the boulder blocking the mouth of the shaft. Yet he'd already tried to move it and knew just how much it weighed. It had taken every ounce of his and Sakakibara's energy as they had strained in unison. There was no way he could push that boulder up while dangling in the pit with no foothold. Moreover, Sakakibara's corpse was dangling down from his trapped head, blocking any space there may have been. The corpse prevented him from even reaching the boulder, and Sugiyama didn't have the courage to pull Sakakibara's gradually chilling body down from between the boulder and the shaft's edge.

Giving up the idea of getting out through the shaft, Sugiyama decided to focus on the opposite direction, making his way downward. In any direction he looked, the interior of the limestone cavern was intricately configured like a labyrinth. It might conceivably be possible to find a way out by a different route. Yet he ended up in a tubular cavern with a radius of about thirty feet. The low portion of the sloping floor was flooded with underground water, forming a subterranean lake. Whichever route he followed ended up at this subterranean lake. He vainly searched every nook and cranny along the edge of the lake for a passageway to another chamber. He realized he was trapped in a sealed cave.

For the past ten hours, he had not switched on his headlamp except to glance at his watch. Although he carried two headlamps, he had long switched over to the spare and could not afford to waste a second's worth of power.

It was now Tuesday afternoon—half past five. Under normal circumstances, he would have been getting ready to leave work and head for home.

He made it a rule to have supper with his family at least

three times a week. No sooner would he open the front door of his home than his son Takehiko would come running up to him. Sugiyama loved to hear his son as he tried to enunciate the words he'd just learned. As he lifted his son into his arms, the boy would utter faltering sounds in an attempt to give his father an account of every little thing that had happened that day. The moments offered great relief and comfort to Sugiyama. The desire to experience the joy of those moments inspired him with the energy he needed to finish up work quickly so he could return home.

Sugiyama remembered that his wife had wanted him to take the oil heater out of storage. He had put the bulky oil heater at the back of the closet and it was more than his wife could handle. It would soon be getting chilly, and all he could think about now was that his wife and son might feel the cold. It was the only heater they had, and he simply couldn't get it out of his mind. He regretted not having taken it out for them before setting out on Sunday morning. It was very cold inside the cave, although temperatures were supposed to remain constant throughout the year. It was probably under fifty degrees where he was at that moment. Although it was odd that anyone in such a predicament should be worrying about others, it didn't occur to him that it was incongruous.

Sugiyama felt the urgent need to get out of there, fueled by an irresistible desire to get back to his family. Once again he pondered all the conceivable possibilities open to him. Although he knew he had covered everything over and over again in his head, there was always the possibility that he may have overlooked something.

He had told his family on the morning of the day before

setting out that he was going "for a little hike in the mountains." He had said nothing about exploring limestone caves. Sakakibara had come to pick him up and they had gone as far as the woodland road at the foot of Mt. Shiraiwa. There they parked the car and walked three or four miles in the countryside before stumbling upon the entrance to the cave. Sugiyama wondered if Sakakibara had told anyone that he was heading this way. It was unlikely. After all, he had lived alone and had no one to tell. They had made no plans to explore any caves; their original purpose had just been to hike in the mountainside to look for new caves.

Given to worrying at the best of times, his wife would be in quite a state by now. She would no doubt have imagined the worst and called the police a long time ago. Yet how could the police go about searching for them? Their only possible clue would be the car left at the side of the road, although there was little chance of the police even finding the car. Supposing they'd found the car, it was all but inconceivable that any rescue party would come his way. Not only was the limestone cave unmarked on the map, its very existence was unknown.

First, it was impossible to avoid the conclusion that the chances of rescue from outside were extremely low. The only alternative was for him to find a way out.

Sugiyama could sit and wait for a rescue team or think of some way of getting out by himself. In other words, he had but one real option. Yet any attempt to escape required so much courage it defied the imagination, and this reality was gradually dawning on Sugiyama. He would need courage, and no ordinary courage at that.

247

Sugiyama may never have thought of a way of escaping had he not discovered the traces left on the walls of the shaft.

A more careful search revealed traces on other parts of the cave as well. The tips of the icicle-like stalactites that hung down over the waterside seemed to be chipped, while the flowstone surface was scratched as if brushed by someone's body. The same kind of damage could be seen in various places around the cave. It occurred to Sugiyama that the interior of the cave had been disturbed by a party of explorers from a caving club or other group. Yet he was not aware of any records of this particular site having been discovered. Caving clubs regularly kept in touch; it would have been big news had any unknown cavern been discovered in the Kanto region.

If the cave hadn't been disturbed by humans, concluded Sugiyama, it must have been an animal. It occurred to him that a sizeable animal could have strayed into the cave and wreaked havoc here and there. Sugiyama slapped his knee the instant the idea occurred to him. The mouth of the shaft had been blocked by the boulder. This meant that any animal must have crept into the cave via a different route. He could not imagine where such a route could be located. Yet some secret route had to exist somewhere; it was just that he had overlooked it.

Though he vainly searched the periphery of the cavern, he failed to find even the smallest crevice. He was at a loss as to how to account for the evidence.

Turning off his headlamp, he sank deep in thought. Immersed in the pitch darkness, he concentrated his thoughts and began thinking hard. The inside of the cavern was not totally silent. There was the constant sound of dripping water. The drips ran down the stalactites of limestone that hung from the grotto ceiling, and fell plip-plopping on the subterranean lake below. Even in the darkness, it felt like he could see the droplets as they rippled the surface of the lake. The sound amplified the notion of water in his mind until he realized that water was the key to the puzzle. Wasn't it possible that water was flowing out from the bottom of the subterranean lake? And what were the implications? Opening his backpack and extracting the lens cap of his camera, Sugiyama set it on the surface of the water. The cap began to float from right to left. He tried floating the cap again, but this time in a different place. It moved in the same direction. Wherever he set the cap on the surface of the water, it made its way from right to left. A current of water was flowing at the bottom of the lake. What was more, the current was flowing quite rapidly. Sugiyama finally realized that, although to all appearances the water seemed to be a subterranean lake, it was in fact an underground river.

Since the beginning of November, two typhoons had swept across the Kanto region, bringing heavy rains. As a result the underground water level was higher than usual, and the route leading out from the cave must have sunk under water. Since the water was flowing from right to left, somewhere down toward the left, he concluded, there should be a tunnel through which the water was draining away to the outside world. The current would not be so rapid if the water had no sizeable hole to drain through.

The more he thought about it, the more certain he felt

that there was an underwater tunnel. That was all well and good, but he still had to find some way of getting out. Although he had found a route out, it was not as if he could just walk along it.

Sugiyama could not yet summon up the courage to take the first step. Once taken, there was absolutely no turning back, and he could have no way of knowing what awaited him along the way.

How inexpressible would be his joy upon seeing the light of day! When he had been trekking across the mountainside, he noticed that the river winding along the eastern side of the mountain had suddenly vanished. According to Sugiyama's compass, east was left. It seemed a fair conclusion that the underground water was flowing into a river on the eastern side. Since they had been making in an easterly direction ever since entering the cave, it was also probable that he was by now quite close to the opening from which the water was draining out.

He frantically tried to imagine the brilliance of the light, how he'd stumble outside into open space from his imprisonment in the cave. He had to invoke his courage by picturing the joy of feeling the light of day radiating down from above. Yet paradoxically, the greater his desire to get out of there, the stronger his fear and anguish, lest what he so longed for should be snatched from him just short of the end.

Sugiyama was a good skin diver. It was quite possible for him to dive into the dark waters and make his way into the underwater tunnel by feeling the water on his skin and gauging the direction of the current. He had no way of knowing, however, how far the tunnel extended. Once on the current forward, there was absolutely no way back. If he found no exit, there was no coming back. If he ran out of air before reaching the exit, there was no coming back. And even if he did manage to find an opening, there was no telling whether it would be big enough for a man to get through. Imagine the agony of flailing about before a tiny opening, fighting for life. All the distress a man could suffer would suffocate him at once in that final moment. The futility, the anguish, the despair, the physical agony...

If he just sat and waited here, he would be spared that agony. Wait? Wait for what? Several years ago, there had been an incident in which a cave explorer had been rescued four days after going missing in some limestone caves in Okinawa. He had apparently dropped his flashlight and lost his way. In that case, not only did the rescuers know which caves he had been exploring, but local spelunkers also turned out in force to search for him. Even then it had taken a full four days to find and rescue him.

Sugiyama wondered which of two options offered the better chance of survival. It was inconceivable that a rescue party would arrive within a few days. Diving in search of an outlet was no doubt the better option in terms of his chances for survival. The question was whether he was capable of facing the suffering that may lie ahead.

Another two days had elapsed. He had now been trapped for a total of four days.

He could afford no more indecision: it was now or never. All he had eaten during those four days had been a box of biscuits that he always carried in his backpack as a precaution.

True, he had lost a great deal of stamina, but still had enough energy left to make the dive, provided he waited no longer. However, his strength would begin to ebb dramatically in another two or three days, whereupon he would no longer have any decision to make, but be left with the default option: a slow but painless death. Any chance of being saved would have run out.

Looking back on his thirty-one years, he began to question whether he had lived a happy life, since the life could be snuffed out at any moment now. Although he would have liked to feel satisfied with the years he'd been given, he felt angry at how thoughtlessly he had lived. There was still so much he wanted to do in life. There were all those adventures that he and his son Takehiko had in store, when his son grew a little older. There was so much he wanted to teach the boy. Sugiyama hoped to instill in him the lessons of life born of his own experiences, so the boy could take advantage of the knowledge and lead a more fulfilling life, supplement the knowledge with his own, and pass it on to the next generation. This, for Sugiyama, was the real meaning of human life. Neither could he help worrying about his wife and the child she was expecting. Yet he would have to try to keep his mind free from such concerns for now. There was no end to the unfinished business that crowded his mind, the insurance settlement, the mortgage, who would take care of his elderly parents, and so on. Still, he wanted to convey his will to his son.

In the fading light of his headlamp, he began to write in the blank space on the back of the map. As if trying to convince himself, he penned each letter and each phrase with firm deliberation. He rolled up the finished letter and put it into an empty film case. He sealed the case with vinyl tape, then inserted it into a waterproof pack on which he had clearly written a name and address. As a final precaution, he sealed the pack and tested it in the water. The test revealed that the little package was both buoyant enough and perfectly water-resistant. What Sugiyama had in mind was what would happen if the outlet was too narrow for him to pass through. If that were the case, he would dispatch the letter to his family in the direction of the opening. He felt that there was little likelihood of it ever reaching outside the cave unless he released it immediately in front of the opening. Even if he managed to push it into the tunnel leading out, there was the risk of the buoyant package getting caught up in the countless stalactites hanging from the roof of the tunnel.

Writing the letter strengthened Sugiyama's resolve. He had to believe that he had a chance. At his best, he could swim about fifty meters underwater without having to surface. With the aid of the current, he could probably cover even more distance. As a precaution against projecting stalactites, he would wear his helmet and keep his overalls and boots on.

Turning his lamp on, he set it on a nearby rock to shine on the left side of the subterranean lake. The light flickered feebly as if it would go out at any second. He gradually lowered himself into the water and waited until he grew accustomed to the cold before submerging his entire body. Swimming over to the left side of the lake, he placed his hand on a ledge and poked his head above water to regulate his breathing. The headlamp on top of the rock was almost out. Sugiyama took several short breaths and filled his lungs with air. The case containing the letter was wedged under his belt so that there was no possibility of losing it. He patted his belt to reassure himself that the letter was still there. The instant he did so, the headlamp went out.

As if this had been his cue, Sugiyama began diving down along the line of the ledge. About six feet down, the current became more vigorous, assailing his face and almost ripping his helmet off. His groping hands found the opening to the tunnel. The water around him was rushing into the tunnel. It was just as he had guessed. His will firm, he entrusted his fate to the current.

Summer 1995

The troupe of twelve pitched base camp on the gentle slope that fronted the entrance to the cave. They were members of the S. University Explorers' Club led by Takehiko Sugiyama.

Although they had been particular about selecting a shaded spot to pitch their tents, no sooner had it passed three in the afternoon than the tents were being directly exposed to searing sunlight. With faces bathed in sweat, the club members shouldered their equipment. Their load consisted not only of caving gear; they also had their full diving equipment to carry, which was no joke. The cars were parked on an empty stretch of ground near the foot of the mountain, about a mile and a half downhill from the camp. Each club member had had to make two roundtrips to carry their two sets of gears uphill.

The screeching of cicadas was so loud that normal conversation was out of the question. The club members devoted their energies to setting up base camp rather than conversing. Their preparations were progressing ahead of schedule. Takehiko gave a satisfied smile as he saw how adroitly the members were handling the preparations. Putting down the tackle he was carrying, he took a brief rest and stretched his back.

The dark mouth of the limestone cave gaped right in front of them. The opening to the grotto had been made wider than it had been back when his father had arrived here two decades earlier. The impenetrable darkness that lay beyond the opening, though, was exactly the same as what his father had witnessed. For Takehiko, the cave was a place that he'd felt destined to visit sooner or later.

Now known by the impressive name of *White Rock Caverns*, these limestone caves discovered by his father had been visited by dozens of research teams. Until the year before, plans had been made to develop the caves into a tourist attraction under the aegis of the local village administration. However, the plans had been abandoned for the most part. Not only had the project been opposed by local environmental protection groups, but the estimated costs of building roads and other tourist infrastructure had been staggering. Thus the limestone caves had been left untouched. The general public was not allowed to enter the caves. The district forest office granted admission permits only to such official groups as research teams.

The caves were only a three-hour drive from where Takehiko lived. He could have come whenever he wanted.

Nor had he lacked specialist friends; he could have dived into the subterranean lake where his father had died whenever he chose.

Takehiko had intentionally kept putting the visit off. Hardly a day had passed during most of his life without him picturing that subterranean lake. It had even figured in his dreams. He had long lost count of the times he had woken in the middle of the night, gasping in panic at the water and darkness as they closed in on him.

At this time in his life, he faced no hardships worth mentioning. It occurred to him that the time had come. Once summer vacation was over, he would have to cut down on activities with the Explorers' Club, and devote himself instead to completing his undergraduate thesis and finding a job. The following year would see him a busy, gainfully employed member of society. He felt that his visit must happen now or never.

Takehiko had just turned three years old when his father's body had been retrieved from the bottom of the subterranean lake. Children of that age do not even understand the meaning of death. That muscular, vital body he had hugged every day had been there one moment and gone the next; the only sensation he had had was that something familiar had suddenly vanished.

Six months after the two men encountered tragedy in the cave, a local exploration team had chanced upon the body of Sakakibara, the friend of Takehiko's father. Immediately after the grisly discovery, the team had also discovered his father's body while surveying the underground lake. Thus they had finally resolved the incident involving the two men who had gone missing about six months earlier. Even after the team had removed the boulder, Sakakibara's decomposing body had remained dangling there. As the team turned their flashlights on Sakakibara's corpse, they had been aghast to see the calcified back of his crushed skull cleaving as one to the limestone.

The police had explained to his mother that his father's death was probably "due to temporary derangement caused by being trapped so long in the darkness."

What the police meant was that his father had become so mentally confused that he'd drowned himself in the lake. Cases of suicide by drowning are apparently not uncommon among desperate people marooned or adrift at sea for a prolonged period of time. Takehiko's mother refused to accept the conclusion offered by the police, although there was no use in contesting it; it was a point of personal rather than criminal bearing. She did, however, doggedly insist that her husband had not been the kind of man to panic in a crisis. She understood her husband's personality better than most.

The club had completed its preparations for diving in the cave by eleven the next morning. Takehiko and five other members would be the first to dive, while the other six members remained on standby. All team members, including the two female members, were certified scuba divers and had plenty of experience diving at sea. Only three members of the team, however, had cave-diving experience. It was the role of the captain, Takehiko, to initiate the remaining nine members into the mysteries of cave diving.

After a meticulous check to ensure that all equipment

was working properly, the six divers lined up on the bank of the underground lake. Takehiko once again ran through the most important points to keep in mind:

"Avoid using your fins as much as possible. If you disturb the sediment, you'll end up with zero visibility. If you panic and try to surface, understand that there's nowhere to surface. The only thing is to avoid panicking. Have you got that? Do not panic, whatever you do. Remain calm at all times. Approach any crisis with calm. Okay?"

Nodding in response, the other divers inserted the mouthpieces of their regulators into their mouths without a fuss. In addition to the lights fitted onto their helmets, all divers carried powerful searchlights. Each diver was tied to the lifeline at a uniform distance from the next diver. Their air cylinders were not fixed to their backs. They were to clasp their cylinders to their breasts if the need arose. The ability to move them this way prevented them from getting in the way in such a constricted environment.

The presence of the divers brought a distinctive aura to the cave as the beams from their twenty-odd lights reflected off the surface of the lake and illuminated the walls of the cavern. They were fitted out with so much equipment and so many lights that they literally dazzled. Takehiko's father had been unadorned with such gear when he made his attempt on the tunnel. If he could see them now, he may well have smiled at the somewhat excessive array of equipment.

The prolonged rainy season had caused the subterranean water level to swell. Takehiko silently dived beneath the surface of the abundant waters of the lake, leading his fellow explorers on their way.

No sooner had he gone under than he became aware of the oval opening to a tunnel, about three feet across, in the left wall. He noticed countless little bubbles moving toward the opening and being drawn in. It had to be a tunnel that led to an outlet. In an attempt to relive his father's experience, Takehiko held in his breath and let himself be directed by the current towards the tunnel, reminiscent as it was of the viscera of some enormous monster.

As he shone the beam of his underwater light in front of him, he could see that the stalactites hanging down from the ceiling made the passageway impracticably narrow. Although the current did provide enough thrust to keep moving him forward, he soon found himself colliding with the projecting limestone if he left everything to the momentum of the current. He discovered that it required considerable adeptness to avoid the projections just above his head and the stelae jutting out from the sides. He could only make his way forward by plowing frantically through the water with his hands, while vigorously moving his flippers up and down. Even with frontal visibility, it was almost impossible to move forward without colliding with the stalactites.

Takehiko lightly closed his eyes in an attempt to recreate what his father must have experienced. Yet no sooner did his eyelids shut than he had to open them again. The instant he closed his eyes, he was overcome by an intense fear as the power of his imagination transformed the stalactites into massive daggers. No matter how many times he tried closing his eyes, the sense of imminent danger forced them open again.

It occurred to Takehiko that it would have been impossible for his father to make it through the tunnel uninjured. He must have suffered innumerable lacerations to his head and arms. As Takehiko pictured his father tenaciously swimming onward in pitch darkness, unable to breathe and bleeding from his wounds, he was overwhelmed by a surge of emotion so intense that he used up all the oxygen in his lungs.

Just as he was about to give up hope of getting any further without breathing, the tunnel suddenly became wider, as if funneling out. Looking up, he saw what appeared to be ripples on the surface of the water. A space seemed to have opened up between the ceiling of the tunnel and the water. Takehiko surfaced and took a breath of air through his mouthpiece. He was sure that his father would have also surfaced here to refill his lungs.

He pondered how he could possibly describe the majestic sight that greeted his eyes. From the gently curved ceiling hung down countless stalactites like so many straws. They descended to almost touch the top of his head, as sharp as a mass of downward-facing needles. The stalactites were up to several yards in length. Yet, sadly, Takehiko's father had been unable to see this impressive spectacle.

A little further ahead, the tunnel once again narrowed to much the same constricting proportions as before. The gap of air between the ceiling and surface of the water disappeared. Takehiko decided to try holding his breath once again. The current began to slope slightly downwards, whereupon the flow of water became swifter. Yet he didn't feel this merited much concern. In his excessive preoccupation with duplicating the conditions that had beset his father, Takehiko had forgotten to take due consideration for his own safety. There was a dramatic surge in the speed of the current, and, to his complete surprise, he found himself swallowed up in a waterfall. No more than ten feet tall, it was tiny as waterfalls go, tumbling him in the water only twice. Yet in the impact of rolling, he lost the searchlight he was holding in one hand and struck his back hard against a rock. Carried along by the current, he skidded jerkily along the tunnel. He could hold his breath no longer, and was on the verge taking another breath when he saw a vertical line rise up about a dozen feet in front of him. Pressing his back up against the wall of the tunnel, he began to draw near to the line. As he drew closer, the true nature of the line became clear. It was a fissure in the rock, measuring about eight inches across. Water was gushing through this crevice and flowing out. This was the outlet! Through a layer of water particularly aerated with bubbles, he could clearly make out the faint light of day seeping through. Inside the fissure, the water on its way out mingled with the incoming light. With his back pressed against the rock by the surge of water, Takehiko thrust his hand into the strip of light from his contorted position. Through here it had been that his father had cast his last words.

A year after the news of his father's death had reached the family, the film case containing a copy of the map had been delivered to the Sugiyamas. On the reverse side of the map were words that testified to his father's final deed. It was a letter from his father, likely written immediately before he died.

There could be no doubt that water linked this underground lake with Tokyo Bay. The water flowed first into a tributary then into the thicker line of the River Tama, which emptied itself out into Tokyo Bay. Yet, what were the chances of a letter delivered this way arriving to the addressee? Surely it could only be described as a miracle. And yet, the sublime strip of light making its way through the aperture had the power to make one believe in just such a miracle.

They had found the letter in their mailbox. It had been delivered in the film case, although the package bore no sender's name, thus making it impossible to determine who had found the letter or when it had been found. They could only imagine that it had been discovered by a resident of the Okutama area; else it had become entangled in the nets of a fisherman plying the stretch of sea near the mouth of the Tama. Whoever the finder, he or she had taken the note from the film case and read it, and appreciated the importance of the message to the family for whom it had been intended. He or she had also been kind enough to send it to the Sugiyamas.

The letter said:

> *Dear Takehiko,*
>
> *Even when we know there is no way out, we sometimes have to press ahead in search of one, no matter how dim the prospects.*
>
> *I know I can count on you to take good care of your mother and the child soon to be born.*
>
> *With love,*
> *Your father*

Without a shadow of doubt, it was his father's handwriting, every letter imprinted firmly. The letter was proof that his father had been prepared to meet his death.

It was clear why his father's body had been found near the outlet below a subterranean lake. Knowing that there was no way out, his father had yet sought a way and tried the submerged tunnel; the attempt could end in failure, but at least he'd send his son a letter willing him a fearless determination to survive. He had not addressed the letter to his wife. He'd wanted to convey to his son—then too young even to read the letter—the message to be strong.

The letter had proved an invaluable source of strength to Takehiko. He'd read it over and over again. When life called for courage, he recalled his father's words and the difficulties he'd tried so hard to overcome. Takehiko had had only two and a half years with his father and now hardly even remembered those days. Yet the darkness that his father had faced pursued Takehiko into his dreams, making him gasp for air. Every time he awoke from the dream, he felt only more determined to be strong. Because he had the letter, there was nothing he feared in life.

He thrust his arm into the crevice up to the shoulder, and slowly pulled it back. If the opening had only been twice as wide, his father's wish would have been granted; he'd have emerged into the radiant light.

Takehiko strove to imprint the sight before him in his memory, so he'd never forget. And he said in his heart, "Dad, I got your will."

EPILOGUE

In the old days, Cape Kannon used to be called Cape Hotoke, or Cape Buddha. Although almost seventy-two, Kayo had never heard the cape called by the older name.

In the dawn of an early spring morning, Kayo briskly walked the route she always took on her strolls. The Buddhist goddess of mercy, Kannon, was supposed to extend the hand of salvation to all who called upon her. Kayo believed in Kannon, and had made it a rule to come this way on her morning stroll for the past twenty years.

Whether "Kannon" or "Hotoke," the name of the cape had welcome associations. If nothing else, the name revealed that the cape was a place marked by history. In fact, the walk along the promenade revealed among the bushes what were either *jizo* roadside statues or tombstones. The things were no doubt originally placed there to appease the souls of the dead who'd been washed ashore on the promontory, but none of the local residents had any idea how or why the artifacts had been installed. In any case, there were surprisingly many of them on and around the cape.

It was not yet fully light as Kayo made her way along the path skirting the sea. In a slightly stooped posture, she walked with her eyes cast down. Once the spring holidays arrived, her granddaughter Yuko would come and visit her, and Kayo would be able to take her granddaughter along on her walks. A walk, she felt, was always a little bit more worthwhile with someone by your side.

Her spectacles steamed up with her own breath; Kayo slowed down and looked at the pedometer fastened to her waist. It was hardly necessary for her to check. She could usually guess how many paces she'd walked and was never off by more than a few paces either way. This kind of accuracy was to be expected. After all, she'd been in the habit of walking this route almost every day for the past twenty years.

Coming to a halt in front of a cave of crumbling rock, she looked at her pedometer, which showed exactly two thousand paces. This meant that she had covered roughly a mile since leaving her home in Kamoi. Stretching her back, she walked toward the sea, bringing her two hands together in prayer as she faced the rising sun. The words of her prayer had not changed much over the past two decades. She prayed for the health of her two sons, the one who lived in Tokyo and the one who lived in Hokkaido, and for their families. Now and then, whenever the need arose, she prayed for something she wanted, but never more than one thing. She'd never pray for too much. Kayo believed that if you stood on the tip of Cape Kannon and prayed to the rising sun, all your wishes came true. She'd been petitioning the sun less than two months when her son called to triumphantly announce that he'd been promoted to section supervisor, at an early age.

"It's thanks to the goddess Kannon," Kayo told him.

"Ha! I think it was thanks to my being very good at what I do," her son replied, laughing.

Originally taken up as a form of rehabilitation, her early morning walks were now undertaken purely for the well-being of her family.

It was now twenty years since Kayo had collapsed on a street corner in Yokosuka. At the time, she had been in her fifties. An ambulance had taken her to hospital, where she had been diagnosed as having suffered a subarachnoid hemorrhage. Her condition required immediate surgery. As luck would have it, the operation was successful, but left her with the temporary inability to walk properly. For several months after leaving the hospital, she had to lean on her husband's shoulder to walk. She had now recovered to an extent that it was no longer immediately noticeable that she dragged her left foot. At one point her spirits sank very low when she thought that, for the remaining years of her life, there would never be a time when she wouldn't have to limp. Yet her success in overcoming the impediment had boosted her confidence so much that she felt she'd gained a new lease on life. She felt more truly alive after the operation than before. As Kayo would have it, this too was a blessing from the goddess Kannon.

While Kannon may have had a hand in Kayo's robust recovery, there was one more reason for her renewed vigor. It began as a strip of light that had caught her eye. She could see it even now, for the scene had imprinted itself on her retina. The strip of light emanating from a tidal pool on the beach

had been one of the main reasons why she'd become so particular about taking her walks every morning like clockwork.
It had happened almost twenty years before, about six months
after she was released from the hospital.

Although the doctor had urged Kayo to walk as a way to
get better, she considered it such a chore that she kept putting
it off. At length, the doctor had told her that she would
become bed-ridden if she did not change her attitude. The
words shook her into action, and one morning she decided to
go for a stroll.

Dragging her bad leg heavily behind her, she nonetheless
managed to walk as far as the tip of the cape. As she paused
to catch her breath, she leaned over the promenade railings.
She was utterly exhausted after having struggled all the way,
forcing her left leg to come forward with the rest of her body.
Ever since leaving the hospital, she had been distressed by her
body's constant refusal to cooperate with her intentions. She
found her disability all the more irksome for once having
been such an active person. Huffing and puffing, she sat atop
the railings and took a wad of tissue paper from her pocket.
After wiping her nose and eyes, she put the tissue paper back
into her pocket, seemingly unwilling to throw the used paper
away. She had repeatedly used the same wad of tissue in the
same way during her walk. The railings gave way to a patch
of rocky coast. The waves were breaking at her feet, and when
the wind suddenly changed direction, it blew drops of spray

onto her cheeks. Directly beneath the railings sprouted tufts of purplish grass. From each short, thick stem flourished a number of sprouts, giving the plant an air of great vitality. The onset of May would see the tips of these sprouts bursting forth in clusters of pale flowers. Yet it was still too early in the year for that. The plant was a species of angelica, known in Japanese as *ashitaba*. Kayo knew the name of the plant as well as its origin. Rendered in Chinese characters, *ashitaba* meant "tomorrow-leaf." Indeed, this plant was named so because if its leaves were picked off today, they would sprout again by tomorrow. As she looked down at the Japanese angelica and pondered how it bore witness to the life force, she felt the urge to bend down and pluck off a leaf or two. She did so not out of some destructive impulse but out of the desire that the plant might share with her some of the life force that flowed within it.

As she looked carefully at the broken stems of the leaves she'd just plucked, she noticed a yellow liquid oozing from the veins. She brought the leaves up to her nose in an attempt to detect a aroma. She could not tell whether she smelled nothing because the plant was odorless or because her runny nose had dulled her olfactory sense.

...I'll have to come back tomorrow and take a look.

She would have to return the next day to see whether the plant, true to its name, sprouted new leaves to replace the ones she'd just plucked. It was an ideal incentive for keeping

at her daily early morning walks. She would pluck off the leaves here every day and return the next day to see if they had sprouted again.

Satisfied with her resolution, she looked up. It was then that she saw it. A small strip of light caught her eye. At first, she could not determine the origin of the light. It did not seem to be radiating directly from the sun as it began to peep above the horizon. It gave the impression of having flashed brilliantly for an instant, leaving a lingering image on her retina, before vanishing again.

She tried training her eye on the spot where she had seen the gleam vanish. Sure enough, there it was once again. From the same angle, the gleam caught her eye, only a little less intense than before. Over there in a hollow on the rocky shore, something seemed to be reflecting sunlight as it bobbed in a pool of seawater. At a certain angle, it sent a sharp gleam to catch Kayo's eye.

Descending to the other side of the railings, she went to the side of the tidal pool. Careful to avoid getting wet, she squatted to take a closer look. She discovered that the source of the reflected light was a plastic bag containing a semitransparent plastic case. It appeared as though the waves had washed it toward the rocks. The cylindrical case tossed in the water as if endowed with a will of its own. She thought she heard a voice nudging her to reach out and pick up the plastic case. Although she was not in the habit of picking up flotsam

washed up onto the shore, she could not resist reaching out and picking up the case. She took the dripping bag between her fingers and held it up to the light of the rising sun. The case it held was securely sealed with rubber tape. She could see in the case, in turn, a rolled-up piece of paper.

...A letter!

With a flash of intuition, she tore open the plastic bag and removed the case. The romantic fancy that occurred to her in that instant was that she had just received a letter that had been washed up after being carried a great distance. Conversely, it could be a child's doing. She recalled having seen her elder son once attach fanciful letters to balloons on sports day at his school, releasing all the balloons into the air at the finale. It did occur to Kayo that it was quite possible that some child had done the same kind of thing by entrusting letters to the sea rather than the air.

Kayo decided not to read the contents of the case immediately, putting the case in her pocket instead and starting back home. She somehow felt that her leg was not dragging as heavily now as it had on her way out.

What she found in the case upon opening it was the neatly folded and rolled up copy of a map of the Chichibu Mountains and environs. She could see that there was some writing on the reverse side; before she knew it, she was reading it aloud. The first time, it failed to arouse the least emotion within her. It simply sounded like a phrase or two from

some homily.

She noticed that the sender was a Fumihiko Sugiyama and that the message bore a date at the bottom, indicating that it had been written over a year ago. It did not seem too fanciful to conclude that Fumihiko Sugiyama had written the letter to his son Takehiko. Kayo was unable to imagine in what sort of circumstances Fumihiko had written the letter. She was also at a loss to understand the significance of the map of the Chichibu Mountains. Meanwhile, the address on the message said Ohta Ward, Tamagawa (River Tama) and even gave the house number. A look at a map revealed the neighborhood to which the message was sent. The locale was roughly on the boundary between Tokyo and Kanagawa Prefecture, at the mouth of the River Tama.

The letter lay in a cupboard drawer for some time after. It had not been put away and forgotten, however. Whenever the fancy struck her, Kayo would take it out and pore over it. The more often she read the message, the more the lines gave off the aura of a powerful will. It occurred to her that this force could become all the greater if the letter were delivered to the intended recipient. She decided to see to it that the letter reached the address it bore. The idea came to her naturally: she'd deliver the letter in person rather than through the mail. During the fortnight or so that she had pored over the letter, she sensed that the letter had imparted strength to her. She felt compelled to seek out the address in order to confirm

what she'd been given and to show her gratitude for it.

At the same time, she felt that this would be a new goal for her. It would involve, for one thing, making all the right train connections from Yokosuka to Tamagawa in Ohta Ward. This was not the kind of plan she could feel sure about implementing unless she could make it around Cape Kannon and back again without any trouble.

After this, her early morning routine was to rise before dawn, set out on her walk round the cape, pluck some leaves from the angelica plant and offer them to the little stone *jizos*, praying that her leg would get well again.

She thought that the delay in getting the letter to its destination was excusable. After all, the message had been written nearly a year and a half ago; surely it could wait a little longer. Yet it was conceivable that the family knew about the letter and was waiting anxiously for its delivery. The thought jolted Kayo out of her complacency and spurred her on in her efforts to rehabilitate her leg.

Around the time the angelica came into bloom, her leg had recovered sufficiently to allow her to travel all the way to Tamagawa and back by herself. Kayo chose a fine, sunny afternoon to put her plan into action.

The condominium of the address was not far from the station, at least as the crow flies. However, Kayo got lost somewhere along the way and had to venture up and down several streets before finally finding the apartment building.

By the time she arrived, she was so utterly exhausted that she did not think she could walk another step. She had to lean sideways with her entire weight on the handrail to make it up the three steps leading to the condominium lobby. At this rate, she couldn't make it back to the station unless she first found somewhere to rest.

Once in the deserted condominium lobby, she saw two sofas set facing each other in the rest area. She decided that was where she'd take her break, but first she had to find the mailboxes.

The names of four people were written on the mailbox to which the letter was addressed: SUGIYAMA, Fumihiko, Kyoko, Takehiko, Akihiko. Kayo felt that the father, who'd sent the message, must be Fumihiko, while Takehiko must be his son. From the content of the message, Kayo had guessed that it was a letter from a father to his son. The names on the mailbox in front of her seemed to corroborate her supposition. She found herself imagining all kinds of possibilities. What kind of circumstances could have made the father write a letter like that to his son? Where was the father now and what was he doing? The father's name was still on the mailbox. Did that mean that he was still living together with his family? Or did it mean…?

Kayo put the letter back in the film case, just as she'd found it. It made a metallic clang as she dropped it into the mailbox. The sound reassured Kayo that it had finally reached

its intended destination.

She had done her part. It was with a mixture of fatigue and satisfaction that her small frame sank to rest on the sofa, there to give herself up to various imaginings. Suddenly, some activity seemed due in the deserted lobby. She looked over to see a little boy of about four or five who'd pushed open the glass door of the entrance with all his might.

"Mom, hurry-y-y!" the boy yelled.

At that moment, his mother was trying to get up the steps to the condominium with a baby carriage containing a screaming infant. As she lifted the carriage, she leaned sideways on the handrail to get up the three steps, just like Kayo. Once up the steps, the mother entered the door her son was holding open. Her son ran ahead again to open up the way for his mother, jumping energetically up and down as he went. Making his way to the mailboxes, he again started jumping, to try to reach the family's box, but fell short. His mother caught up, quickly retrieved the contents, and held them up high. The boy let out a cry of protest; his eyes fixed on the film case as though it were some treasured prize, he started jumping higher than ever. The mother stood there staring suspiciously at the film case that she'd just taken out of the mailbox, while the little boy, leaping up by her side, howled "I wannit!" and "Show it!"

Then the elevator doors slid open, and the three of them disappeared inside, leaving the lobby to be completely

engulfed in the same deserted silence that had pervaded it before their arrival. In the silence, the baby's screams and the little boy's howls lingered in Kayo's ears. Before the sounds could die down completely, Kayo stood up laboriously.

The clamor that pressed itself into that brief instant in time must have left a deep impression indeed. A full score years later, Kayo could still see that little boy springing up and down. *I know I can count on you to take good care of your mother and the child soon to be born.* These had been the final words of the father to that little boy, and even now it was with a poignant delight that Kayo remembered his vibrant little face, so full of life.

Naturally, Kayo had memorized the whole letter. Towards the end of the previous summer, she had recited the letter to her granddaughter Yuko, telling her that it was a piece of treasure washed up by the sea. After listening to the words, her granddaughter had stared backed at Kayo dubiously. The girl clearly didn't understand how the words amounted to any kind of "treasure." Indeed, even Kayo could not say for certain that she understood the truth that lay behind the message. Yet there could be no denying that no matter what that truth may be, it had suffused every inch of her body and provided spiritual support. She'd started to take morning walks every day, and her left leg had begun to heal ever since and was by now almost fully recovered.

It would soon be the spring holidays. It would not be long

before Yuko would arrive to stay with her. Kayo plucked off a leaf from an angelica and offered it to a roadside statue. As she hurried home, she bounced with life.

ABOUT THE AUTHOR

Koji Suzuki was born in 1957 in Hamamatsu, southwest of Tokyo. He attended Keio University where he majored in French. After graduating he held numerous odd jobs, including a stint as a cram school teacher—an unorthodox one who loved telling scary stories to entertain his students. Also a self-described jock, he holds a first-class yachting license and has crossed the U.S., from Key West to Los Angeles, on his motorcycle.

The father of two daughters, Suzuki is a respected authority on childrearing and has written numerous works on the subject. He acquired his expertise when he was still a struggling writer and househusband. Suzuki also has translated a children's book into Japanese, *The Little Sod Diaries* by the crime novelist Simon Brett.

In 1990 Suzuki's first full-length work, *Rakuen* (Paradise), won the Japan Fantasy Novel Award and launched his career as a fiction writer. *Ring*, written with a baby on his lap, catapulted him to fame, and the million-selling sequels *Spiral* and *Loop* cemented his reputation as a world-class talent. Often called the "Stephen King of Japan," Suzuki has played a crucial role in establishing mainstream credentials for horror novels in his country. The author is based in Tokyo but loves to travel.

LIFE BEGAN
IN THE SEA
AND
IT WILL END
BY THE SEA

At a bookstore near you...

SPIRAL

You don't know what the Ring is yet.

In this award-winning sequel, the story we thought we knew in *Ring* is broken down and twisted into a new reality. Ryuji wasn't who we thought he was. And Sadako is back.

Ando, a medical doctor haunted by dreams of his drowned son, faces a choice at the end of *Spiral* more sinister than Asakawa's.

Coming in 2005: *Loop*, the trilogy's stunning conclusion.

Whether you like Japanese stuff

READ

For those unfamiliar with contemporary Japanese fiction, here is a quick overview of some of the most absorbing writing in Japan today – all available in translation from Vertical!

Gangster noir
Ashes by Kenzo Kitakata

"*Ashes* depicts yakuza life with a unique understanding and edge-of-your-seat reality."
–*Midwest Book Review*

New Age mystery
Outlet by Randy Taguchi

"Her sexual encounters may have a healing power...and the novel's dark twists and turns should keep readers hooked until the surprising climax."
–*Publishers Weekly*

r just like good books,

DIFFERENT
READ

V
E
R
T
I
C
A
L.

Comedy of manners
Twinkle Twinkle **by Kaori Ekuni**
"This book is simple. This book is a pearl. This book is like water, clear and loose and natural and fluid." *–BUST magazine*

Ghost story
Strangers **by Taichi Yamada**
"An eerie ghost story written with hypnotic clarity. He is among the best Japanese writers I have read." –Bret Easton Ellis, author of *American Psycho*

Fantasy epic
The Guin Saga **by Kaoru Kurimoto**
"Readers should be cautioned that once you start this journey, it will be nearly impossible to leave it unfinished." *–SFRevu*

BUDDHA

OSAMU TEZUKA

Fall 2004

Vol.**5**: *DEER PARK*

Vol.**6**: *ANANDA*

IN VOLUME 5, THE BUDDHA
ACCEPTS A DEER AS HIS
FIRST DISCIPLE. DEVADATTA,
NOW A CUNNING YOUTH, PAIRS
UP WITH THE EQUALLY
STREET-SMART TATTA.

IN VOLUME 6, THREE BRAHMIN
BROTHERS TEST BUDDHA'S
WISDOM, AND DEVADATTA'S
HALF-BROTHER ANANDA, A
CRIMINAL PROTECTED BY A
SHE-DEVIL, JOINS THE FRAY.

THE GUIN SAGA

KAORU KURIMOTO

In a single day and night of fierce fighting, the Archduchy of Mongaul has overrun its elegant neighbor, Parros. The lost priest kingdom's surviving royalty, the young twins Rinda and Remus, hide in a forest in the forbidding wild marches. There they are saved by a mysterious creature with a man's body and a leopard's head, who has just emerged from a deep sleep and remembers only his name. Guin.

Kaoru Kurimoto's lifework will enthrall readers of all ages with its universal themes, uncommon richness, and otherworldly intrigue. New installments of this sterling fantasy series, which has sold more than twenty-five million copies, routinely make the bestseller list in Japan.

Visit us at www.vertical-inc.com for a teaser chapter!